A Hard Favored Death

Frank Zafiro

Other Crime Series By Frank Zafiro

River City Series
Police procedurals with ensemble cast, begins with *Under a Raging Moon*

Sandy Banks Thrillers
Vigilante assassin who targets bad men, begins with *The Last Horseman*

Stefan Kopriva Mysteries
Private detective mysteries, begins with *Waist Deep* (set in River City)

SpoCompton Series
Hardboiled underside of Spokane, begins with *At Their Own Game*

Cam & Bricks Jobs (with Eric Beetner)
Two competing hitmen – action and dark humor, begins with *The Backlist*

Ania Series (with Jim Wilsky)
Hardboiled noir with a femme fatale, begins with *Blood on Blood*.

Charlie-316 series (with Colin Conway)
Police procedurals full of action and intrigue, begins with *Charlie-316*

Jack McCrae Mystery Series
Retired detective solves mysteries, begins with *At This Point in My Life*

Frank also writes mainstream fiction and non-fiction as Frank Scalise and science-fiction and fantasy as Frank Saverio!

A Hard Favored Death

A Sandy Banks Thriller

Frank Zafiro

A Hard Favored Death: A Sandy Banks Thriller #3

Frank Zafiro

Copyright © 2025 Frank Scalise

All rights reserved. No part of the book may be reproduced in any form or by any electronic or mechanical means, including information storage and retrieval systems, without permission in writing from the publisher, except by a reviewer who may quote brief passages in a review.

Published by Code 4 Press

The characters and events in this book are fictitious. Any similarity to real persons, living or dead, is coincidental and not intended by the author.

Cover Design by Zach McCain

ISBN: 978-1-962889-64-3

For Ozzy,
Who taught me that being a weirdo outcast
wasn't just okay, but actually cool.

> *"Do you wonder ever if you're a bad man?"*
>
> *"No, I don't wonder, Marty. World needs bad men. We keep the other bad men from the door."*
>
> —Martin Hart and Rustin Coehle,
> True Detective, Season 1

PROLOGUE

2013

Alexandros Dimitrakos shielded the boy from the man leveling the gun at them.

Were it not for the gun he held, the man would have been almost completely immemorable. His build was average, though fit. His short hair may have been a dirty blond but was too short for Dimitrakos to be certain. It could have been graying. The man was old enough for that to be the case. Forties, certainly. Perhaps fifties.

And American. Dimitrakos had seen enough tourists on the islands to make that assessment almost immediately. Not just from the clothing but there was a subtle demeanor most Americans exhibited, like a bad scent, and Dimitrakos never failed to notice it.

He'd also seen enough killers to recognize one when he stared into the man's hard eyes.

His instincts were hardly necessary, however. The gun the man pointed at his chest was adequate proof. The shots he'd heard as he passed the guest room Bogdan was staying in now made sense. A pair of bare feet extended past the end of the nearby bed. The rest of his guest's body lay on the far side of the bed.

Dimitrakos knew what he'd find if he were to look there. Or, worse yet, if Andrej did.

The frail boy was sixteen and stronger than he looked. Even as the man held the pair at gunpoint, Andrej tried to surge past Dimitrakos to get to his fallen father. Dimitrakos kept his arms outstretched, blocking Andrej's attempt and clutching a handful of the boy's shirt. He turned his head to the side, his gaze never leaving the face of the gunman.

"Andrej, no." He injected as much gravity and urgency into the two words as he could.

The boy's efforts subsided but did not stop entirely.

Dimitrakos braced for the inevitable. This man was a professional, he could tell. Bogdan had been his target, no doubt. The Bosnian was reportedly an activist, reviled by political opponents. That was apparently why he'd sought sanctuary with Dimitrakos here among the Greek isles. Or so Dimitrakos had been told by his contact. He hadn't asked for details, a situation no different than dozens of others he'd encountered over the years. Offering a safe haven without question was part of his livelihood.

We've seen his face, Dimitrakos thought. *Surely, he will kill us both now.*

Yet, the man hesitated. As Andrej's frantic efforts wilted and the boy dissolved into tears, the assassin did not move.

What was he waiting for?

Dimitrakos matched his motionless stance. Held his breath. Waited. Seconds passed. How many, Dimitrakos did not know. The only sounds were Andrej's muted sobs and the cry of birds and the light crash of waves on the nearby beach. Dimitrakos concentrated on the birds and the waves. If those were the last echoes he was to hear in this life, at least they were beautiful ones.

The barrel of the gun dipped toward the ground. Dimitrakos tilted his head slightly in confusion. His gaze drifted to the man's eyes. The hardness there had softened, albeit minimally. When the man spoke, his voice was flat. Even so, Dimitrakos could detect the American accent.

"You were never here," he said. "Do you understand me?" Realization dawned on Dimitrakos. He nodded slowly.

"I need you to say it."

"We were never here," Dimitrakos said.

The man appraised him, still not completely lowering the weapon. Then his gaze flicked to Andrej. "The boy was never here. You take him, and you both go far away for a long time."

Theé mou. We may yet survive.

Behind him, Andrej's choked sobs were punctuated by immature curses and what must be threats, spoken in the boy's native tongue. Dimitrakos recognized only the profanities. He hoped the man in front of him did not understand what was being said or hear anything other than grief in the boy's tone.

"We will go far away," Dimitrakos repeated, speaking slowly, grateful for his command of English. "For much time."

The man considered for another moment, then nodded. He gestured toward the bedroom door.

Dimitrakos moved, dragging Andrej roughly along with him. The man marched them into the hallway. He raised the gun again and kept it leveled at them the entire time.

"Stop," he ordered. He motioned toward a closet door. "Inside."

Dimitrakos didn't argue. He opened the door and pushed Andrej inside. The boy grunted as he crashed into the wall, his string of wailing curses suddenly interrupted. Dimitrakos followed him, stepping into the closet. His eyes met the gunman's one last time as he reached for the knob.

"Count to one hundred," the man told him. "Slowly. If you come out any earlier, I will shoot you both."

Dimitrakos dipped his chin in acknowledgment. Then he pulled the door shut and started counting.

The wind in Sandy Banks's face felt good. The moon glinted off the Aegean sea as the boat sped toward the mainland.

"Any complications?" Lori Carter asked him.

The supervising agent sat opposite him while one of Szoke's tactical operatives drove. The vessel cut across the waves like a knife, hopping slightly as it crossed each swell.

Sandy shook his head. "None."

Carter watched him for a moment. Then she shrugged and looked away.

Sandy knew why. She still wasn't accustomed to the enormity of what they did. She'd been FBI before being recruited – no, *drafted* was a better term – by Danforth into the Agency-funded dark project to which they now belonged. Once, as an agent, she'd hunted Sandy and the Four Horsemen. The vigilante group of former cops had visited justice on the worst of criminals, those who managed to escape due to technicalities and gaps within the system. Two members of the team left before the end, leaving only Sandy and the youngest of the crew, Brian. Sandy had no idea how long the feds had been investigating the operation, but somewhere along the way, Carter managed to compromise Brian and flip him. His former partner-in-crime gave him up to Carter, and the agent was instrumental in almost bringing Sandy down.

Not that any of that mattered now, however. Today, they all served the same master, Lori Carter included. Former CIA agent Mark Szoke cracked the whip but everyone knew the orders came from the shadowy Danforth. Sandy was unsure which of them resented the pair more.

Probably Carter, he decided. She'd lost her illusions more recently than him. Perhaps she still clung to some of them.

Sandy's own were stripped away long ago. *Except that's not entirely true, is it? If it were, you never would have let the boy and that man live.*

Sandy shifted in his seat. He'd been forced to eliminate witnesses on several occasions but those men—and one woman—were accomplices who just happened not to be the actual target. Dimitrakos was different. He was no saint, Sandy knew. But the briefing had been clear: the man was largely naïve about the people he sheltered—more host than accomplice. The terrorist label the U.S. government hung on Bogdan Marković did not extend to Dimitrakos. Or Marković's son, for that matter.

Hell, Sandy ventured a guess it probably barely fit Marković. More and more, terrorist was a term Sandy had seen Szoke apply to anyone Danforth wanted dead. The briefings he and the rest of the team received were never in-depth enough to determine the validity of the intelligence. They were required to accept the determination of enemy status on faith.

And Sandy had little faith in Szoke, Danforth, the Agency, or his government.

But he was trapped.

Dimitrakos was ignorant and Andrej Marković still barely more than a child. Even if Bogdan was a terrorist and deserved to die, neither of them shared that distinction. They weren't accomplices. Sandy didn't need their blood on his conscience.

Like it matters, he thought grimly. With all the deaths he'd delivered, first as a soldier, then a vigilante, and now as an assassin, did sparing these two lives really make a difference or balance the scales? They were two drops of water in a deep, wide sea of death, indistinguishable and unnoticeable. He could spare another hundred lives and not make a dent in the karmic debt he'd incurred.

Sandy stared at the approaching shoreline, knowing this was true.

Even so, that doesn't mean it wasn't the right decision, he told himself.

He chose to believe that.

1

2024

Sandy sat down in the chair across from Agent Mark Szoke's desk.

"What is it?" Szoke asked, sounding put out at the interruption and not looking up from his paperwork.

"I want to retire," he said calmly.

Szoke glanced up at that. "Retire?" he asked, his tone disbelieving.

Sandy nodded.

"Get the fuck out of here," Szoke said dismissively.

"I'm serious," Sandy said. "I've done enough."

Szoke set down his pen and leaned back. He folded his hands and gave Sandy a frustrated look. "I thought things were pretty clear when we all started this little journey together. Once you're in, there's no getting out."

"That sounds more like the mafia than the federal government."

"Officially, this isn't the federal government, and you know it."

"Then who signs your paycheck?" Sandy asked. "Where does my pitiful stipend come from? More to the point, who pays for our operations? Santa Claus? The Salvation Army?"

Szoke didn't reply. He only stared at Sandy, as if waiting to hear something worth responding to.

Sandy turned up his hands. "Mark, it's been over thirteen years. I've paid my debt."

Szoke scoffed. "Three lifetimes isn't long enough to pay off what you owe."

He's right about that.

"Look at me," Sandy said. "I'm getting old. My knees are halfway shot. I can't keep doing this."

"We'll let you know when *we* think you're too old to handle the job," Szoke said. "We'll even give you a pair of new knees if necessary. Until then, you keep yourself fit and trained and do what you're told."

"And if I don't?"

Szoke cocked his head. "You really need me to remind you what happens then?"

"Send me to prison. I don't care."

"There is no prison. There's a deep, dark hole at a black site that doesn't exist and, once you disappear in it, you stop existing, too."

"It's still a cell," Sandy repeated. "And I don't care."

"You would once you were there." Szoke eyed him knowingly. "Anyway, it isn't just about prison. Did you forget about Janet and her family?"

Sandy glared at him. "You've been threatening me with that since the beginning. I've heard it enough."

"It's not a threat. It's a reality. You do what needs to be done and Janet and her family get to keep living their happy lives. Otherwise, the IRS gets very interested in them and that's just for starters. It's that simple."

"See?" Sandy said. "Like the mob."

Szoke lifted his shoulders and dropped them. "Effective motivational techniques are universal, Banks. Probably the Romans used the same methods, way back when. The ancient Chinese, too."

"Fuck them, and fuck you, too."

"Don't be that way," Szoke chided. "Accept your fate. It makes the day to day living much easier."

Sandy stood up to go.

"Where are you off to?"

I'm going to the indoor range to shoot at targets I will imagine are you and Danforth.

"Back to the grind," Sandy told him.

"Attaboy," Szoke said.

Sandy left without another word.

2

"He's right, and you know it."

Sandy glanced over at Agent Lori Carter, who sat in an overstuffed chair with an open novel in her lap. He'd been watching the television on low volume, using captions to keep up with a story that was somehow boring and convoluted at the same time.

"I didn't ask you," Sandy said.

"You did," she argued back. "At dinner."

"I *told* you at dinner," he corrected. "It's not the same."

"There's an implied question when you share something like that."

Sandy scoffed and turned back to the television. "That sounds like a distinctly female perspective."

He could almost hear the scowl he was certain her face bore. "Guess it's a good thing I'm female, then," she said coldly.

"Guess so."

"You ever think of coming back from the 1980s, Banks? You know, stop being sexist for maybe thirty seconds and have a real conversation?"

Sandy didn't look her way. "I'm not stuck in the Eighties. And even if I were, at least the music was good."

"If you're not stuck, then why avoid talking about this?"

Sandy exhaled in frustration. He had no energy—no will—to argue. "In the past thirteen years, I've talked to maybe five different people outside of being on an op. Every possible conversation I'm willing to have has played out several times."

"And how many of those were real?" Carter pressed.

"Pretty sure sound waves left their mouths and invaded my ears in each case, no matter how irritating or irrelevant those sounds were." Sandy shifted in his seat, still watching the nonsensical action on the screen. "Like now."

"Oh, please," Carter said, her own tone exasperated now. "You won't say three words to Brian even now. Barely more than that to Szoke, except to argue. And on the rare occasion Danforth has blessed us with his presence, you clam up like you're being charged ten grand for every sentence."

Sandy shrugged. She wasn't wrong. "There are reasons for each of those."

"I get it. You have grievances against each of them. But—"

"Grievances?" Sandy's gaze snapped to hers. "Brian betrayed me. He sold me out to save his own skin. To *you*, by the way. Szoke is a shameless tool to his master. And Danforth—"

"Ensnared us all," finished Carter. She turned up her hands. "I know. I'm here, too, remember?"

Sandy stared at the woman who had so relentlessly pursued him while she was still an FBI agent. Throughout their long game of cat-and-mouse, they'd only crossed paths a few times, but he still recalled the blazing hatred in her eyes each time. Over the past decade-plus, however, some of that bile had burned away. Carter's stance toward him had softened into something less than camaraderie but no longer adversarial. The pragmatic nature of it reminded him of what a broken marriage might feel like in the aftermath of a betrayal. Tenuous trust. Strained civility. Reluctant consideration. Most of all, a sense of resigned surrender.

He wondered what emotional journey brought her to this

point. His own weariness needed no explanation. He'd been killing "enemies" since his youth. First the abusive step-father who drove his mother to drink herself to death. Then the enemies his commanders set him against. Eventually, the vigilante kills in Spokane as one of the Four Horsemen and since being drafted into this unit. The cumulative weight of all those deaths was expected.

But, until Danforth manipulated them all into the trap that had been their existence for well over a decade, Carter had been an idealistic FBI agent. She saw Sandy and his vigilante work in Spokane in black-and-white terms; it was murder, not justice. She'd made that clear to him on more than one occasion. She saw his military service in similar terms, though he sensed her outrage lay more with the policymakers than soldiers like him who carried out their directives.

But things were different now.

Time has a way of wearing us all down, he thought. Perhaps this was simply how Carter reacted to this truth. Or maybe it had something to do with how her partner, Agent Scott McNichol, had survived the gunshot wound Sandy gave him. His survival made it more difficult for Carter's rage toward Sandy to remain white-hot.

"Are you just going to stare at me and say nothing?" Carter asked him.

"Maybe," he said.

Deep inside, he thought he knew the truth. It wasn't time or the diminishing rage about McNichol's shooting that softened Carter's stance toward Sandy.

It was her own complicity.

Thirteen years of operations. Carter was the lead in the field. She may not have pulled the trigger in each of those instances but her actions supported Sandy, who did the dirty work. Her hands were bloody and she knew it.

She's starting to understand.

It wasn't just the weight of the killing, either. Each killing didn't feel the same. Even accounting for the hyperbole of the government position on each of the targets they'd eliminated, some of them clearly deserved their fates. One could almost feel good for taking them out.

And that emotion felt a different kind of bad.

Was that what was happening with Carter? Sandy suspected so. With the two of them alone in the day room, she seemed to want to talk about it. In typical fashion, however, she masked that desire by trying to get Sandy to talk about his own feelings. This was something he had no intention of doing.

"You know," Carter said flatly, "studies have shown, if two people stare at each other in silence even as briefly as one minute, it sparks feelings of love." She tilted her head. "Are you going to try to kiss me now, Banks?"

"You wish."

"Truthfully, I'd rather kiss a chainsaw," she said. "But I knew that would get you talking again."

Sandy noticed the lines at the corners of Carter's eyes and mouth. They hadn't been there when this dark journey began. Her hair had changed, too – it appeared more brittle. Telltale signs of age were beginning to show in her hands and throat, as well.

He knew his own age was even more apparent. Not that anyone other than a handful of necessary personnel saw him.

Sandy grabbed the remote and flicked off the TV. "Everything ends," he told her. "Why not this?"

"It will end," she assured him. "Just not until Danforth decides he's gotten every ounce of usefulness out of us."

Usefulness? My life has been a net negative, he thought. The justice he'd doled out as part of the Four Horsemen, was questionable. Worse, he'd now become a government tool for nefarious use. He had zero doubt he'd leave this world a worse place than the one he'd entered.

"Acceptance is like forgiveness," Carter said, her tone turning quiet. "It sets you free."

"Now you sound like a religious nut."

"It's not religion, it's philosophy."

"Then you sound like a philosophical nut."

She turned up her hands. "I've had to accept my fate. You have to accept yours."

Sandy narrowed his eyes. "Are you trying to handle me, Agent Carter?"

"When a team member goes to see the boss to try and quit, it's something to address," she admitted.

"Did you learn that in FBI supervisory school?"

"I was never a supervisor."

"Probably a reason for that."

"Don't deflect. I'm the team lead now. If you're distracted out in the field or half-assed in your motivation, it puts all of us at risk. You might not care if something happens to Brian—"

"I don't."

"—but I'd like to see retirement someday."

"You won't," Sandy assured her. "That hope is an illusion. Szoke made that pretty clear today."

"Then why keep doing this?" she asked him. "It's not about staying out of prison. At least not entirely."

"Why do you?" he shot back. "Last I checked you were a free woman."

Carter gave him a resolute shake of her head. "This is about you. Why *you* keep on."

"You know the answer."

"I do. Janet."

"Exactly." Sandy waved his hand. "Are we done, then?"

Carter was quiet for a few moments. Then she asked, "You don't check up on her anymore, do you?"

"How would you know that?"

"I don't. Not for certain. But you never talk about her."

"You don't talk about Scott, either."

"But I know he's doing well," she said. "Still married. Even has grandkids now."

Sandy watched her carefully. "You're in touch?" He'd assumed all of the contact rules in place for him applied to the rest of the team as well. Did Carter get an exemption?

"No. Between stalking his wife's Facebook and Instagram, though, it's pretty easy to keep up."

No exemption, then. She's as trapped as the rest of us.

"Good for him," Sandy said flatly. Despite his tone, his sentiment was genuine. He hadn't wanted to shoot McNichol that day. It had been an operational necessity. Even so, he opted to wound the agent to facilitate his own escape. He could just as easily have killed both him and Carter.

"Was I right?" Carter asked. "Do you check on Janet?"

Sandy hesitated, then shook his head. "Not anymore."

"When was the last time?"

He didn't reply, but his mind supplied the answer. It had been at least a decade since he'd sought any information on Janet Griggs. Seeing images of her happy life with a husband and children made him happy for her at first. It validated his surrender to Danforth. Then, as time passed, those images on a computer screen that cast a cold light on the bare walls of his bedroom left him with a sense of longing. One that rose up and almost drove him to fight his way out of the secure compound where he lived with the team. He wanted to go to her even though he knew he couldn't. When the compulsion eventually passed, he was overwhelmed with a sense of loss.

He knew there was no way he could spend the rest of his life feeling that way. So he vowed to let her live her life without him poking in, even from afar. All of the darkness he brought to the equation would only sully whatever good was in her world, anyway. He had to accept the sacrifice he made.

Accept. There was that word again. First Carter said it, now he'd thought it. He was suddenly glad he hadn't answered her question.

"It's been a while, I bet," Carter said.

"What if it has? It doesn't change why I keep up my end of the bargain."

"Yet you asked to retire. Did you think the agency was suddenly going to be seized by a sense of fairness or mercy?"

Sandy shrugged. "Can't blame a guy for trying."

Carter leaned forward, setting aside the paperback. "Except I can. When we go out on an op, I need everyone fully engaged, Banks. These people we're dealing with are dangerous. They—"

"I'm fully aware of the kinds of targets we go after," Sandy interrupted. "And you don't have to worry about me."

She watched him carefully for a while. Finally, she said, "Take my advice: accept the facts. We're all here until the agency decides we're no longer an asset."

"Or we die," Sandy added, thinking, *Not a bad option.*

"Or that," she agreed. "Either way, it's for the long haul."

"I get it."

"Yeah?" Carter asked. "Well, as long as we're clear on that."

"Crystal."

Carter continued to watch him, as if trying to ascertain how complete his understanding was. Sandy gazed back at her flatly. When Carter opened her mouth to speak, she was interrupted by Brian entering the day room.

"Hey, guys," Brian said, his oddly jovial tone jangling Sandy's nerves. "We gonna watch a movie tonight or what?"

Sandy didn't look in Brian's direction. His eyes remained locked on Carter as he dropped the TV remote on the couch next to him and stood. "I'm going to bed," he said, and left the room.

3

"Did you handle it?" Szoke asked her.

Special Agent Lori Carter sat in front of his desk, feeling once more like she'd been called to the principal's office.

"I reinforced his reality," she said.

"That's not what I asked."

She turned up her hands. "How am I supposed to know, Mark? I won't see how he handles field work until he's back in the field, will I?"

"Should I bench him?"

"Bench?" The euphemism clanged in her ear. "You mean ship him off to some black site to live out the rest of his days, don't you?"

"Don't be dramatic."

"I'm not. If anything, I'm underselling. You probably had something more permanent in mind."

"Come on, Lori," Szoke said. "This is me we're talking about."

"I know," she said, surprised at how sharp her own words sounded. In what felt like a lifetime ago, she and Agent Mark Szoke had a brief romance, followed by a long friendship. All the vestiges of that relationship were gone, however, seemingly along with much of Szoke's humanity. Over the past decade-plus, the man she'd once thought of as a good person had turned into a robotic bureaucrat, a mindless tool for

Danforth's machinations. Worse yet, he seemed to take a perverse joy in the power he wielded.

"Look, I know this has been hard on you," Szoke began, but she cut him off.

"You don't know shit, Mark. Except for ops, I'm essentially a prisoner on this site. At least you have a life in the real world."

"Don't be so jealous," Szoke cautioned. "That's not all it's cracked up to be."

"Bullshit. If your life sucks, at least that's on you."

His eyes narrowed. "Need I remind you *you're* the one who pulled *me* into this mess. If you hadn't called asking for intel and help on your goddamn manhunt, my career would have stayed mainstream. I'd be a legit supervisor by now, if not a division head, instead of laboring in the dark."

She gaped at him. "*If?* You want to play the what-if game with me?"

"I'm just pointing out you had something to do with your own situation. And you're not the only one who's been impacted."

Carter let it drop. For Szoke this was, at most, a difficult assignment. In her case, Danforth changed her life trajectory.

"Besides, you still have your pension," Szoke continued, not letting it go. "I know you already hit your twenty-year-mark, but this is a special assignment. When it ends, you can retire and live out the rest of your days comfortably. Go buy a condo in Mexico or something."

"Who are you kidding? Danforth isn't letting any of us go."

"What did I say about being dramatic?"

"Mark, I tried to quit, remember?"

Szoke pursed his lips. "Vaguely."

"Oh, bullshit. You remember. I tried to resign and *you*—" she pointed at his chest. "You told me Danforth was unlikely to accept my resignation. That I might find his reaction unpleasant."

"I don't think I said that."

"You insinuated I'd be incarcerated. And that he'd mess with Scott's medical pension."

"Incarcerated is a strong word. A friendly detention for a debrief, maybe."

"Do you even know when you're just swapping out euphemisms?"

Szoke shook his head. "Danforth is fine with either of us retiring. We can both leave, when our time comes. But the timing is on his terms, that's all."

She gaped at him. Retirement was a carrot Danforth would use until it didn't work, then he'd switch to the stick. That was apparent in how he managed Banks. Szoke either knew that and was lying to her, or he actually believed it, in which case he was stupid. Neither possibility changed her attitude toward the man.

She dropped the matter and moved on. "We'll know whether Banks is re-engaged or not when we go on the next op," she said, bringing the focus back to the purpose of this meeting. "My recommendation is no, *don't* bench him—whatever that means. If you do, you're benching all of us. Without him, our entire purpose here disintegrates. He's the trigger man."

Szoke shrugged. "He can be replaced."

"Then why haven't you?"

The CIA agent glared at her. "You might want to remember who asks the questions in this relationship, Agent Carter."

She turned down the corners of her mouth and nodded knowingly. "And there it is. Pulling rank. The first sign of great leadership."

"Keep your sarcasm to yourself." He leveled a finger at her.

A Hard Favored Death

"Just make sure your team is ready for the next op. You're accountable for the outcome."

And you're not? Carter thought, but decided she was too weary to poke the bear any more than she had already. Besides, Szoke's humorless, predictable demeanor sapped any of the satisfaction she might otherwise get from doing so.

"We've done how many missions now, Mark? Dozens?"

"Not all of them successful," he chided.

"Maybe not," she conceded. "But our readiness was never a factor."

Szoke gave her a disappointed look. "Readiness is all there is. It is the only aspect we can control."

4

"Listen up, people," Szoke barked from the head of the table.

The small group was assembled in the briefing room. Sandy sat as far away from Szoke as the seating arrangement allowed. Brian and Carter flanked the ex-CIA man. Brian's lap dog appearance set Sandy's teeth on edge. Carter's pinched expression was more resigned, making her look like someone about to do an undesired but necessary task, like scooping dog leavings from the back yard.

Szoke tapped a key on his laptop. A photo appeared on the screen behind him.

"This is Héctor Maravilla. He's a top lieutenant in one of the Mexican cartels. He will spend two days—"

"Which cartel?" Sandy asked.

Szoke shot him an irritated glance. "That information is not mission essential."

"Who decides that?"

"I do."

"It seems pretty essential to me."

"Well, let me consider that input for a moment, Banks. I'll balance it against the collective weight of U.S. Intelligence and let you know which one wins out." He gave Sandy a withering look before continuing. "Maravilla will be in El Paso tomorrow for two days. We think he may have an American mistress there—"

Sandy scoffed.

Szoke stopped and stared at him. "What is it?"

"This is the incredible power of the intelligence you were touting not two seconds ago? You *think* he has an American mistress?"

"It's our best guess," Szoke said through gritted teeth. "Maravilla has only become a target of intelligence gathering very recently. And the cartels are famously opaque."

"That's a fancy way of saying your intel is shit."

Carter sighed and dropped her chin. "Can we please just get through this?" She glanced at Sandy. "Let's just get briefed, huh? No amount of cock-waving is going to change the end result." She pointed toward Szoke. "He's going to send us on the mission and we're going to go. What does it matter which cartel or how thick the dossier is on this guy?"

"Easy for you to say," Sandy told her. "I'm the point of the spear. If things go wrong, it's not you or anyone else who's exposed."

"By anyone else, you mean Brian?"

Sandy didn't answer nor did he allow his gaze to shift to Brian for even a moment.

"We're in the field, too," Carter continued. "Right alongside you."

"You're in support," Sandy corrected. "*Behind* me. And sitting in a panel van a block away isn't exactly being in the line of fire."

Carter shook her head in frustration. "Jesus, when did you become such a diva?"

"Diva? I'm not asking for fruit plates and caviar here. I don't think solid intel is too much to ask for when it involves—"

"Enough!" snapped Szoke, dropping his fist onto the conference table.

Brian started at the sound. Carter frowned. Sandy eyed

him coolly and waited.

Szoke leveled a finger toward Sandy. "You want to make this difficult, Banks? Because I can do difficult."

"What I want is competence."

"You have no idea what that word means in this context."

Sandy pointed up to the screen. "I know, if this guy is a top lieutenant in a Mexican cartel, he's likely both smart and brutal. He's also twenty years younger than I am." He glanced at Carter and Brian. "And at least ten years younger than anyone else at this table. He looks fit. He's almost certainly familiar with firearms and probably carries one more frequently than you think. He'll be armed. There's no way he comes to the U.S. and doesn't have a weapons depot of some kind. Now, if you're going to send the three of us out to kill this guy—"

"I haven't given you the mission parameters yet."

"Please," Sandy scoffed. "I can count the times it wasn't a kill mission on one hand and still have fingers left over to tell you exactly what I think of your intel."

Szoke smirked. "For all you know, all the intel you could ever want is forthcoming, if only you'd stop with the dramatics and let me brief you."

"If you're sending us to kill Maravilla," Sandy continued, ignoring Szoke's comment, "then the only potential advantage we have is superior intelligence. Whatever mastermind fantasies you might have aside, we simply don't have the physical skills or the razoo devices of *Mission Impossible*. We're nothing more than an old man, a failed FBI agent, and a turncoat." He shook his head in disgust. "But you don't even know if he definitely has an American mistress. He could just as easily be meeting a drug dealer or a rival gang."

"Intelligence is an inexact science at times," Szoke said bitterly, his jaw tight. "But, regardless of the purpose of the trip, we have an advantage you seem to have forgotten."

"What is that?"

"The element of surprise."

Sandy waved a hand dismissively. "If you think you can surprise a member of a drug cartel, you're nuts. He's survived long enough to rise to whatever position you think he's in precisely because he *doesn't* get surprised."

Szoke stared at him with naked hatred. "I think you've forgotten your place, Banks. You are not a member of some elite team. No one is waving a flag and praying for you."

"Believe me, I know."

"You are a prisoner of the federal government," Szoke continued, ignoring Sandy's response. "Your life—and the livelihood of certain other people, I may remind you—depends upon your performance. Part of that performance is not being a pain in my balls." He smiled tightly, malice radiating toward Sandy. "Your performance at the moment is inadequate. So, you have two choices. Close your mouth and listen to the briefing, keeping your questions to valid operational considerations. Or I'll have you strapped to a chair in another room, where you can watch the briefing on a computer monitor. Which would you prefer?"

The question hung in the air along with the tension that crackled between the two men. Carter and Brian watched on, she with frustration and he with rapt fascination.

Sandy was briefly tempted to choose the second option. At least he'd be out of Szoke's officious presence. But Carter was right about one factor. The end result would be the same. He knew it was true, but his frustration had been building for years now. Discipline was difficult when there didn't seem to be a point to it.

Finally, he flicked his fingers toward Szoke. "Whatever," was all he said.

A satisfied look crossed Szoke's face, as if he'd just scored a major victory. "I thought so," he said smugly. He turned his gaze back to his laptop. "Maravilla will be in El Paso tomorrow for two nights. He's staying at the Stanton House Hotel downtown."

"How do we know this?" Carter asked.

A ripple of irritation crossed Szoke's face. Sandy wondered if he'd tear into her, too. Instead, he said, "We scraped it from a DEA intelligence report. They've got a couple of insiders on the payroll. May I continue?"

Carter waved for him to do so.

Szoke hit a few keys in succession, showing photos of the location and the schematics. He outlined the roles for each team member. As Sandy expected, Carter was in near support while Brian was relegated to tech support.

Despite his earlier grousing, Sandy actually preferred the op this way. He didn't want to rely on Brian. He couldn't trust him. At least he knew Carter's sense of duty drove her actions. She'd once been a competent FBI agent, despite what he said to Szoke about her being a failed one. Sandy could count on her if he had to.

But he never wanted to have to count on anyone.

As Szoke dictated the plan, Sandy listened for the subtext. Not much was revealed, but he was able to fill in the backstory. Maravilla's star was clearly on the rise. He wasn't so big yet he traveled with a massive entourage or was a publicly recognized figure. Szoke's masters wanted to take advantage of this opportunity, when the man was exposed, to get to him while they still could. Kill the baby in the cradle, as it were.

It wasn't the first time Sandy had seen this. In fact, he'd first been sent on this sort of pre-emptive strike way back when he was a soldier. A different time and a different role, but he suspected the same people had been pulling the strings.

That mission hadn't gone well. Sometimes he still woke from dreams about it. In the dark, it was as if he were surrounded by jungle once more, the dead weight of Lloyd's slack body heavy upon his shoulders, the man's blood in his hair. He could almost hear Brophy's labored breathing as they pushed through the brush. The remnants of the ache in his own lungs burned. Faint voices rattled off in rapid, staccato Spanish, drawing closer.

He almost died in that jungle. In a very real way, a version of him did pass from existence and, in his place, Sandy Banks was born.

"Any questions?" Szoke asked, his tone sharp.

No one spoke. Despite the weak intel on the purpose of Maravilla's trip, Szoke's presentation had been comprehensive. No plan survived intact once in the field, but Sandy had no questions. Thankfully, neither did Carter or Brian.

"Very well," said Szoke. "Get some rest. We gear up at zero seven hundred tomorrow."

5

"*Status check.*"

Brian's voice in his ear grated on Sandy's nerves. He knew the man was only relaying an order from Szoke but that somehow made it worse.

"*Exfil still clear,*" Carter replied.

She was parked on the street, half a block from the hotel. Her role was simple—pick Sandy up as he exited the hotel after the mission was accomplished. Her secondary responsibility was to lend direct support if he was somehow trapped within the building.

"Approaching," Sandy muttered. He spoke loud enough for the mic to pick up his voice but low enough to avoid being overheard. There was little danger of that in the empty hallway, but Sandy had learned to adhere to caution. You never knew what surprise lurked in the next moment, what ears might catch a stray word. All it took was one element to go wrong and the operation could be compromised.

"*Hotel comms are clear,*" Brian stated. "*Access to video coming through now.*"

At times, it was hard for Sandy to believe the young, brash patrol officer who'd joined the Horsemen after an unfortunate incident had somehow become the security system expert he was today. Brian had never struck him as a particularly tech-savvy individual. Yet he'd developed the knowledge and skills to provide technology support. Most of it involved surveillance networks, frequently ones Brian had to hack into in order to use.

In another world, another life, Sandy might have admired his talent, his adaptability.

None of it changed Brian's betrayal however. That one fact continued to burn coldly in Sandy's gut, like he'd swallowed an icicle that would not melt away.

"Hotel security?" Sandy asked, keeping his voice low.

Brian's reply was immediate. *"One's in the break room, chatting up some girl. The other is still in the lobby."*

Sandy didn't answer. He kept walking down the hallway, an envelope tucked under his arm. His shirt was emblazoned with the name and logo of an international courier chain whose stores and trucks and delivery people were ubiquitous. When he'd entered the hotel lobby, no one had so much as looked twice at him.

The hotel security being out of the way wasn't surprising. Szoke's briefing while en route detailed the advance team's assessment of the crew, pegging the small group as mediocre at best. Penetrating the hotel was never the largest obstacle to getting to Maravilla. The man's own security detail was a much greater problem. He usually traveled with a team of eight, its members drawn from an array of backgrounds; some ex-military, some longtime cartel soldiers deemed well-suited to the task.

Sandy knew why this trip to El Paso was when the Agency chose to target Maravilla. In an attempt at subtlety Sandy found almost amusing, Maravilla had slipped across the border with only two bodyguards. He registered at the hotel under an assumed name. For a man who was, at times, very loud in his activities, this trip was clearly meant to be clandestine.

When Sandy had asked why, all he got from Szoke was a dismissive shrug. "Who cares? He'll be where he'll be, mostly unguarded. That's the important part."

"Maybe he wants to keep his American side piece on the down low," Brian had offered.

Sandy hadn't responded. He wasn't anywhere near convinced a romantic tryst was the reason for Maravilla's trip. It seemed odd to him someone in that life would have any reservations about something as straightforward as a mistress. Then again, Catholicism was prevalent south of the border, wasn't it? So was resentment toward Americans. As much as Sandy didn't want to admit it, perhaps Brian had a point. Maravilla might want to keep his affair low-key and off everyone's radar for any variety of social or political reasons.

If that was his intent, he'd failed. Szoke's intel included all of the man's movements from his home outside El Ciudad Juarez to the Stanton House hotel. His bare bones security complement was noted and this operation quickly scrambled. Sandy knew it was Danforth, operating from some shadowy location, who gave the order. For whatever reason, he—or his masters, though Sandy wondered if Danforth answered to anyone at all—had decided Héctor Maravilla was a bad man who threatened national interests and therefore needed to come face-to-face with his God.

And they're sending me to arrange the meeting.

The thought didn't make him angry or leave him cold. Instead, it was a sense of weariness that flickered inside him.

"Second man?" he asked quietly.

"He hasn't left the room across the hall since being relieved," Brian responded in his ear.

Good. Most likely the other bodyguard was sleeping, preparing for coverage in the evening hours. With only two men on the detail, he reasoned they'd take twelve-hour shifts for the duration of the stay. The only variance would likely be during travel to and from El Paso.

Still, he couldn't count on that. He'd need to remain as

quiet as possible to avoid rousing the resting bodyguard. He didn't want to deal with reinforcements.

Sandy turned the corner into the hallway that housed the executive suites. Near the end, he spotted the single Hispanic male standing near the door to Maravilla's room. Inside, the cartel lieutenant was no doubt enjoying the company of his American mistress, though Szoke's surveillance team hadn't caught her arrival. Once Brian had hacked into the hotel's security system, he'd likewise seen no one arrive at Maravilla's suite.

This fact bothered Sandy. Forget the incompetence he'd railed about during the earlier briefing. He accepted Maravilla's potential mistress had been a low priority and so her identity was unknown to the Agency. But how hard was it to note any young female who entered alone and headed up to the top floor?

Sandy doubted the other agents were lazy. Then again, he didn't know any of them. Human nature was always prone to cutting corners, to not doing work that didn't seem essential, particularly if the job itself was overly broad. Perhaps Maravilla's mistress was older or unattractive and the agents made an assumption they shouldn't have. Maybe his mistress was actually a man, which would have escaped their notice entirely.

No, he decided. The world of Mexican cartels was hypermasculine. If Maravilla were gay or bisexual, Szoke would know it.

Then again, that *would* account for all the secrecy, wouldn't it?

It didn't matter, he knew. His first task was to neutralize the bodyguard. Once inside Maravilla's room, he'd eliminate the cartel lieutenant. If whoever he'd taken as a lover was with him when Sandy took out Maravilla, his orders were also clear on that point.

She was to be terminated, as well.

No witnesses. That was the protocol and it was ironclad.

The bodyguard was alert. He'd already noticed Sandy's approach. The man was shorter than average, with the broad shoulders of a man who'd spent many hours in the gym. Sandy wondered briefly if that gym was at the cartel compound or a prison yard somewhere. Then he pushed the thought aside, bringing his mind into laser focus.

"Hola, amigo," he said, giving sound to the 'H' in the first word to ensure his Spanish had the taint of a non-native speaker. He held up the delivery envelope as he continued to walk forward.

The bodyguard eyed him coolly, saying nothing.

"Tengo una entrega," Sandy added, butchering the pronunciation once again. He shook the envelope and smiled solicitously as he drew closer. "Sorry," he said in a West Texas twang. "*Mi Español* ain't so good."

The bodyguard stepped forward, holding out a hand to stop. "*No puedes—*"

Sandy dropped the envelope. As soon as the man's eyes lowered to follow it, Sandy took the final step to close distance. The knife edge of his left hand lashed out, crashing into the tip of the bodyguard's nose. The man grunted in surprise and pain. His hands flew to his face.

Without pause, Sandy struck again, this time driving the heel of his right hand into the man's groin. He pivoted his hips as the blow landed, bringing the full force of his body mass to the technique.

A low moan escaped the man's mouth. His hands dropped to the injured area.

Sandy snapped his left hand out once more. This time the knife edge caught the bodyguard squarely in the throat. The burly man sank to his knees. His expression was one of paralyzed panic.

A Hard Favored Death

Sliding behind the man, Sandy drew the thin knife from his boot. He grasped the man around the neck and thrust the blade between his ribs, aiming for the heart. His opponent's body stiffened, then became dead weight in Sandy's arms.

Sandy dragged the limp body backward. He leaned the dead man against the wall where, to the casual onlooker, he might appear to be sleeping. Then he wiped the blood from the blade and slid it back into his boot.

A quick search of the bodyguard revealed the room keycard Sandy had hoped to find. He was prepared to force the door, if necessary, but the accompanying noise of that action raised the risk considerably. It would also warn Maravilla he was coming.

Sandy drew the forty-five caliber from beneath his fake delivery shirt. He took a moment to listen for any response in the hallway. There was none. Then he pressed his ear to the door. He heard a pair of voices, too muffled and distant to make out any words.

"Going in," he murmured for the benefit of the team. None of them responded.

He held the keycard to the lock. A green light appeared and the mechanism whined and clicked.

Sandy opened the door.

As soon as he pushed it open, he was met with a small, tiled foyer. The voices, one male and one female, suddenly broke off.

So it was a mistress, after all.

Sandy stepped inside, closing the door without slamming it.

Footsteps approached, the soles of someone's shoes clicking on the tile.

That's good, Sandy thought. *Come to me. Make it easy.*

He leveled the gun and waited.

"Manuel?" a man's voice asked as he neared the foyer. His

tone sounded irritated.

Sandy didn't reply.

The footsteps stopped.

"Manuel?" The tone shifted to something more wary.

Sandy didn't hesitate any longer. He strode forward, rounding the corner to a large living space. In front of him stood Héctor Maravilla. Surprise flared in the cartel lieutenant's eyes before they narrowed.

"*Hijo de puta*—" he began.

Sandy fired three times. Two to the chest, one to the head. The silencer on the muzzle muffled the sound but the report was still loud. The sharp, metallic clack of the slide echoed through the room.

Maravilla flopped heavily to the ground and lay still.

Sandy turned to the blond woman on the nearby loveseat, who stared at him with shocked, disbelieving eyes. Her mouth hung open. She was older than Sandy expected—mid-thirties at least—and attractive. Not in the garish way of a trophy girlfriend, though. Rather, she seemed to him to be much more… normal.

No matter. Protocol was clear.

He was to leave no witnesses. And she'd seen his face.

Sandy moved the gun to point it at her. The woman's shocked expression didn't change.

"No!"

The shrill shriek came from his right. Sandy swung the pistol that direction. A streaking form crossed the room, hurling itself toward the woman on the loveseat.

Not a man. Not fully a woman, either.

Smaller.

By the time it registered with Sandy that it was a kid, a young teenager at best, the girl was already clutching at the woman on the couch, crying. Her eyes were screwed tight and her face was pressed against the woman, burrowing into the crook of her neck.

He looked at them both, hesitating. The girl couldn't be more than thirteen, maybe fourteen years old. *No witnesses.* He could almost hear Szoke's voice in his ear. *Protocol.*

To Hell with that, Sandy thought.

He made his decision in an instant.

6

The first thing he did was immediately pull out his earpiece and drop it to the floor. Then he stepped on the device, crushing it.

"Listen to me," he said to the woman. "Do not scream. If you scream, I will have to shoot you. Do you understand?"

The woman stared at him in shocked disbelief.

"Do you understand?" Sandy barked.

The woman jumped at his voice. Frantically, she nodded. Silent tears streaked from her eyes.

"And keep her quiet." Sandy motioned toward the girl.

The woman pulled the child tighter, cupping her hand behind the girl's head.

Sandy lowered the gun. "What's your name?"

The woman swallowed. When she spoke, her voice quavered. "Allison."

"Allison what?"

"Allison Dell...Dell... Delancey." Her wavering tone stretched out into a half-sob as she finished the sentence.

"Listen to me, Allison. I'm going to leave this room. Thirty seconds later, you need to follow—"

Allison's gaze dropped to Maravilla. "Oh my God. Héctor." Her expression dissolved into a twisted sob.

"Héctor's gone," Sandy snapped. "If you don't listen to me, the same thing is going to happen to you and your girl."

Allison looked at him as if struggling to comprehend his

words. "Why?"

"There's no time for that. You need to listen to what I'm about to tell you."

The girl in the woman's arms sobbed into her mother's side. Sandy pointed at her. "How old is she?"

Allison looked down, then back to Sandy. "Don't hurt her. She's only thirteen. She's a baby."

"What's her name?"

"Angelita," she said, the Spanish name rolling off her tongue with near-native fluency. "Lita."

"You want Lita to live?"

Allison bobbed her head frantically. "Of course, but—"

"Then shut up and listen. We all need to leave this room."

Allison's mouth worked silently, then she sputtered, "But Héctor—"

"Héctor's dead!" Sandy barked.

Allison recoiled at his words. She cradled her daughter's head, fresh tears spilling down her cheeks.

Sandy considered for a moment. Then he said, "I know you don't want to listen to me because of what I just did. But think about it, Allison. If I wanted you and Lita dead, it would have already happened. We wouldn't be talking now. So, if I'm trying to keep you alive, it only follows that you should listen to me. You should do what I tell you."

Allison stared at him. Fear and confusion swam in her eyes.

"I am not supposed to leave witnesses," Sandy stressed to her. "If you wait here for the police, the men I work for will find you and kill you. So might Héctor's people. Your only choice—"

At Héctor's name, Allison's gaze snapped back to his crumpled, bloody form. Her face dissolved into grief-stricken tears once more.

"We don't have time for this," Sandy said. "We all have to go, now. First me, then you and your daughter. Don't take the elevator to the lobby – use the stairs. You walk out of the hotel like nothing is wrong. Do not go home. Get some cash and go to a motel. There's one just off of I-10 on the west side of town called The Texan. Check in and pay cash for the room. Stay there until I contact you. If you don't hear from me in two days, you take your girl and you run. Drive as far away from Texas as you can get. Do you understand the plan?"

"Y-y-yes," she sputtered.

"Say it back to me."

Allison hesitated, thinking. Then she swallowed nervously. "Take the stairs to the lobby. Leave and get money. Go to the motel. Wait for you there."

"No," Sandy corrected. "Wait there until you hear from me."

She tilted her head at him as if she couldn't understand the difference.

Sandy didn't bother explaining. He could feel time slipping away. Every moment he stood there added to the chance someone might see Manuel propped against the wall in the hallway, or that his gunshots were heard and drawing a response. Moreover, the sudden loss of comms might spur Carter to leave her position as the getaway driver and come to his aid.

"How long do you wait to hear from me?" he asked Allison.

"Two days," she answered immediately.

"And if you don't?"

"We run." She looked up at him, her expression lost. "Run where?"

"Far away, like I said. Fucking Alaska or something." Sandy peeled off the delivery uniform shirt and tossed it aside. He found the zipper on the side of his uniform pants and hurriedly unzipped first one leg, then the other. He stepped out of the disguise. He now wore a conservative business suit. Just another middle-aged white executive among many.

"Count to thirty after I go, then leave," he instructed her. "And this is important, Allison—don't look back. You understand? This is life and death now."

Allison swallowed hard but she gave him a surprisingly resolute nod while she held Lita's head to her chest. "Thirty," she repeated.

Sandy slipped the gun into his waistband below his suit jacket, turned and left the room.

The hallway remained empty. Manuel slumped against the wall where Sandy had put him. Affecting an easy gait, Sandy headed down the hallway. He took first one turn, then a second. Once he found the stairwell, he started down to the lobby. As he passed a fire alarm, he reached out and pulled it. He was rewarded with the immediate trilling sound and emergency lights snapping on. The screech of the alarm reverberated throughout the stairwell.

Sandy continued down the stairs.

7

"*I lost him.*" Brian's voice sounded slightly panicked to Carter's ear. "*He went into the stairwell.*"

Carter frowned. Banks's transmission had been garbled right before it cut out. She didn't know what to make of that. The technology could have simply malfunctioned but that was rare with this equipment. More likely, Banks had been physically attacked and the earpiece dislodged in the struggle.

She debated going in for almost a minute. By the time she reached for the door handle, Brian had come back on, informing them that Banks was exiting the suite. But now the assassin was using the stairs.

Why?

A piercing alarm burst in on her thoughts. The high-pitched warble came from the hotel.

A fire alarm.

Coincidence?

Carter didn't think so.

Why the hell did he pull the alarm?

People began spilling out of the lobby of the hotel onto the sidewalk. Carter glanced around to make sure she wasn't too close to get hemmed in by the fire department vehicles she expected would arrive shortly.

"You seeing this?" Brian asked her.

"I am."

A Hard Favored Death

Szoke's voice broke in, something the team leader rarely did during an operation. "What the fuck is going on?" he demanded.

"Stand by," Carter said. "We're still figuring that out."

Several men in business attire appeared on the sidewalk, glancing around in a cross between curiosity and mild confusion. A blond woman with a dark-haired teenager emerged from the front doors of the hotel and strode away. The girl clung to her mother with a ferocity that surprised Carter.

She looked closer at the two. She doubted the alarm was for an actual fire. No, Banks was almost certainly responsible.

Maybe the child was autistic or otherwise sensitive to loud noises.

Carter watched them go while more people streamed out onto the sidewalk. Most stood and looked around. Only a few walked away.

Sirens wailed in the near distance, echoing off the buildings of downtown El Paso. Carter spotted motion in the passenger side mirror. A moment later, Banks pulled open the door and dropped into the seat.

"Go," he said.

Carter didn't argue. "I've got him," she said, for the benefit of Szoke and Brian. She put the car into gear and pulled from the curb, glancing toward Banks. "What the hell was that?"

Banks stared forward. "A diversion," he said flatly.

"Why'd you need a diversion?"

Banks didn't answer. Behind them, a fire engine rolled around the corner, blasting its air horn. Along the sidewalk, pedestrians turned toward the noise.

Everyone, Carter noticed, except the woman and child, who strode purposefully forward, eyes fixed ahead.

Carter frowned but kept driving.

"What the mercy fuck was that?" Szoke demanded.

The team was clustered in a plain conference room in a secure building on Fort Bliss. Szoke had shared enough of the overall plan with Carter that she knew they were now scheduled to remain at Fort Bliss for twenty-four hours, perhaps as long as thirty-six, before exfiltration back to their home installation in Idaho.

"A successful mission?" Banks answered. He spoke in the same flat tone he'd used with her in the car, but the sarcastic intent was unmistakable.

"Don't give me that," snapped Szoke. "This wasn't supposed to be noisy. Operational plans were designed to give us enough lead time to be out of the region before Maravilla's body was discovered."

"It was a shitty plan," said Banks.

"I'm not asking for your critique of the plan. I'm demanding an explanation for how you fucked it all up."

Banks eyed him coolly. "If you wanted extended lead time, there should have been a contingency for taking out the other bodyguard. Even if things went smoothly, he'd still be up in less than twelve hours and checking on his partner."

Szoke ignored the criticism but Carter noticed a light redness creeping up his neck. "What... the ...fuck... *happened?*" he demanded, his voice low and perilous now.

Banks didn't seem to notice the danger. "I took out the bodyguard. Propped him against the wall. Used his door card to enter the room. It was quiet inside, except for the television. I started my search for Maravilla. He surprised me. We struggled. I shot him."

Szoke peered closely at him. "A little more detail, please," he growled.

"What do you want, a play by play of the fight?"

"How did he surprise you?"

"He was waiting around a corner. He was fast. I was fortunate he didn't have a gun."

"What happened to your comm piece?"

"It must have popped out while we grappled."

"How convenient."

Banks seemed unruffled at the accusation. "It was pretty *in*convenient, if you ask me. I couldn't update the team or get any further intel during my exfil."

Szoke appeared unconvinced. "What happened next?"

"After I left the room, I wasn't halfway down the hallway when the other bodyguard came out. He saw me."

Szoke shrugged. "So? Your orders are clear in that scenario. Terminate him."

"It was a long shot. I elected to run instead."

"With your knees?"

Banks smiled acidly. "They hurt but they still work." He glanced to the side. "But he was either going to chase me or check on his boss. Either way, things were going to get loud very soon. I pulled the alarm to create camouflage." He returned his gaze to Szoke. To Carter, his expression was clearly challenging the agent-in-charge. "It worked."

Szoke snorted derisively. "It worked in calling a ton of attention to a scenario that should *still* be under wraps right now. Hell, if the bodyguard made the discovery, he might have called in Cartel assets and kept it quiet. Instead, we've got firemen tromping all over the place and discovering dead bodies."

"That was the mission," said Banks. "Besides, no plan survives contact with the enemy. If you'd been a soldier, you'd know that."

Carter watched Szoke take several breaths before replying. It amazed her how much Mark Szoke had changed over the past decade. The man she once knew and briefly dated had been a solid analyst and then field agent for the CIA. He'd been someone she'd trusted to reach out to, someone who had a grounded sense of values. Those seemed to be gone now, along with the even keel personality once so prominent.

Casualties of this program, she thought. No one escaped unscathed, it seemed.

"The mission was what I say it was." Szoke spoke through gritted teeth. "And don't give me that soldier of fortune bullshit. Our plans do frequently go like clockwork."

Banks shrugged. "This one didn't."

Szoke worked his jaw. "Can you confirm Maravilla's termination?"

"Yes." Banks pointed to his chest with two fingers extended, then tapped his forehead with his index finger. "Zero doubt."

"Was anyone else there?" Szoke pressed.

"No."

"He wasn't meeting anyone? A mistress?"

"Apparently not."

Szoke flexed his jaw. "Then why was he in El Paso?"

Banks shrugged. "How should I know? And who cares? Wasn't that what you said? Maravilla was the target. Maravilla is dead. Mission accomplished."

Szoke stared at Banks with what looked to Carter as something approaching abject rage. Banks reflected back only stoicism. After a brief battle of wills, Szoke said, "That'll be all, Banks. For now."

Banks rose from the table and left the room without a word.

As soon as the door closed behind him, Szoke turned to her. "Anything to add?"

Carter waited a moment before she shook her head. She was thinking of the blond woman and her child, walking purposefully away from the hotel. Perhaps it was nothing but it seemed worthy of follow-up, even though Banks said there'd

A Hard Favored Death

been no one else in Maravilla's room. That said, it wasn't anything close to concrete. If she mentioned it now, without any other supporting information, all it would serve to do was to send Szoke into a speculative rage.

Szoke noted her hesitation. "You sure?"

"Yes," she said, though she wasn't entirely certain.

Szoke pinched his nose, sighing.

"What now?" Carter asked him.

Szoke didn't open his eyes but only frowned. "We'll see," he said. "Loud is not how we like to operate but it's not unmanageable. We'll get some disinformation out there, then lay low and see how things proceed."

8

Sandy sat in the chair in the small barracks room he'd been assigned. The entire wing was empty, likely a result of military downsizing over recent years. Guards were posted at the doors at the end of the hallway, but outside of that, he, Carter, and Brian had free reign of the day room, a kitchen, and showers, in addition to their own private rooms.

The furnishings were sparse and offered a modicum of comfort. Sandy didn't mind. He folded his hands on his lap and stared at the wall. If he'd been operating on his own, he might have taken out a pen and paper and written out his thoughts in order to better examine them. He could burn them when he'd finished. But there was always the chance Szoke had cameras in place, watching him. If he was seen writing something, Szoke might burst in with those guards to seize Sandy's notes.

Then, as they say, the gig would be up.

So, instead, he stared at the wall and worked through it in his head.

How long did he have before Szoke discovered his lies?

The story itself was plausible. It fit the known facts. The critical weakness was the video. Brian's hacked in presence gave him access to the hotel security system. What had he seen? Could he tell Szoke the other bodyguard never left the room across from Maravilla's? Worse yet, that a woman and her daughter fled from Maravilla's room thirty seconds after

Sandy exited?

He'd have to be watching the hallway to have seen that, Sandy realized. And didn't it make more sense that he'd track Sandy's movements? That was the standard tactical procedure. So, it was possible Brian had seen nothing that might contradict Sandy's official version of events.

It was also possible the fire alarm canceled or rebooted the security network. Brian may have been forced out of the system, at least temporarily. This was part of the reason for his decision to hit the alarm in the first place, though the primary purpose was to provide Allison and her daughter camouflage in their escape.

Lita. The daughter's name was Lita.

Sandy was momentarily grateful he'd not seen the young girl's eyes. The eyes of the young man in Greece—Andrej, he reminded himself—still haunted him all these years later. Sure, he had spared the boy's life. But what life had he left the kid? One with the trauma of a murdered father. And now, he'd laid that same curse at the feet of Allison and Lita. At least he'd been spared from seeing the hurt in the child's eyes this time.

How long, he mused gain. *How long until Szoke knows? And what will he do then?*

The answer was simple and one Sandy didn't doubt. Szoke barely controlled his rage at Sandy earlier today when it came to going off plan in the slightest. The man had no tolerance for the realities of what occurred in the field. He'd become an absolutist when it came to protocol. The number one protocol for this little group was they did not exist. Maintaining that fiction required no witnesses whatsoever. They moved anonymously and did nothing memorable, so as to be invisible. Any witnesses became collateral damage. Szoke was brutally insistent on this point. If anything, his ardor had increased as the years passed.

In the past, Sandy had been more engaged in the planning

process. With a mind toward Szoke's rigidity regarding witnesses, Sandy influenced the structure of the ops plan in ways that minimized witnesses. His reasoning—that such an approach was quieter and therefore more effective—usually resonated with Szoke, who reluctantly accepted his suggestions and incorporated them. This minimized the amount of collateral damage Sandy was forced to cause. Usually those witnesses were hip deep in the dark activities that brought the mission target to Szoke's attention in the first place, so Sandy didn't feel especially bad about punching their tickets. But he always wondered what would happen if he came across another truly innocent witness.

As his relationship with Szoke grew more contentious, the agent-in-charge was less open to input from Sandy. For his part, Sandy's own bilious stance toward Szoke got in the way of a more strategic approach, such as giving his thoughts to Carter instead. Variations on the plan coming from her would always be more palatable to Szoke.

If this tenuous venture were to continue, Sandy knew he'd need to be smarter.

If.

Would Szoke discover his lies? Sandy thought so. If that happened, their already frayed interactions would fracture completely. Perhaps it would spell an end to the operation, at least for him.

Sandy was at peace with that. If it meant Janet continued to live her life, he didn't mind if the rest of his was spent in a cell somewhere. Despite Szoke's threats, he didn't believe it would be in a dark hole at some black site. Nor did he think Szoke would target Janet. Not if it was Szoke who pulled the plug. In the end, it was all too much effort for no tangible gain. People may act out of spite, but bureaucracies were ultimately practical. Szoke had proven himself every inch a bureaucrat.

No, Sandy believed Janet would go on living while he'd

end up in a black site, almost certainly. Overall, though, the experience was unlikely to be much different than what he experienced between missions now. Less room, less movement, but otherwise much the same.

The only problem with this scenario was Allison and Lita. He thought of the two of them hiding at the motel even now. If Szoke discovered their existence, Sandy knew what he would do. Allison would be targeted for certain. Would they kill a thirteen-year-old girl, too?

Sandy didn't want to think so, but he wondered.

He needed a plan. Two plans, actually. One for knowing and, depending on what he discovered, a plan for doing.

9

"Sit down," Szoke told Carter. "We have a problem." Carter took the seat opposite Brian. Szoke sat at the head of the small conference table. "Where's Banks?" she asked.

"Never mind him," Szoke said. He motioned to Brian. The former cop-turned-technician hit a key on the laptop in front of him. The monitor behind Szoke flickered to life.

Carter looked up. The screen was split into multiple images, each displaying paused security footage from the hotel.

"We recorded the feed," Szoke said. "At least, until the alarm trigger interrupted the hack." He cast a slightly disapproving look toward Brian before returning his gaze to Carter. "Tell me what you see."

Szoke twirled his finger toward Brian, who tapped another key. Carter watched as the images sprang into motion. A cursor made rapid circles around the screen showing a hallway with a single Hispanic man posted near the end.

"The bodyguard," Brian explained needlessly. The cursor lighted on the door to the left. "Maravilla's suite."

Carter didn't answer, only watched as Banks appeared in the frame, dressed in the delivery uniform.

"Hola, amigo."

The sound of Banks's voice momentarily surprised her. She glanced at Brian.

"I synced the comms recording to the video feed," he explained.

Carter nodded and returned her gaze to the screen.

"*Tengo una entrega,*" Banks said. His pronunciation was horrible, but rang true to her ear. More importantly, it provided a distraction as he drew closer to the man. Banks might be a pain in the ass, but she had to admit he was skilled at what he did.

"Sorry," Banks said, slipping into English with a Texan accent. "*Mi Español* ain't so good."

The bodyguard finally reacted. He stepped forward and held out a hand to stop Banks. He said something in rapid Spanish but she didn't pick it up. The earpiece's mic range was purposefully limited so the wearer's voice was the primary sound that came through.

The envelope fell from Banks's hands. Another distraction. Things moved quickly after that. Banks slid closer to the bodyguard. Three quick blows stunned the man. A moment later and Banks had drawn a knife from his boot and grasped the man from behind, stabbing him.

"What do you see?" Szoke prompted her.

"He's efficient."

"And?"

"Everything is going according to plan," she said.

"And what did you hear?"

Carter considered the question as she watched Banks prop the man against the wall and quickly search him. "Minor scuffling sounds," she said. "Like something from a cop's body camera."

In her peripheral vision, she saw Szoke nod.

On the screen, Banks found what he was looking for. The video resolution wasn't high enough for her to see the item he took but she knew it had to be the keycard for the door to Maravilla's suite.

Banks drew his pistol and pressed an ear to the door.

"Hear anything?" Szoke asked.

"No."

"Neither do I. But I wonder if he did."

Carter wasn't sure of Szoke's point. She continued to watch the video feed. After listening briefly at the door, Banks said, "Going in" and used the keycard to open the lock. He slid past the open door and into the suite.

The camera didn't follow. Carter stared at the door as it snapped shut behind Banks. She listened, wondering if the audio feed was still running.

After a second or two, a man's voice called out, sounding very distant. The single word was muffled and unintelligible, again due the acoustic settings of the earpiece. She squinted and listened harder.

Whatever the man said, Banks didn't answer. A few seconds passed, then the voice came again.

"Manuel?"

This time she picked out the word. She'd barely processed it as a name, likely that of the bodyguard, when the same voice snarled something in Spanish, followed by a series of concussive reports accented by the clacking of the metal slide action of Banks's weapon.

Carter glanced at Szoke, who was watching her expectantly. She didn't know why. So far, Banks had been swift and sure in his infiltration. Now, it sounded as if he'd taken out the target. Why was Szoke—

"*No!*"

The voice was loud and shrill, even when dampened by the mechanics of the earpiece. Carter's eyes narrowed. She listened to the silence of the feed for one beat, then two. Suddenly, there was rustling sound, similar to when Banks had taken out the guard.

Similar but different, she thought.

A Hard Favored Death

Then silence.

Szoke watched her while he twirled his index finger to Brian. The images on the screen twitched as the tech fast-forwarded. "Almost sixty seconds," he told Carter. "Then this."

Brian returned the video to regular speed. Banks exited Maravilla's suite, now dressed in a business suit. He walked with purpose but avoided looking hurried.

"Notice no second bodyguard in the hallway?" Szoke asked.

Carter nodded distractedly while she watched. When Banks left the camera range for the hallway, Brian used his cursor to call attention to which feed had coverage. Carter watched Banks push open the door to the stairwell and disappear.

The cursor moved back to the hallway where Maravilla's suite was located.

"In about eight seconds, the video feed will be interrupted because Banks pulled the fire alarm," Szoke said. "But pay attention to the target's door."

Carter shifted back to the first camera feed. The cursor danced a slow circle around the door while Carter counted down silently in her head. When she reached two, she drew a sharp intake of breath.

The door to Maravilla's suite opened. A blond woman and a dark-haired girl stepped through. They made it only a few feet into the hallway when the image went to static.

I've seen them before.

It was the same woman and daughter she'd noticed walking away from the hotel while most everyone else was gawking. The woman had the same purposeful gait as Banks used, only it was unpracticed and therefore failed to appear casual.

"This is bad," Carter muttered.

"Yes," Szoke said. He pointed to the screen. "Turns out our intel on the mistress part wasn't all bad, though."

Congratulations, she thought sarcastically, but held her tongue.

"What's your assessment?" Szoke asked, though his tone had an element of a demand to it.

Carter turned to him. "You don't need my assessment. The situation is plain. Banks left witnesses."

"Yes, but why?"

"Let's ask him."

Szoke waved a hand. "He's grown petulant. I don't expect him to be honest."

"He might surprise you."

Szoke frowned. "Little to nothing surprises me anymore, Lori."

Carter didn't like it when he used her first name. It was a relic from the person she used to be, tossed out by a man who wasn't the same one she used to know. She preferred it when Szoke was officious and demanding. It wasn't pleasant but it was easier that way.

"Look," she said, "they were probably hiding somewhere in the bedroom or something."

"Then he did a shit search."

"Maybe they hid well."

"Or maybe he let them go."

"Either way, it's doubtful they saw anything." She pointed toward the screen. "Besides, you've got bigger problems. Once the cops get a look at this recording…" She trailed off as a sly, knowing smile appeared on Szoke's lips. He motioned toward Brian without looking at him.

"When I hacked in, I uploaded a virus," Brian explained. "It's set up to trigger when I break contact."

"What kind of virus?"

Brian's expression had a hint of pride in it when he answered her. "The kind that deletes all recordings."

"Deletes them? Couldn't a tech like you recover a deleted

file?"

"*Shreds* them," Brian corrected. "I should have been more specific. Unrecoverable."

"What about the cloud or whatever?"

Brian smirked and made a snipping motion with his first two fingers. "Completely gone, all the way to their previous system backup. And before you ask, they back up every twenty-four hours, at three a.m." He shook his head. "As far as the hotel is concerned, the video is gonzo."

Carter considered that. "So, unless one of the security personnel was watching it live..."

"They weren't," Brian confirmed. "One was in the lobby, the other in the breakroom."

She remembered hearing that during the mission. "Won't the missing files make the cops suspicious? It's awfully convenient with there being two bodies and all."

Brian glanced at Szoke for an answer.

"They'll blame the fire alarm for the glitch," the agent-in-charge said. "As for the bodies, it doesn't matter how suspicious the local police are. In a few hours, a combined unit of DEA and ICE agents will swoop in and take over the investigation."

"A cover-up, then," said Carter. Despite her tenure as part of this shadow team, such subversions still left a bad taste in her mouth.

"Not at all," Szoke assured her. "The agents assigned will legitimately work the case. Their knowledge is compartmentalized."

"Meaning they don't know it was a hit carried out by their own government."

"*Meaning*," Szoke said, his voice tone taking on a slight menace, "they will play their role, unwitting or no."

Carter glanced away, feeling dirty inside. The idea that good men and women—people she once called colleagues—

would waste their noble efforts running down blind, dead-end alleys disgusted her. Szoke usually kept these details from her. Now she knew why.

"The investigation isn't our problem," Szoke continued. He pointed to Brian, who hit a key. A still image of the woman and her daughter exiting Maravilla's suite appeared on the screen. "She is."

"What's the solution?" Carter asked, dreading the answer.

"First we identify her, then we find her."

"Then what?"

Szoke stared at her impassively. "We find out what she saw."

"No shit," said Carter. "But it doesn't matter, does it? Because you'll never be convinced she didn't see Banks pump those bullets into Maravilla. You'll kill her just to be safe. You've done it before."

"*I* won't do anything," Szoke said mildly.

"Don't play word games with me. You'll have it done. She'll be executed."

"It's a possibility."

"What about the girl?"

Szoke peered at the screen. "That is a thornier question, isn't it?"

"It shouldn't be. She's a child."

"That depends."

"Depends? On what?"

"Whether she's above or below the Escobar line."

"The *what?*"

A shadow of a smile lighted on Szoke's mouth. "Not a baseball fan, Lori?"

"What the hell does baseball have to do with this?"

"In baseball," Szoke explained, "the Mendoza line is a batting average of .200, so-named for a player named Mario Mendoza." He leaned forward slightly, as if explaining an historical importance to her. "Hitting below the Mendoza line represents a threshold for failure for a batter. It's a line of demarcation. An unofficial one, but it gives a manager a benchmark when considering his options concerning whether to send a player down to the minors or not."

Carter stared at him. "I have no idea why you are telling me this. We're talking about killing civilians and you bring up *baseball?*"

"Stay with me a moment," said Szoke, clearly enjoying his professorial moment. "In Colombia, during the Pablo Escobar era in Medellin, the cartels had to make difficult decisions about who lived and who died. All of this was according to their own codes of conduct and included children who were either witnesses or might potentially grow up to seek revenge for a parent's death. But where do you draw the line when it comes to killing a minor?"

Carter drew in a heavy breath and let it out. She muttered an expletive.

Szoke continued, ignoring her reaction. "Do you kill a baby? A two-year-old? Of course not. The cartels were ruthless but not inhuman. No one acted in those instances. But what about a fifteen-year-old, especially a male? They didn't hesitate there, either. But, again, where is the line? What age?"

"I can't believe you are quoting cartel ethics to me," Carter muttered. She wanted to add how it only confirmed to her how messed up the entire situation was, but she knew that would only invite trouble.

"Their ethics are actually quite utilitarian," Szoke told her. "And, amongst the cartels, often democratic in their formation. The rumor is it was Escobar himself who set the age at twelve. Under twelve, the child was spared. Twelve and older, he or she was treated as an adult."

"And *that* is how you intend to handle this?" Carter demanded. "According to the ethical code of a criminal organization that murders hundreds of people—no, probably thousands—every year? *That's* your moral compass?"

"There's a certain logic behind it," said Szoke.

"It's a logic I'm sure Hitler and Stalin would both have found entirely reasonable."

"Let's not be hyperbolic."

Carter gaped at him. "You're talking about murdering a child. Not only that, an uninvolved American citizen on our own soil. If anything, I'm underreacting here."

"The woman is hardly uninvolved," Szoke said dismissively.

"What about the daughter?" Carter asked.

Szoke didn't answer.

Carter shook her head. "No. You can't do it."

Szoke stared at her, that impassive expression returning. "Don't be naïve, Lori. I can do anything that needs to be done." He turned to Brian. "Now, go get Banks. Let's see what lie he chooses to tell us."

10

As soon as he realized both Brian and Carter were summoned to meet with Szoke without him, Sandy acted. He left his room and headed down the hall to where Brian was quartered. The door was locked, which didn't surprise him. The wide-eyed, good-natured image Brian tried to portray hid what Sandy knew resided beneath—a traitor.

He moved to Carter's and found the door standing open. This did surprise him. As both an FBI agent and a woman, he'd expected her to put a premium on privacy.

Perhaps it was a trap. Sandy considered the possibility but rejected it. To what end? Lure him into her room? And then what?

He went inside.

Her laptop was open on the small military-issue desk. The screen was dark. Sandy touched the space bar and was met with Carter's virtual desktop. Unsurprisingly, it was tidy, with only a half dozen or so icons.

He didn't bother with the ones he knew accessed government files. Those would be password-protected. He'd once had access to those databases himself, albeit briefly. Szoke began winnowing down the range of his allowed information, compartmentalizing it more and more as time passed. For the last several years, he'd been limited to the same level of Internet access as any civilian.

Or so he'd thought.

Earlier, when he ran the name of Janet Griggs on his own laptop, he realized his web connection was being filtered. The search return included all sorts of unrelated Janets and unrelated Griggs, both real and fictional, but not Janet herself. It was as if she didn't exist.

Sandy knew that was wrong. Even someone who strove for peak personal privacy left some kind of an online footprint. It was impossible not to do so in this day and age. Even if a person limited their own activities, posts from their friends and family pinged them. Plus, Janet had been a realtor. He'd seen the website for her agency, years ago, along with photos of her and her business partner. Now, if the internet were to be believed, neither she nor that agency existed any longer.

He could believe the agency shut down. What he couldn't believe was no trace of it ever existing remained online.

No, his access was being blocked somehow.

He'd found her name in listings claiming to have phone numbers and addresses—all for a cost, of course—but none of those Janet Griggs resembled his Janet. The same happened when he tried to find her via social media platforms. Plenty of profiles for a Janet Griggs, but none of them *his* Janet.

How long had Szoke been filtering his online access? And to what degree? Were stories referencing the political fallout from their missions blocked as well?

More importantly, *why* was he narrowing Sandy's access to information? What did Szoke fear he would learn?

He needed to find out.

In Carter's room, Sandy called up the search engine she had on her desktop. He was immediately met with a password prompt.

He cursed. So much for that.

He stared at the blinking cursor for a few moments. Getting her password was impractical, but perhaps he could ask

Carter to access the web for him. Their relationship didn't approach friendship but there was a grudging respect that had slowly developed between them, if for no other reason than they seemed to be the only two people whose involvement in this endeavor was a reluctant one.

In the end, though, he suspected Carter would act to protect her own interests. That meant not crossing Szoke.

Sandy rose from the desk chair. Once in the hallway, he headed back toward his barracks room. He knew he needed a plan, because it was only a matter of time before—

"Sandy!" Brian Moore called out to him from the end of the hallway. The small man trotted his direction. "Mark wants you."

Sandy eyed him coldly. "Now?"

Brian appeared hurt at the reaction, a response he somehow still managed to conjure up despite the fact that Sandy's treatment of him had ranged from hostile to frigid for the entirety of their time in this enforced assignment. Sandy had long ago decided the man had to be an optimist.

"Yeah, he said now."

"What for?"

"Round two of the debrief, I guess," Brian said, but Sandy heard the shift in his voice and saw the way his eyes cut away briefly.

Sandy stood. *He's lying. Szoke knows about Allison and Lita.* "All right," he said. "Let's go."

He'd expected a bit of showmanship from the CIA agent. It seemed to Sandy that Szoke had devolved over the past decade into a man who clung to pettiness as a way to cope with his own version of captivity. Sandy guessed the way Szoke treated him and the others gave him the illusion he wasn't every bit as trapped by this situation as they were.

Yet, Szoke surprised him. Instead of putting on some grand charade, the man simply asked him, "Tell me the truth about what happened in that hotel room."

Sandy maintained an impassive expression. He felt no qualms about the lie he'd told before, nor about repeating it here. "I told you what happened."

"We know you lied," Szoke insisted. "We have the video."

Sandy curled his lip doubtfully. "What video?"

Szoke waved impatiently at Brian who hit a key on his laptop. The black screen came to life, showing the hallway of the hotel. Sandy watched carefully. He saw himself exit Maravilla's room and stride away. That exposed his lie about encountering the second bodyguard. A few moments later, he heard the trilling of the fire alarm.

"You doctored the video?" he asked.

"We synced the audio, that's all. Keep watching."

Sandy waited. Before long, the door to Maravilla's suite opened. Allison and Lita stepped through. After a few steps into the hallway, the screen dissolved suddenly into static.

"How do you explain that?" Szoke demanded.

Sandy shrugged. "They must have been hiding."

"You didn't sweep the place?"

"Briefly. I didn't look under beds or in closets. There wasn't time."

"Seemed like you were in that room for plenty of time," Szoke said, his tone accusing.

Sandy glanced at Carter, who was watching him with an expression he couldn't read. He had little doubt the former FBI agent was as suspicious of him as Szoke, however.

"I was inside long enough to find Maravilla, struggle with him, and make the hit." Sandy kept his voice even. "I did a brief sweep of the suite while I tore off my cover clothes. Then I left."

"That's interesting, because it sounded to me like there

was a scream on the tape." Szoke stared at him, his eyes hard.

"A woman's voice, or a girl's, screaming *No!*"

Sandy shrugged. "The TV was on. Maybe you heard that."

Szoke scoffed. "I doubt it."

"Doubt all you want. I told you what happened. If you want to weave some sort of Q-Anon conspiracy theory about it, that's your decision."

"Don't gaslight me, Banks." Szoke jabbed a finger at him, then shifted it toward the static-filled screen. "Something happened in that room other than what you reported. I know it. You don't want to admit it? Fine. I'll deal with you and your dependability issue after I've cleaned up this mess."

"What's to clean up? Maravilla is dead."

"You left *witnesses!*" Szoke snapped at him.

"If I didn't see them, they didn't see me."

Szoke shook his head slowly. "I'd call you naïve if the truth wasn't that you are just a bad liar."

It was Sandy's turn to scoff. "I'm the farthest thing from naïve. Trust me."

"That's the problem. I *can't* trust you. You're lying to me and I know it."

"I'm not lying."

"I'm supposed to believe you didn't see this woman and her child inside that suite?"

"I didn't."

"Bullshit. But let's say for a microsecond that's true. It isn't, but I'll entertain the idea for the sake of discussion." He leaned forward slightly and spoke in a slow, deliberate voice. "It still doesn't mean they didn't see you."

"If I didn't see them—" Sandy began, but Szoke cut him off.

"Oh, stop. You sound like a child covering himself with a blanket." He mimed a child's tone. "If I cover my head, the monsters won't see me." Szoke smirked. "You hear yourself?

It's ridiculous."

And there's the showmanship I was expecting.

"This whole conversation is ridiculous." Sandy glared coldly at him. "You think I'm lying? Then bench me. Or throw me in that hole you keep threatening me with. I don't care."

"Deep down, I think you *do* care."

"You don't want to know what I think deep down," Sandy told him. He motioned toward the static-filled screen. "They're not witnesses. They're bystanders who saw nothing."

Szoke eyed him carefully, his tongue pressing against his cheek while he did so. It was an odd tic, and one Sandy had only noticed developing over the past couple of years. Perhaps the cumulative weight of this long mission was getting to him, too.

"Do you remember your work in Nicaragua?" Szoke asked him. "From your time in the Army."

Sandy sat back slightly. He tried to remember back to his first conversations with Danforth, the mastermind behind this unit. The man had known everything about him. Not just what he'd done in Spokane as a vigilante ex-cop, but his previous identities as well. That included his military service.

If Danforth knew the details, surely Szoke did, too. There seemed to be little use to deny anything. Even so, Sandy didn't like the idea of giving in. "I was never stationed in Nicaragua," he said.

"Don't be pedantic. I know that. But you were stationed in Honduras." He smiled slightly. "*Keegan.*"

Sandy didn't react to the name, though it was as familiar to him as the face he wore for the entirety of his military service. Sergeant Keegan Anthony Fuller, detailed to Honduras for a special operation that, not unlike Danforth's shadow unit, did not officially exist.

"I can't talk about that," Sandy said evenly. "It's classified."

Szoke laughed. "I have a security clearance. In fact, it's so high the existence of this level of clearance is itself classified."

He sounds like a braggy fifteen-year-old.

"Then you know, regardless of clearance level, there's also the compartmentalization factor." It was Sandy's turn to smile, but his was cold and humorless. "The need to know."

"You have no idea what my need to know is or isn't," Szoke told him.

"You're right. I don't. Which is why I can't talk about whatever it is you're referring to."

Szoke waved away his objections. "It doesn't matter. My point is all from open-source material anyway."

"You have a point?" Sandy jabbed.

"I always have a point."

"Then get to it."

Szoke cocked his head mockingly. "Why? You have someplace important to be, Banks? A hot date? Or just can't wait to get back to staring at some crack on the ceiling in your barracks room?"

"Even that would be better than listening to your bullshit."

Szoke's eyes narrowed. "You really are probing for my limits, aren't you? Well, get ready to find out what they are. *Soon.*"

Sandy shrugged. "You said there was a point?"

"My *point* is your little operation in Nicaragua that went bad ended up going much worse in the years that followed. Oliver North and all that?"

"That had nothing to do with me."

"Bullshit. It had everything to do with you. *We* were able to keep your operation, and a few others, from getting pulled into the shit show, that's all."

"Good for you."

"It was good for you, too. Oh, I know you were already Sandy Banks by then. Probably still in a police uniform and not a full-fledged vigilante yet, but you probably felt safe and far away from what happened in Central America. But if we hadn't done our job, your cover wouldn't have held. You might have found yourself in front of Congress right alongside the good Colonel."

"I doubt that very much."

"That's because you're ignorant of how the larger world works."

"So what are you saying?" Sandy asked. "I should be grateful to you?"

"Yes," Szoke said adamantly. "You should. But that's not what I'm trying to explain to you here. My point is your failed mission in that jungle and the trouble it caused—specifically, the witnesses you left behind—is where the entire operation began to unravel. Your mission never came fully to light, but its failure still provided part of the catalyst that brought down the entire enterprise. The end result was not pretty. A presidency was almost toppled. We're talking huge stakes here."

"Why the history lesson?" Sandy asked. "Are you trying to draw some sort of parallel here?"

"You don't see it?"

"Frankly, no. A cartel member was killed at an El Paso hotel. Not an uncommon event, except it happened on American soil. It'll be a news item for a day or two, and then disappear into the mists of the Internet." He resisted adding it seemed lots of things disappeared on the Internet these days. Cueing Szoke that he knew his own access had been curtailed served no purpose other than the immediate joy of further tweaking the bureaucrat.

"Except there were witnesses," Szoke said. "Witnesses who saw a white American male do the killing." He shook his head slowly, meaningfully. "It's a stray string that could easily be the first to be pulled. The one that eventually undoes the entire enterprise. And this one makes your mission in Nicaragua look as harmless as a boy scout camp-out in comparison."

"They didn't see anything."

Szoke drew in a deep breath and let it out. "You're lying, Banks. I know it and you know it. So now I have to decide how to handle that. But first, I have to clean up your mistake."

"I told you, they didn't see me."

"It doesn't matter. Even if you were telling me the truth, I can't take the chance. There's too much at stake."

Sandy motioned toward Brian. "Bring up the video again," he ordered. "Stop when the two of them show up."

Brian glanced at Szoke. When the agent-in-charge didn't object, Brian did as Sandy bade him. A few moments later, the hallway filled the screen again. The image of Sandy in a business suit walking confidently down the hall was followed by the door opening and both Allison and Lita exiting the suite. Brian paused the feed, freezing them in place.

Sandy stared up at the screen for a second or two, then turned back to Szoke. "That girl is, what? Thirteen? Fourteen?"

"She looks at least twelve," Szoke said, a hint of a sly smile touching his lips. Sandy was struck with the strange but fitting comparison of a sexual predator announcing his intended victim had achieved puberty.

"At least twelve?" His stomach clenched. "So what? She's a child. A child who saw nothing. What are you going to do? Kill her mother, then her?"

"You don't have to worry about that," Szoke said. "As I said, I'll clean up your mess."

"Don't do it," Sandy said. "They didn't see me."

Szoke shrugged. "You can go. We're finished here. We leave for home base in the morning." He pointed at Sandy. "I'll deal with you once we're back there."

"Don't do it," Sandy said again. He glanced at Carter, who he'd almost forgotten was there. She sat as still as stone, discomfort etched on her face. Sandy swung his gaze back to

Szoke. "You don't have to do anything. They saw nothing. They couldn't have."

Szoke scoffed. Sandy could hear the deep-rooted condescension in the sound. "I don't know what world you live in, Banks, but it's clearly not the real one. Jesus, you're like some kid worried about his ant farm while the house is on fire." Szoke tapped his own chest. "I'm the fireman in this scenario. And I have larger concerns."

Sandy's jaw tightened. He had held out little hope he'd convince Szoke but he had to try. Now, though, it seemed like silence was his best option.

He stood and left the room.

11

Lori Carter watched Banks walk out of the room, shutting the door behind him with enough force it would have slammed if the pneumatic hinges hadn't engaged.

"That went about as I expected," Szoke said. He let out a long sigh and looked over at Carter. "When we get back to base, we're going to have to decide how to handle him."

Carter didn't like the sound of that, but there was another matter more pressing. "You don't really intend on going through with it, do you?"

"Decommissioning Banks? I don't see another choice."

Carter doubted Szoke's word. She was almost certain he had no intention of giving up an asset like Banks so easily. Maybe someday, but not yet. But that was a problem for a different day. She had a more pressing issue to address in the moment.

"Not Banks," she said. "The woman and her daughter."

"Oh." Szoke shrugged. "Nasty business, to be sure. But it is a compromise in the operation that must be terminated."

"Terminated? Call it what it is, Mark – murder."

Szoke scowled. "What we do isn't murder."

"What is it, then?"

"What we do isn't murder," he repeated firmly. "We're soldiers, Lori."

"Last time I checked, we're not at war with Mexico."

"Don't be naïve," he said.

You like throwing that word around, don't you?

"This *is* war," Szoke continued, "if an undeclared one. Not on Mexico, per se, but on all of those enemies within her borders who pose a threat to our national security. You don't think drug cartels fit that criteria?"

"That's not the point."

"It is exactly the point. We're at war. And, in case you weren't aware, in war, soldiers kill the enemy. That is their primary purpose." He narrowed his eyes at her. "Jesus, when did you get so squeamish? How many ops have we run in the last ten-plus years? How many of those had unscheduled terminations?"

Carter ignored his questions. "Fine," she allowed, her voice laced with sarcasm. "Let's agree we're in some secret war against all the bad guys in the world. We're the last bastion of freedom or whatever. Even if that's so, *this* killing still doesn't make sense."

"I don't know that I like your tone, Agent Carter," Szoke growled. "Or your sentiment."

Carter leaned back. By using her former title, Szoke was once again emphasizing their relative authority and position in this shadow entity. The prudent response from her would be to withdraw her objections now, before she found herself alongside Banks, facing "decommission." She wasn't certain what that entailed, but she had a few ideas. None of them were good.

Even so, the words tumbled out of her mouth before she could stop them. "You know what? You sound more and more like Danforth every day. Your mouth moves, and I hear his words coming out. It's like he's got his hand up your ass and is making your jaw flap."

Szoke's face reddened. His jaw tightened. He shot a glance to Brian, who stared on in shocked amazement. "You are dismissed, Mr. Moore," Szoke said, his words clipped with barely controlled rage.

Brian rose and hustled from the room. Once again, the door bounced languidly on the pneumatic hinge before easing shut. Szoke waited for the clicking sound before he turned back to Carter.

"Don't disrespect me in front of other members of the team," he growled. "In fact, don't disrespect me at all."

"I was stating a fact."

"You were stating an *opinion*," Szoke snapped, his voice rising to a shout. "And I didn't ask for your fucking opinion!"

Carter shifted backward slightly at the sudden outburst, but otherwise held her ground. When she spoke, she kept her voice calm, trying to come in below his anger. "You said we're at war. Fine. You said we're soldiers and soldiers kill the enemy during war. Also fine. But these aren't enemy combatants. They're civilian bystanders, not aiding and abetting."

"They are witnesses. They represent a threat. I already explained this to Banks. You and I talked about it before that. So, are you being dense or purposefully defiant right now?"

Carter remained quiet for a few moments. Then she said, "Mark, it's a *child*. A woman and her *child*."

"I recognize that. I don't relish what must be done."

"Then don't do it."

"I don't have that luxury," said Szoke. "The need for success—and continued secrecy—of this unit outweighs individual concerns. What we do is critical. You hold Danforth in contempt, I know. But, trust me, he isn't sending us to the grocery store for milk here. The missions he assigns are crucial. Lives are saved. Terrorist acts are thwarted. Wars are averted. This is high-level shit that goes beyond you, me, Banks, or anyone else." He paused, then shrugged. "It's unfortunate, but these two people are collateral damage."

"Not yet, they're not."

"They represent a compromise to the op and all compromises must be eliminated."

"That's not the only option. It can't be."

"What do you want me to do?" he asked. "You know this is too great a risk not to act."

"Take them into protective custody," she urged. "It's not like this operation lacks the funding for it."

"Oh, sure," Szoke replied, his voice laced with sarcasm. "Great idea. We'll snatch them up and send them to live on a nice farm somewhere. How would that be? Maybe the kid could play with all the family dogs people have sent there over the years." He gave his head a shake. "Newsflash—that farm doesn't exist. Not for old dogs and not for people who see shit they shouldn't. You know why? Because it *can't* exist. Because, as far as the outside world is concerned, *we* can't exist." He paused a beat, then added, "And witnesses can't exist, either."

Carter scrambled for some sort of argument that would dissuade him. "What if this gets out?"

"You're making my case for me. The need for secrecy—"

"Not the operation against Maravilla," Carter interrupted. "The fact government assassins murdered a mother and her daughter?"

"It won't get out," Szoke assured her. His eyes narrowed further. "Unless what you're saying constitutes a threat."

"Of course not. I'm not a traitor, and what's more, I'm not stupid. But think about it for a second. In every government scandal that's happened over the past hundred years, it wasn't the actual act that did the most damage. It was the cover-up that followed that landed people in the most trouble and, worse yet, eroded even more public trust in government. Think Watergate, or even what you threw up in Banks's face earlier—Iran/Contra."

Szoke shook his head. "Your argument is ass backwards. Eliminating the witnesses ends the threat. You know I'm right."

"Mark, they're innocent."

He scoffed. "Come on, Lori. This woman was banging a lieutenant in a Mexican drug cartel. That makes her far from innocent in my book."

So I'm Lori again. He was giving her whiplash with this. Still, she took the slightest bit of hope in his use of her first name, wondering if there was still a chance to convince him to forgo his plans.

"What about her daughter?" Carter asked softly. "At least, she *is* innocent, right?"

Szoke considered, then reluctantly nodded. "I'd say so. Probably."

The spark of hope flared in Carter's chest. "Then—"

"The child is collateral damage," Szoke interrupted, his tone now dismissive. "As I said, it happens in every war. Stray rounds fly through walls, bombs miss their target, whatever. It's unavoidable."

Carter was crestfallen. The hard look on Szoke's face made it clear he was resolute on this path. Nothing she could say would dissuade him. All she could do now was appear to accept his decision.

She let her shoulders collapse and sighed. With an effort, she was able to force her eyes to mist over with tears. "All right," she whispered huskily, and glanced away. "All right."

Szoke watched her for a while. Then he said, "I'm sorry it has to be this way."

The conciliatory tone in his voice sounded wooden to her ears but she nodded anyway. "So am I," she said.

"It has to be done."

She swallowed. "I know."

"Good," Szoke replied. He waited another beat, then added, "And then, after, we need to deal with Banks."

Yes, we do, Carter thought. *Yes, we do.*

12

Will they kill me?

Sandy let the question roll around in his mind as he lay on the bottom bunk in his stark barracks room. The facility was a step down from the small base at which they usually operated. Sandy knew their home base was located somewhere in northern Idaho. He probably wasn't supposed to know this fact but, over the years, he'd picked up more than enough clues to deduce the location. Besides, Szoke wasn't so tight-fisted with information early on. The man had let more slip back then than he did now.

Not that it mattered where "home" was. The secrecy from the public of both the location and the existence of the base was key. He found it ironic that, for a decade, he'd operated from a black site less than an hour's drive from where he'd spent all those years as one of the Horsemen. Years of dispensing a form of vigilante justice he knew was legally wrong and yet still struggled to call morally wrong. The men he'd killed over those years in Spokane were all unquestionably bad men. They'd been thoroughly investigated. The facts were all present. Only a technicality of law or a failed procedure by the police or the prosecutor had resulted in their unjustified freedom.

They deserved the death that found them. Probably deserved it much sooner than it actually came at his hands. And, while their deaths left a psychic weight on him, it had been a weight he'd been able to bear for a long time. Right up until the end, in fact.

His mind flashed to the final life he'd taken as a Horseman. A surge of guilt fell over him. Kelly Merchant. *She* had been innocent. He'd been tricked into the act by someone he'd trusted but that didn't change the fact that she hadn't deserved to die. Her death was a mistake.

His mistake.

One he never wanted to make again.

Sandy recalled the panic-stricken eyes of Allison in the hotel suite. Her daughter's face pressed into the crook of her neck, sobbing in fear. Neither of them deserved to die, either. But he was convinced that was the fate Szoke had planned for them. The man had been eminently clear on that point.

I have to stop it.

But how? He knew his own run as an assassin was likely over. Once they returned to Idaho, he'd be transferred into a prison somewhere. Perhaps it'd be a black hole like Szoke threatened, but more likely it'd be a federal prison under a false name. Or maybe they'd revive the Sandy Banks identity. Throw him in federal prison and let it leak he used to be a police officer. Let nature take its path.

Szoke might not even wait for the return trip. Sandy half-expected to hear the tramp of feet on the tiled floor of the hallway at any moment. A trio of guards to escort him to an SUV with darked out windows, and then to whatever fate awaited him.

He could escape. He didn't know exactly how at this moment, but he knew he could. Escape or die trying. Either outcome was better than rotting in a cell for the remainder of his life.

But there was also Janet. Both Danforth and Szoke made no bones about what would happen to her if he refused to carry out his missions. The full weight of the federal government would fall upon her and her family.

It still might, but Sandy thought, if he accepted the sentence Szoke and Danforth meted out, Janet might be spared. Hell, it was even possible he was engaged in catastrophic thinking at the moment. Szoke may yet take another run at "taming" him, wiping out his resistance and so-called insolence over a stretch of weeks back in Idaho.

Sandy thought it was possible. He was a tool for them. A valuable and effective tool, at that. Szoke and Danforth were unlikely to throw that away easily. An attempt at rehabilitation would be their first inclination.

Then again, maybe his departure would mark the dissolution of this team. If that occurred, Brian would be destined for a jail cell, no doubt, but Szoke and Carter could return to some semblance of a normal life. Did Szoke secretly hope for that outcome?

Sandy stared up at the wire frame of the bed above his, considering the question. Was Szoke searching for a way to usher in the change, to hurry it along? Somehow, he doubted it. Carter might welcome a release but Szoke seemed to have warmed to his task after the first year or so. He clearly liked who he was now and what he did. Worse yet, he truly believed in it.

In any war, Sandy knew, the zealots were the last to surrender, if they gave in at all.

Besides, what was to stop Danforth from reconstituting the team with new members? Nothing, Sandy realized. He might be an effective tool but he was far from the only person with his skill set. There might not be many who they could also blackmail into keeping on such a tight leash, but he felt certain Danforth was resourceful enough to find someone. For all he knew, other teams existed and operated independent of this one. Where the federal government was concerned, he'd long ago learned not to discount any possibility.

He returned to the main question—what awaited him? Rehabilitation or incarceration?

Sandy shook his head. It didn't matter what Szoke chose to do with him. Neither option helped Allison or Lita now.

I could get out, he thought again. *I know where they are. I could get to them first.*

Maybe he could. But doing so condemned Janet and her family. The reason he was still here, still doing these missions, was to keep her safe.

That's not the only reason, a voice deep inside him whispered. *Don't kid yourself.*

Sandy let that thought simmer for a few moments. Was it true? Sandy knew the threat of prison kept Brian fully engaged in these missions. It was at least partially so for him, as well. Throw in Janet's well-being as hostage, and that was more than enough leverage to keep him in line.

Wasn't it?

Maybe. But no one held a Sword of Damocles over his head in Spokane when he was one of the Horsemen. There, he took solace in knowing he was distributing justice. He was a willing member of that team, all the way up to the end. Was that really any different than what Danforth was doing here?

Sandy pushed the thought away and focused on his immediate problem. It was a lady or the tiger scenario, wasn't it? A choice devoid of any good options. Save Janet and her family or save Allison and Lita. No matter which door he chose, suffering and death occurred.

Did Janet's potential suffering outweigh Allison and Lita's lives? He didn't like to think so, but his own heart got in the way of his thinking.

But I can't just let them die.

He heard footfalls in the hallway approaching his door. His eyes narrowed and he sat up on the edge of the bed. If they were coming for him, he'd have to make his decision quickly.

Once they got him into handcuffs—

But the steps were singular and lighter than the boots a soldier might wear. He doubted it would be Szoke, but it might be Brian, either acting as messenger again or once more trying to bridge the chasm between the two of them. He seemed to desperately want to return to a time when they were like brothers.

That would never happen. But Sandy let him try. It gave the man something to do.

A light knock came at the door.

"It's open," he called.

The door swung open and Lori Carter appeared in the doorway, alone. Her expression was resolute. She stared at him for a few moments, saying nothing. Sandy returned her gaze.

Finally, she said, "Come with me."

Sandy didn't move. Had Szoke sent Carter to escort him on the first stage of his journey to prison? Perhaps march him to the pair of guards who were posted in the lobby and turn him over? Somehow, he doubted it. "Where are you taking me?"

"To my room," Carter said. "Let's go."

Sandy stared at her, trying to discern her purpose. Carter reflected back nothing but determination. When he didn't get up from his chair, she repeated her order.

"Let's go."

Carter turned and left. Sandy waited another beat, then rose to his feet and followed.

Sandy hesitated at the door to Carter's room. She stopped once inside, crossing her arms. When she noticed his reluctance, she motioned him inside with a jerk of her head.

He stepped across the threshold. "What is it?"

She worked her jaw, glancing down at the floor. "You know what he has planned?"

"Szoke? Yeah."

"Say it, so I know we're on the same page."

"He's going to send someone to kill that woman and her daughter."

Carter drew in a deep breath, nodding. "That's right."

"Is it you?" Sandy asked her.

Carter looked at him sharply. "No! I'd never do it."

"Somebody will, though."

"Somebody will," she agreed.

They stood in silence for a few moments. Then Carter stepped past him and closed the door. Sandy waited, unsure what to expect.

"We need to talk," Carter said, once the door clicked shut.

Sandy put a finger to his lips. With his opposite hand, he pointed up and twirled it slowly.

"If we were back at base, I'd be worried about that," Carter said. She paused, then added, "I'd be sure of it, in fact. But we were originally only supposed to be here for a couple of hours. I don't think they thought to bug the place."

Sandy cocked his head and gave her a look of caution.

Carter ignored his warning and forged ahead. "I know you don't agree with what he's planning to do. You think it's wrong. So do I. We have to stop it."

Sandy watched her while she spoke. Everything in her manner told him she was being genuine. Yet, years of suspicion kept him wary.

"How are we supposed to do that?" he asked. "We're not on the op. And as soon as we get back to base—"

"Do you know where she is?" Carter asked.

Sandy leaned away slightly, lifting his chin and narrowing his eyes at her. "That's what this is about? Szoke sent you to interrogate me for intel?"

"No."

"What were his instructions? To trick me? Torture me? Or were you supposed to try to seduce me, if necessary?"

"Oh, please," Carter scoffed. "Get over yourself." She pointed at him. "I brought you here because we're both still human enough to believe a woman doesn't deserve to die simply because she was in the wrong room at the wrong time."

"With the wrong person," Sandy added.

"Even that. And her daughter certainly doesn't deserve to be murdered alongside her just because she's above the so-called Escobar line."

"The what?"

She waved her hand. "It doesn't matter. It's some arbitrary bullshit Szoke and his ilk use to justify their actions. Point is, I'm talking to you now because we're on the same side with this. I don't want them hurt and neither do you."

"If you care so much," Sandy said, "why don't you do something about it? You have way more freedom than I do."

She nodded grimly. "I could probably get off base," she agreed. "But where would I go? I don't know where these two are. I don't even know *who* they are yet, although Szoke has Brian and the gang working on that. They might have identified them already. But I'm not in on that op. I'd be playing catch-up the entire way." She pointed at Sandy. "You know where they are. I know you do."

Sandy didn't react. "Even if I did, I wouldn't tell you."

"I know. You think I'm trying to trick you. That I'm doing Szoke's bidding."

"You're not?"

"No. But we don't have enough time for me to convince you. Once Szoke figures out who this woman and her daughter are, how long before he sends his goons to take care of business?"

"His goons?" Sandy mused. He shook his head in disgust.

"*We're* Szoke's goons, too, you know."

"Fine," she snapped. "I'm not here to argue semantics. He has other teams for other purposes. Where we might be the scalpel, he has others that act as a sledgehammer. That's who he'll send."

Sandy considered that for a moment. Then he nodded. "You're probably right. He said as much in our meeting."

"He said even more in the meeting before that," Carter told him. "And after you left." Her gaze bored into him. "We have to get you out of here so you can reach those two before that sledgehammer unit does. Take them somewhere safe."

He eyed her suspiciously. "You help me do that, you know what happens, right?"

Her jaw was set. "I'll deal with those consequences when they come."

"Let's say I trust you, just for the sake of discussion," Sandy said. "And that I know how to find them before the hit team does." He turned over his hands. "What can I do? You know the leverage Szoke has on me."

"About that..." Carter motioned toward her laptop. "Take a seat."

Sandy hesitated, then settled into the desk chair. He didn't reach for the keyboard, however. He kept his eyes on Carter.

She returned his gaze evenly. "I figured out a while ago they must be limiting your search access. You probably suspect why that is, but here's your chance to confirm it." She turned over her hand and waved it toward the laptop like a game show hostess presenting a prize.

Sandy turned to the computer. Gingerly, he reached out and typed in Janet's name followed by "Nashville" and hit enter.

The return was almost instantaneous. A full page of entries. Some of them were the same false Janets he'd seen on his own computer, but others were clearly his Janet. The real estate agency she worked for. Facebook.

He scrolled downward half a page and stopped. The title of the link blared at him.

Local Family of Five Dies in Tragic Accident.

Oh, no.

A tendril of despair sliced through Sandy's gut. Woodenly, he clicked on the link. He read the short article from a Nashville TV news station in disbelief as his chest tightened.

The names of the local family that perished last week in a single-car traffic accident have been released by police now that next of kin have been notified.

The family of Trent and Janet Griggs were on a skiing trip near Paoli Peaks, Indiana, when their Range Rover slid off an icy road and tumbled down a steep slope. In addition to the husband and wife, their adult children, Elizabeth, Trent Junior, and William, also did not survive the crash.

The individual words made sense but he struggled to believe their collective meaning.

Yet, he couldn't deny it.

Janet was dead.

For the first time in a long while, Sandy felt thrust back into real life. Visceral grief washed over him like a flash flood in the desert. The weight of a life unlived crashed down onto him. His shoulders slumped forward and his mouth opened in a silent groan.

She was the reason—the *entire* reason, he sometimes told himself— he'd kept on with this terrible charade. Every time Szoke ordered an op, he told himself that was why he geared up and went out. For her. To keep her and her family safe.

Sandy took in a hitching breath. Tears stung his eyes. He wiped at them before any could fall.

Get a grip. She's gone.

The coldness of the thought hurt almost as much as knowing the truth about Janet and her family. He stared at the words on the screen through eyes slightly blurred with unfallen tears, wanting to read more but knowing it didn't matter.

Who had he become?

What had he become?

Something less than who he was all those years ago, back when he was William Sutter, sitting on the sandy creek banks with her beside him. A world of promise awaited them both. He'd destroyed that promise for himself, of course, though not without cause. Others had played a role in his downfall, as well. But he took some measure of comfort in knowing he had at least kept his actions from stopping Janet from realizing her own promise.

She did, he reminded himself. *For years, she did.*

He wiped at his eyes again. Then he scrolled back up to see the date of the article.

It was three years ago.

Sandy's jaw tightened. Three years. For three goddamn years, he'd been running operations for Szoke and Danforth, doing the dark, dirty work for men in suits who never left the comfort of their homes and offices but decided who must die. He'd choked down those orders and he carried them out for one reason—Janet.

That's a lie, a voice whispered inside his mind. *And you know it.*

"Shut up," he murmured aloud.

"What?" Carter asked him, but Sandy barely heard her. The voice in his head grew louder. The genie was out of the bottle. He knew Janet wasn't the only reason he'd kept on. Sure, the threats Danforth made to destroy her life if Sandy didn't cooperate were the largest part of why he'd initially capitulated. The looming specter of life in prison factored in heavily as well. But he was too old and too far down this path not to admit there was something else. Something that had taken root in Spokane, when an old lieutenant took him aside and told him about the Four Horsemen.

"I'm talking about justice," Cal Ridley explained as he laid it all out. And Sandy listened, first in disbelief, then in righteous anger. He joined the shadowy four and together they brought justice to those worst of criminals who somehow managed to slip through a broken system due to a technicality.

He quickly discovered it was a role for which he had a knack. Then, somewhere along the line, he realized that, at times, there was something he liked about it.

The sentiment was one he pushed back against. That resistance, coupled with some weariness, was no doubt the reason he decided to call it quits when four horsemen became two and finally just the one—him.

If he were being honest, though—and it was far too late in life for him to try to find comfortable lies to make living easier—his desire to bring bad men extrajudicial justice was at least part of the reason he let Danforth blackmail him into this position. Protecting Janet was a real consideration but it also made for a comfortable excuse, didn't it?

An excuse that no longer existed.

"I'm sorry," came Carter's soft voice from beside him. "I know you loved her."

Sandy whipped his gaze back to Carter. He'd nearly forgotten she was standing there. Now, a cold fury enveloped him and he stood suddenly, clenching a fist at his side.

Carter didn't react. She simply waited as if she knew the question that was coming.

"How long have you known?" he asked her, the words slipping out through his clenched jaw.

"About four months," she said, answering immediately. "Once I figured out they were compartmentalizing your access, I wanted to know why." She motioned toward the screen. "As you can see, it wasn't hard to find." She waited another moment, then repeated, "I'm sorry. Like I said, I know you loved her."

"Don't act like you care." Sandy spat the words at her. He glanced around, but avoided looking at the laptop. Then he said, "I'm not falling for your charade, *Agent* Carter."

He turned away, stepping toward the door. Carter's hand fell onto his upper arm. Just a light touch, not a grip, but Sandy shook it off all the same.

"Wait," she said. Her tone was laced with both urgency and confidence. The combination gave him pause and he stopped, not looking back at her. "Think it through," she said. "This isn't a ruse. I'm not working with Szoke."

Sandy didn't move. His mind clicked through the scenario, but images of Janet flashed in front of him, disturbing his focus. "I don't believe you," he said stubbornly.

"*Think*, Banks. Szoke would never give up his leverage over you. Not even for this."

Sandy took a deep breath and let it out. He considered what she said. The more he thought on it, the more he realized she was right. Janet was Szoke's unbeatable trump card, his nuclear option. The threat of it was what made it valuable. Expending it took away its power and left him with nothing. Besides, the revelation wouldn't convince him to cooperate. It was more likely to strengthen his resolve to resist.

Unless Szoke sent Carter to get the information from him.

He turned to face her again. Her expression was resolute, reminding him of the one she'd worn more than a decade ago when he'd faced her and her partner, all of them staring at one another down gun barrels.

"I'm not telling you," he said, leaving no doubt in his voice.

"I'm not asking you to tell me. I'm asking you to save them."

He eyed her for another beat before speaking. "All right," he said, finally. "What's your plan?"

13

Lori Carter looked at herself in the bathroom mirror. The harsh light of the military latrine was less than flattering to her eyes. Not that she'd spent a lot of time over the past decade worrying about her looks. Fitness, sure. But looking good in order to attract a man had barely ever come across her radar. Even when it did, the goal usually revolved around a fleeting encounter. Her current circumstances didn't allow for a relationship to develop.

However, tonight was going to require dusting off that particular playbook. Show some charm, a little allure.

And prepare for the shit storm that would follow.

Carter drew in a deep breath.

I'm making the right decision.

Szoke and all his justifications didn't shake her from that resolution. She could accept collateral damage when it involved confederates but not innocents like this woman and her daughter. Szoke's plans went a bridge too far. She couldn't follow him there. *Wouldn't* follow him there.

Instead, she'd help free a man who'd killed dozens of people in his lifetime, most of them extralegally. Some of those assassinations happened with her full support.

My hands are just as bloody. After a certain point, numbers stopped mattering. Once a person's hands were coated with blood, more of it stopped making a difference.

Except maybe on the soul.

And her soul was dark and heavy these days.

But maybe she could do something about that. Do her part. One good deed didn't balance the karmic scales, but it still made a difference. Especially to that woman and her daughter.

That would be enough.

Wouldn't it?

Carter stared into the blackness of her own eyes. Then she reached up and undid an extra button on her blouse.

Wouldn't it?

She turned away from the mirror and strode from the bathroom.

14

Sandy lay atop the blankets on the bunk bed. The room was dark except for a sliver of light that came through the cracked door to his room. He resisted the urge to look at the small digital clock on the three-drawer chest to his right. It would only confirm how slowly time was crawling toward midnight.

The soft tread of boots passing his door had occurred forty minutes prior, though it seemed like hours. That had been Carter, headed to distract the two soldiers guarding them.

Guarding *him*, Sandy corrected. And Brian, too, he supposed. Carter's status was different, though he doubted she was entirely free herself. Certainly, she was part of this team under some measure of duress.

The oddity of his ad hoc alliance with Carter should have struck him more forcibly than it did. Perhaps he was inured to any kind of strangeness at this point in his life. Or maybe the pact made a sort of sense. Either way, it didn't matter. He was committed to a course of action now. They both were.

The lingering images of the words he'd read kept flashing in his mind like some cruel neon sign.

Local Family of Five Dies in Tragic Accident.

Over and over.

Again and again.

Grief and anger melded together into one, sitting in his gut like a cold ball of lead. The loss of Janet. The weight of what he'd been doing here for Szoke, and for Danforth, the man behind it all. And, deeper in the background, the quiet mantra of self-accusation.

A sense of futility threatened to settle in, but Sandy pushed it away. He couldn't let himself feel that. He pushed away the grief and most of the anger in the same mental motion. Tamped it down into that heavy ball in his stomach and compartmentalized it there. All of those emotions would cloud his judgment. Slow his actions. He had to focus now if he wanted to complete the mission before him.

They planned to find and murder both Allison and Lita.

He had to stop them.

Get the two to safety.

And then he was done.

Whatever that means.

He glanced at the clock again.

Eight minutes to go.

Sandy swung his legs over the edge of the bunk. He reached beneath the bunk and retrieved two items. The first was a compact nine-millimeter in a tactical holster. He stood and unbuckled his belt. Expertly, he slipped it out of the first two loops and threaded the tip through the holster connection plate. Then he slid the belt back through the loops of his pants and re-buckled it snugly.

The second item was a short knife with a clip on the back of the sheath. Sandy slipped this into his front pocket on the left side, leaving the clip exposed for an easy draw.

Both items belonged to Carter. According to plan, she'd claim he stole them but, in reality, she'd handed both of them to him in her room as she detailed her simple intent.

Sandy lifted a light jacket from the back of the nearby desk chair. He put it on. Most civilians wouldn't realize he was armed but any cop or soldier would notice the small bulge on his hip or note the slight imbalance in his gait. Certainly the guards at the end of the hall would be able to tell. Once he left this room, anyone he was likely to run into would know he was carrying.

He left the jacket unzipped. He had no doubt the reaction of the guards would be to shoot him without further questions. As much as Danforth and Szoke likely valued his expertise to accomplish their dirty little missions, neither man wanted him to escape. Their orders to his captors would be clear and brutal.

Sandy looked at the clock once more.

Six minutes.

He stared at the thin, full-length mirror affixed to the far wall. In the dim light, all he could make out was a shadowy figure.

Somehow, that felt right.

He breathed deeply. In, then out.

A minute passed.

Five to go.

Sandy clenched and unclenched his jaw, his mind racing with indecision. Finally, he made a choice.

If I'm never coming back, then it's time to take care of some unfinished business.

He slid the knife from his pocket and flicked open the blade. Then he slipped out of his room and headed down the hall.

15

"Here comes the bitch," said Sergeant Steve Richter.

He grinned at Carter and dropped the queen of spades into the center of the table.

Carter groaned and gave her eyes a dramatic roll. Then she wagged her finger at him. "You're a very bad boy, Sarge."

Richter's mischievous grin broadened. "That's what my momma always said."

Richter was in his late thirties, a thick-bodied white man with ruddy features. His caterpillar mustache was within military regulation, Carter believed, but just barely. Though he wore a thick gold band on his finger, she knew his wife and daughter were at home in Michigan while he was on this tour. She also knew he frequented the local bars when not on duty.

All of this made him the easy part of her plan.

The tougher bit was Private First Class Medgar Atherton. The athletic black soldier was at least a decade younger than Richter, though Carter thought he looked younger than he actually was. He'd been hesitant when Carter approached the two of them almost an hour ago, a deck of cards in her hands.

"Idle hands," she'd said, presenting an expression of mock apology. "And I can't sleep. You fellas know how to play Hearts?"

Richter had been eager enough and followed her into the small kitchen area nearby. Carter made sure to select the chair with the best view of the open doorway. Once they'd settled at the table, Carter frowned.

"Where's your partner? We can't play Hearts with less than three people."

Richter called Atherton in. The PFC lingered in the doorway, clearly nervous.

"You two play," he suggested. "I'll keep watch."

"We need three for this game," Richter insisted. He flashed a grin at Carter. She smiled back encouragingly.

"Sergeant—" began Atherton.

"Everyone else is asleep," Carter said. "But, if you aren't comfortable, I get it." She tapped the deck of cards to straighten them and slid them back inside the box.

"Hold on now," said Richter. "Me and you, we can play something else. Rummy, or some poker maybe?"

Carter smiled sadly. "Hearts is the only game I know. I don't think I'm up to learning something new tonight." She stood. "It's all right. I shouldn't have bothered you."

"It's no bother," Richter assured her. He turned to Atherton. "Med, don't be rude. Have a seat."

Atherton hesitated, then reluctantly did as his sergeant bade him. The chair he selected gave him a narrow view of the hallway, but Carter realized he'd see Banks coming before she did.

"Here," she said. "Take my seat. That way you'll have a good line of sight out the doorway."

She saw some relief flicker across Atherton's face, but he clearly remained conflicted.

"Thanks," he said.

Carter vacated the seat and Atherton lowered himself into it. Out of the corner of her eye, she watched the soldier shift in the chair and test his field of vision.

He's a good troop, she thought. She hated doing this to him.

Richter, on the other hand, she wasn't so conflicted about.

As she shuffled and dealt out the cards, the veteran sergeant gave her another grin, this one borderline lascivious. He'd taken the bait wholeheartedly.

"Everyone know the game?" she asked. "First one to a hundred points loses?"

Richter snapped his fingers and pointed at her. "Let's do it."

Next to her, Atherton remained glum and silent.

They played the first hand. Carter made sure to play smart but did her best to make sure Richter took the fewest points. Then she lifted her hand to her head, pretending she'd forgotten something.

"What is it?" Richter asked. "Regretting the challenge already?"

"You wish," she teased back. "No, I forgot a notepad to keep score."

Richter reached for the small notepad in his uniform pocket. "I'll do it."

"Hell you will," Carter said, keeping the flirtation in her tone restrained but still present. "You'll cheat."

"I won't," he protested. "I'd never."

"Yeah, you will." She eyed him from underneath her lids, the beginnings of a smile simmering on her lips. "And you would."

Richter raised his hands in surrender. "If you say so. But now I think you're up to something."

Carter forced her smile to broaden. "Like what? Rigging a game of Hearts? Trust me, I'm not that ego-driven." She turned her gaze to Atherton. "He should do it."

"Me?" Atherton looked unhappy. He glanced between them. When neither said another word, he suppressed a sigh and removed his own notepad. Carefully, he tore out a single page, replaced the notepad in his pocket, then wrote three initials on the paper. "What's the score again?"

"The score is, I'm winning," said Richter.

Carter shrugged. "He's not wrong." Then she told Atherton the actual score from the first hand. The soldier scribbled it down. She waited until he'd finished, then pushed the pile of cards toward him. "Your deal," she instructed.

Atherton gathered up the cards, shuffled and dealt.

They played.

As the cards flew, Carter kept an eye on Atherton. For his part, the soldier made consistent glances toward the empty hallway, checking every few seconds. After a few hands, though, she noticed him doing so slightly less frequently. She did her best to keep both men engaged and distracted—Atherton with the game, and Richter with her attention.

Shift change was at zero two hundred hours. As midnight approached, she kept a close eye on the sliver of hallway she could see. By her estimation, she would see Banks perhaps a foot or two before Atherton could. While the young soldier's eyes flicked toward the doorway less often, he remained alert and at least partially focused on his duty.

Carter worked them both. After Richter dropped the queen of spades on her, her score hovered perilously close to one hundred. One more hand might put her out. She might be able to convince them to go again, but there was no guarantee.

Where are you, Banks?

She gathered the cards together and took her time shuffling. Then she began to deal slowly.

Richter noticed and shook his head. "You deal slower than anyone I ever played with."

Carter paused, then shrugged. "Some things are better when you go slow." She cocked her head at him.

Richter grinned knowingly.

Let him chew on that for a while.

That was when she spotted Banks in the hallway. Her heartrate kicked up slightly.

"But you want speed?" she asked. "I can do speed. Watch yourself."

She spoke the code words she and Banks had settled on earlier in as close to a joking tone as she could summon. Then she resumed her deal, zipping the cards across the table. Richter caught his deftly, but she made sure to send one of Atherton's cards skittering off the edge of the table.

"Oops," she said. "Sorry."

Atherton didn't complain. As he bent to retrieve his errant card, Banks passed through the space where the soldier's field of vision used to be and, just as quickly, out the other side.

Carter slowed down and waited for Atherton to finish picking up his card. Then she said, "Sorry about that. I guess that's another good reason to take it slow, huh?" Her eyes flicked to Richter for the briefest of moments.

Atherton shrugged, still uncomfortable. "It's all right."

For his part, Richter said nothing, but his thinly disguised leer told her all she needed to know.

The door. Banks will need some cover for the sound of the door.

Carter cleared her throat and adjusted her position, causing the chair to squeak on the floor. Then she resumed dealing.

"Okay, here we go, boys." The cards slid across the table as she spoke. As soon as the words left her mouth, the irony of them struck her. "Time to see if you can knock out the dumb civilian or if she can manage to stay alive."

In more ways than one.

16

Sandy slipped through the darkness between buildings, avoiding the empty streets of the Army base.

He knew the Military Police would have a nighttime patrol by default, and it was entirely possible Szoke had arranged for extra diligence due to their presence. The request—or demand, more likely—would have gone through several layers of bureaucracy to hide its source but Sandy had no doubt Szoke could get it done.

The question was, had he?

He opted to keep close to the buildings. If he were in a city, he might stick to the sidewalk and try to blend in as just another pedestrian out for a late-night walk. But on the base, there was less foot traffic at this time of night. The rules were different, too. A city cop might pass him by, but an MP patrol could and would stop anyone strolling down the street. They didn't need probable cause. Sandy couldn't risk that.

He moved without dashing but slipping along with deliberate speed. Most of the buildings he passed were administrative, open during business hours and shuttered for the night. As he rounded the corner of the dentist's office, he took the time to consult a signpost and get his bearing.

The residential zone lay one direction. Sandy went the opposite way. Residential meant too many people, not to mention dogs. No one was looking for him yet, but they would be soon enough. A neighborhood of sharp-eyed soldier families and barking dogs would only lead to his recapture.

The chokehold Szoke had clearly applied to Sandy's web access hadn't extended to something as benign as a map of the base. When Sandy studied it earlier, he knew his best option was to make for the firing range. The large swath of land gave him an opportunity for cover and the easiest way off base.

As he passed the personnel office, Sandy heard the rumble of a vehicle nearby. He ducked behind the concrete steps that led to the front door. Powerful high beams swept over him, painting the area with white light. Sandy stilled his breath and froze, waiting for the car to lurch to a stop. But the patrol rolled past without so much as a hitch in the hum of the motor.

He let out his breath and resumed his trek, picking along next to the buildings until he finally reached the firing range.

The range building was bathed in bright light and secured behind a fence and what he was sure were strongly locked doors. He saw shadows of movement through the shade-drawn windows.

Someone is up late, counting bullets.

Sandy gave the building a wide berth, skirting around the edges of the apron of light cast by the powerful bulbs on the side of the place. The range itself wasn't locked, protected only by an off-set fence opening he had to weave through, reminding him of the entrances to baseball diamonds he'd played on as a kid.

The first firing course was ranged at twenty-five yards, designed for pistols. Sandy broke into an easy lope, covering the ground quickly. It took only a short time to reach the rifle range, a much larger field of fire. Here, Sandy increased his speed. He doubted the MPs patrolled here often, if at all, but the possibilities of cameras occurred to him. If he was spotted, the response would be immediate. There was no good reason for anyone to be out here alone at night.

If they came for him, he didn't like his odds. They'd have

greater numbers and superior firepower. The small pistol at his hip was a poor answer to the rifles the soldiers carried. That was if he decided to fight at all. Getting caught at this stage might just be the end of it. Why shoot it out with soldiers who were unwitting dupes for Szoke? They were innocent, just doing their jobs. To them, he was a dangerous criminal.

Sandy breathed deep as he ran, sucking the cool night air into his lungs. The thought of dying for nothing burned in his stomach. That's what it would be, if he failed here. There had been many times in his life where death had come close enough for him to feel its hot breath on his neck but, so far, he'd slipped its grasp. He knew he was only putting off the inevitable, just like everyone did. But if the official story was going to see him die as a fugitive and a traitor, he wanted to be certain he did something worthwhile to balance it out.

When the open area gave way to light forest, Sandy slowed his pace. He could hear his breath over the top of the night sounds that surrounded him. His knee twinged with every stride. Keeping his bearings, he headed forward.

Always forward.

It wouldn't be long now.

When he found the fence at the edge of the base, it was surprisingly decrepit. Sandy was able to lift and bend the bottom high enough to roll underneath. Just like that, he was off the base.

There was little transition between the base and the city of El Paso. Even so, Sandy slowed his gait, walking with purpose. Hopefully, his theory regarding civilian cops held true. By his estimation, it had to be nearing one o'clock in the morning. How long would it be before Szoke discovered he was missing? Or found the mess he left behind?

Once he did, the man would go on the warpath. Local cops

would join the hunt.

Sandy kept his pace brisk but avoided the temptation to run. He made his way to an arterial and kept heading east. There were a few more people out and about, especially as he passed through a short bar district. Their presence camouflaged his. He avoided eye contact and kept moving forward.

He passed a bank. Blood red numbers told him it was now fourteen minutes past two. In a couple hours, the sun would start to threaten the horizon.

We need to be out of town before that happens.

Thirty minutes later, he saw the sagging sign for The Texan motel. The 'X' in Texan was replaced with a star. Part of the lighting had failed, giving the star a broken, incomplete look.

Sandy paused outside the coffee shop across the street and surveyed the scene. The motel parking lot was half-filled with an assortment of aging sedans and battered trucks. Sandy tried to guess which car might be Allison's but there were several candidates.

If she's even here.

She'd be there. He believed that. If she'd been rounded up by Szoke already, the man wouldn't have hesitated to gloat about it, regardless of what time it was. The more likely reason she might not be there was she didn't trust Sandy and ran on her own.

If she did, then that was that. She'd made her choice and he'd done his part.

But he didn't think that was the case.

He waited and watched another ten minutes before making his decision.

The bell above the office door let out an anemic ding when Sandy stepped inside. The front desk was empty, but he could hear some rustling behind the curtained doorway. A moment later, a slender man in dark-framed glasses stepped through. He was chewing on something and wiping his hands on a napkin.

Sandy nodded to him.

The man nodded back as he swallowed. "Need a room?" he asked.

"Not exactly." Sandy glanced down at the desk, looking for a name plate but didn't see one. "I'm hoping you can help me."

"No," the man said sharply. He pointed to the door. "Out."

Sandy held up his hands. "Wait, you haven't heard—"

"Mister, if you're selling, I ain't buying. And if you're looking for girls or junk, you can go two blocks either direction and find whatever you want. Just don't bring it here."

"It's not like that."

"Oh, it's not, huh?" The man sounded dubious. "Then what is it?"

"I'm looking for my sister," Sandy said. The lie came easily enough. Hell, his entire life had been surrounded by lies for the past two decades. "Her and my niece are supposed to meet me here."

The man's eyes narrowed with suspicion. "I can't tell you anything about our guests, if that's where you're heading with this."

Sandy heaved a sigh, trying to avoid being too dramatic. "Listen, what's your name?"

"What do you care?"

Sandy turned over his hands. "Come on."

The man continued to stare at him, barely yielding. Finally, he said, "Greg."

"Greg," Sandy repeated. "Thanks, Greg. Look, here's the situation. My sister Allison has an asshole boyfriend. He's abusive and controlling. She's been trying to leave him for a while now. Earlier tonight, she called me to say she was taking

Lita and getting out. I told her to meet me here. Then she went dark. I think he took her phone from her or something."

Greg's gaze softened slightly but still held some skepticism. "He beats her up or what?"

"Sometimes. Mostly, he keeps her in fear of it. And he controls everything, like I said."

"Why don't you just kick his ass and be done with it?"

Sandy let out a pained laugh. "I wish it were that easy. Every time I take him to the woodshed, he ends up going with some kind of sympathy play with her. She takes him back and we're right back at where we started."

Greg crossed his arms. "Sounds like she wants to be with him."

"You ever hear of the cycle of violence, Greg? Psychological dependency?"

Greg's eyes narrowed again. "Of course. I ain't stupid. I'm just saying she's a grown woman making her own choices."

"Maybe," Sandy allowed. "But this time is different."

"What do you mean, different?"

"She said she doesn't like how he's been acting toward Lita," Sandy said.

Greg cocked his head. "How's he acting?"

Sandy frowned. "He's making the girl feel uncomfortable. I gotta spell it out for you, Greg?"

The two men stared at each other for several moments. Sandy watched for micro expressions on Greg's face. When he saw what he thought was a shift in attitude, he made his play.

"Are they here, Greg?"

Greg hesitated. "How do I know you're not him? Just telling me some bullshit story?"

"Fair enough," Sandy said. "How about you walk me to their room and see for yourself?"

There was another long pause before Greg grabbed a set of keys. "All right," he said. With his other hand, he grabbed a sawed-off baseball bat. "If you're lyin', I'm gonna thump you upside your head and call the cops."

Sandy held up his hands in surrender. "No problem."

Greg waved at him with the bat. "Stay in front of me."

Sandy turned and walked out of the office.

Greg came behind him. He gestured with the bat. "That way."

They climbed up a single flight of stairs and halfway down the row before Greg told him to stop. He rapped lightly on the door. "Miss?" he called, keeping his eye on Sandy. "Are y'all awake in there?"

It remained quiet for a few seconds. Then Sandy heard Allison's wavering voice. "What is it?"

Greg cleared his throat. "It's the front desk, Miss. I'm out here with a man who claims to be your brother."

There was another pause. Then the lock rattled and the door opened a crack. Allison stared out, looking harried.

Greg motioned toward Sandy with the bat. "Is this your brother, Miss?"

Allison's gaze slid toward Sandy. Recognition blossomed, but did little to lighten her expression.

"Allison—" Sandy began, but Greg tapped the bat to Sandy's chest to cut him off.

"You be quiet," Greg growled. He turned back to Allison. "Miss? You know this man?"

Now we'll see if she trusts me more than she fears them.

Sandy gave her a beseeching look, imploring her to play along. He shifted his feet slightly, prepared to take control of Greg if she didn't. One way or another, he and Allison were at least going to have a conversation in that motel room.

She stared at Sandy for another long moment before she swallowed hard and bobbed her head. "Yes," she rasped. "He's my brother."

17

"Wake up."

Lori Carter recognized Richter's muffled voice when the brusque knock came at her door. She hadn't been sleeping, but waiting for what she knew was coming.

When she didn't answer Richter right away, he said, "Boss wants you in the briefing room."

"Now?" Carter asked.

"Five minutes ago," he snapped back.

A moment later, she heard his boots stomping away.

The sharpness of his tone didn't surprise her, considering the likely reason for the sudden meeting. He'd been played a fool and wasn't pleased. Several people were poised to be unhappy, to say the least.

But probably mostly me.

She swung her legs off the bed. Her jeans were draped over the nearby chair. Light filtered in through the high window, so she didn't bother with the desk lamp. She slid into her pants and pulled on the shirt that lay beneath it. A simple pair of flats were at the foot of the chair and she slipped them on mechanically. Then she grabbed her bio-watch and left the room.

As she strode down the hallway, Carter fished a hair tie from her pocket and pulled her hair back into a stubby ponytail. She glanced at the watch on her wrist.

Just a few minutes past four.

That gave Banks roughly a four-hour head start. Hopefully, he made good use of the time.

She found Szoke in the briefing room, staring intently at a tablet. He glanced up when Carter entered.

"So glad you could join us," he smirked.

"I'm too tired for snotty bullshit, Mark. What's going on?"

Szoke shook his head emphatically, his lip curling into a snarl. "No, I'm the one who's tired, *Lori*. Tired of all the foot-dragging and disloyalty in this unit."

Carter stopped at her customary seat but remained standing. "What are you on about?"

"Don't act like you don't know. Banks is gone. And you helped him."

Carter considered continuing to feign ignorance, but in that moment, she was too tired to do so. Not sleepy, but bone-weary and ground down from a decade of the work she'd been doing.

If this is where it ends, so be it. Fire me or arrest me, but at least it will be over.

"No denials?" Szoke asked her. "No sassy retort?"

She shrugged. "What do you want from me?"

"The truth, for starters."

"Fine. I ran interference for Banks so he could slip out."

"Why would you do that?"

"Because you are planning to murder an innocent woman and a child," Carter said acidly.

"She's a drug dealer's mistress," said Szoke. "Hardly an innocent."

"What about her kid?"

Szoke shrugged. "Sometimes we have to accept that civilian losses are necessary for the greater good."

Carter gaped at him. "The greater good? How... I mean, seriously – how can you even say that?"

"It's not as difficult as you think. Not once you realize what we do is the dirty work that keeps this country safe. Because, in case you didn't notice, the world is about forty times more fucked than most people realize."

"And murdering innocent people will solve that? Tell me, how exactly does that math work?" Carter pressed her lips together and gave her head a single, emphatic shake. "No, it wasn't hard in this situation for me to make the right choice."

Szoke mirrored her motion, but shaking his head in disappointment. "Still the idealist, aren't you?"

"It isn't idealism. It's human decency. Something you used to have, once upon a time."

"I recall," Szoke said. "That was before I knew how bad things were and what extreme measures were required for us to even have a chance to maintain our national security. It's worse than you think. I've kept you insulated from much of it. Trust me, quasi-ignorance is definitely bliss."

Carter stared at him, trying to remember the man he was a decade ago, when she called him friend. She saw no vestige of that person in him tonight. It was as if Danforth had possessed his entire being. "What happened to you?"

"You."

"Me?!"

"Yes, you." Szoke leaned forward, his expression tight. "You dragged me into this mess with Banks and I got pulled into Danforth's orbit. Right through the fucking looking glass, Lori, and you know there's no going back."

"Of course, I know. I'm right here with you."

Szoke wagged a finger. "Except you're not. Not entirely. You've been operating at a level of malicious compliance, at best."

"I've done everything asked of me," Carter said. "I've done my job, no matter how distasteful. But I draw the line at killing innocent people because they happened to be in the wrong place at the wrong time."

"You don't get to draw the lines. That's not your role."

"We all draw our own lines, Mark. We make our choices."

"And you certainly made yours."

Carter didn't answer.

Szoke motioned toward the chair. "Have a seat." He glanced down at the tablet. When she didn't sit, he spoke without looking at her. "We have a few things to go over, Agent Carter. Sit down."

Carter slid out the chair and settled into it. "What do you want from me?" she asked again. "I figured you have Richter and Atherton in here to arrest me."

"There's still time for that. But I'm faced with a bit of a leadership conundrum here. Maybe you can help."

"I'm no leader."

"True enough." Szoke traced a finger across the tablet. A faint smile touched his lips. "But you're smart. So, I want your take."

Carter crossed her arms and waited.

"What do I do," Szoke said, still intent on the tablet, "with a team member that performs well even though her act was disloyal? Do I reward the outcome or punish the intention?"

"Don't be so vague. I know you mean me, but..."

She stopped, suddenly uncertain. An unease rose in her as she watched the smile grow on Szoke's mouth. He lifted his gaze to hers and raised his brows.

"Are we having an epiphany?" he asked her.

Carter stared at him, her mind whirring. Szoke seemed angry but his demeanor remained confident. Banks escaping should have made him more than angry. He should be livid. On top of that, her betrayal should have further outraged him. And yet...

Realization dawned on her and her stomach sank.

"You *planned* this...?"

"I did." Szoke sounded like he had difficulty containing

his own glee.

"And I…"

"You performed brilliantly, albeit unwittingly." His smile was cruel and his eyes cold. "You thought you were *so* smart, Lori. But everything that has occurred happened exactly as I intended."

"How did you know?"

"It wasn't rocket science. I *knew* Banks and his warped sense of justice wouldn't lay down for this. I *knew* your tender sensibilities wouldn't accept it, either. Once that's out on the table, the rest becomes pretty easy to predict. All I had to do was put a few simple matters into play, and all the cards fell into place."

At the word *cards*, her eyes narrowed.

Szoke smirked at her again. "Oh, I'm sorry—did you think your feminine charms were actually that powerful?"

She shrugged off the insult. "Why? Why let him escape?"

But as soon as the words left her mouth, she knew the answer. Szoke did it to follow Banks, believing he would lead them directly to the woman and the child.

Szoke seemed to sense she'd answered her own question. He lifted the tablet. "We've been tracking him since he left. I've got top men on this."

"Brian?"

Szoke snorted. "I don't know where his loyalties lie any more than yours. No, Easton is accessing multiple public camera systems and Paulinus is on drone duty. We've been up on him every step of the way."

Carter stared at him, partly in disgust but also with a grudging respect. Szoke might have turned into someone she despised but she had to admire his effectiveness.

"Well played," she muttered.

You bastard.

Szoke's smug expression remained cold. "Don't be that

way, Lori. Everyone gets duped once in a while. I might even allow you to remain on the team, provided you get your priorities back in order."

Carter opened her mouth to reply. The words forming in her mind were ones that would sever her connection to Szoke and this program forever. For all she knew, they would send her into the same black hole prison he'd often threatened to send Banks. But before she could utter them, a knock came at the door, then it burst open without waiting for Szoke's response.

Richter's bulky frame filled the doorway. His expression was a mix of worry and anger. "Sir?"

"What is it?" Szoke asked him, his eyes narrowing at the intrusion.

"Sir, you better come. It's Moore."

"Brian? What's his problem? Why isn't he here yet?"

Richter swallowed nervously before he replied. In that moment, Carter knew what he was about to say.

"That's why I'm here, sir. It's Moore. He's dead."

Carter's shoulders sagged. Her relationship with Brian was a strange one. But despite her own contempt for his vigilantism, they'd worked together for the past ten years. She couldn't entirely identify the exact emotions she felt toward him, but hearing he was dead sent a lance of sadness through her.

Szoke gaped at Richter. "Dead?"

"Yes, sir."

Szoke continued to stare at Richter, suddenly at a loss for words.

Apparently, Carter thought, *he didn't see that coming.*

18

Sandy stepped inside the motel room and closed the door behind himself. Allison opened her mouth to speak but he held up a hand to silence her. Then he jerked a finger toward the door before putting it to his lips.

Allison followed his movements. She scowled but seemingly understood, as she remained quiet.

Sandy cocked his head, listening. Outside the door, Greg the hotel manager remained motionless for several moments. Then Sandy heard the light tramp of his feet as he moved away.

"Okay," he said. "He's gone."

Sandy glanced over at one of the queen-sized beds in the room. A hunched figure lay beneath the blankets, perfectly still.

Lita, he thought.

Before he could turn back to talk to Allison, he saw motion out of his peripheral vision. An open hand lashed out and caught him on his cheek. The force of the slap surprised him more than it hurt.

Allison reloaded for another swing, but Sandy caught her wrist as it flew toward his face.

"Easy," he cautioned her.

"Who the fuck are you?" she growled. Her voice was low but the tone urgent.

"I'm the only friend you've got right now."

"*Friend?*" Her mouth twisted and her eyes burned with anger. "Bullshit. You murdered Héctor."

"I did," Sandy admitted. "That was the mission. But I saved you." He jerked his head toward the form on the bed. "And her."

Allison's gaze followed his motion before snapping back to him. "Who *are* you?" she repeated.

"I'll tell you whatever you want to know," Sandy said. "But not now and not here. Right now, we have to get the hell out of El Paso."

She stared at him, her eyes searching his. Sandy reflected back impassivity, waiting for her to make her decision.

"Who sent you?" she asked. "Was it Ortega?"

"It doesn't matter," Sandy told her. "Not right now. All that matters now is that we move. If we stay here, we're dead."

Allison glared at him without reply. After a few moments, she jerked her wrist free of his grasp. "How can I trust you after what you did?"

"We've already had this conversation," Sandy said. "If I wanted to hurt you and your daughter, I would have done it at the hotel We don't have time for this. You already made your choice when you played along with the desk clerk and told him I was your brother. Hell, you made it when you came here instead of going to the police."

She continued to glare at him, crossing her arms.

"Okay," he allowed. "Maybe not. Either way, wake her up while I check outside to see if it's clear."

Allison didn't move.

Sandy shrugged. "Do what I say or lock the door behind me. Call the police. If that's what you decide, then so be it. We go our separate ways. But understand there are people looking for you right now. If they find you, they won't hesitate to kill you or Lita."

"Don't say her name like you know her!" Allison snapped.

"You don't have that right. Not after what you did."

Sandy held up a hand. "Fine. I'm going outside. Make your choice."

He turned and exited the room.

As he stood on the second-floor walkway, the cool of the night accentuated the warmth on his cheek where she'd struck him. Sandy scanned the parking area below, watching for shadowy figures. He saw nothing. He listened, expecting to hear the crunch of tires nearing the motel, full of armed men. The hiss of distant traffic was all he heard at first. Then, he caught a slight buzzing sound, barely above a whisper.

Sandy looked up.

19

The scene was one of the cleanest homicides Lori Carter had ever encountered.

Brian Moore sat at the simple wooden desk in his barracks room, hunched over with his head on the desktop. He looked like a high school student who had fallen asleep in class.

Except, that was, for the thin stream of blood that had pooled near one leg of the chair.

"Knife," Richter announced, though the method of assassination was clear to everyone in the room. "Right under the ribs and into the heart."

At least he didn't suffer, Carter thought. *Hell, he may have even welcomed it.*

Szoke stood in the doorway, fuming. He glared at Brian's dead body with barely controlled rage. "Get this cleaned up," he instructed Richter. "Bag his body for our return to base."

Richter gave him a surprised look. "Sir…?"

"Was I speaking English, Sergeant?"

"Yes, sir. But…"

"Then do it."

Szoke wheeled around and left the room.

Carter hesitated, her gaze returning to Brian. The man had been her confidential informant at one time. She and her partner ensnared him and turned him against Sandy Banks. As much as she loathed what he and the other vigilante cops had done, once he became her CI, Brian was her responsibility. That obligation didn't end just because Banks was captured.

And now Brian was dead.

Goddamn you, Banks. Why did you do this?

She knew the answer. Banks felt betrayed by Moore. This was his revenge. But he clearly hadn't thought through the consequences. If he had, he'd have known she wouldn't be able to let this stand. It was the one action that all but assured she'd be back to square one where he was concerned, hunting him once again.

It seems our fates are intertwined.

"Maybe that's how you want it," she muttered.

"What?" Richter asked.

"Nothing," Carter said. "Do what Szoke said."

She left the room and headed back to the makeshift command room. The walk was brief. By the time she arrived, Szoke was already there, staring at the big screen TV at the end of the conference table. Easton and Paulinus were present as well. The two technicians were familiar to her but she hadn't interacted with them much over the years. Brian had always been her tech guy. Szoke tended to keep operations compartmentalized.

"You're sure that's the room?" Szoke asked Paulinus.

The chubby man with a trimmed mustache nodded. "The desk clerk walked him up there."

Szoke lifted a radio to his mouth and pressed the button. "How far out are you?"

The brisk reply came a moment later. *"Under two mikes."*

Szoke frowned. "Step it up," he ordered.

"Roger."

Szoke glanced up at Carter, then over at Paulinus. "I want a closer view. Can you get any lower?"

"Sure," Paulinus said. "But—"

"Do it."

Paulinus hesitated. His hands rested on a pair of joysticks inside an oversized briefcase. The portable drone piloting gear was frequently deployed on team operations. Carter had learned to appreciate the advantage of the eye in the sky.

"Sir," Paulinus began. "I'm already at—"

"Jesus, am I surrounded by imbeciles?" Szoke interrupted. "Just do it."

Paulinus complied. On the screen, Carter could see the target door growing larger as the drone descended. Then the door opened and a male figure stepped out onto the walkway. Carter recognized Banks almost immediately. Given recent events, she didn't know whether to be disappointed or elated.

Szoke suffered no such turmoil. "Got you, you son of a bitch," he crooned.

On the screen, Banks seemed to be scanning the parking lot.

"He's getting ready to run," Carter said aloud.

Szoke waved a hand. "Good luck with that. I've got an SUV with four hardcore shooters less than a minute away."

It was more like ninety seconds, she knew. Or longer. The difference might not matter. Then again, it might. She'd learned not to underestimate Sandy Banks. First as an adversary and later a teammate, he'd proven to her he was resourceful.

The figure of Banks grew larger on the screen as the drone descended. Suddenly, Banks looked up sharply. It seemed as if he were staring directly at them.

"Shit," Carter muttered. "You just got made. He sees the drone."

"So what?" Szoke shook his head dismissively. "It's all but over now."

In one smooth motion, Sandy Banks drew his pistol and

pointed it upward. There was a flash of light, followed by a second one. The view on the screen skewed for a brief second, then dropped to static.

"What the fuck?" Szoke demanded.

"He shot down the drone," Paulinus told him.

"I know that, you idiot!" Szoke glared at him. "You went too low."

Paulinus stared back, confused. "But you…"

"Idiot," Szoke repeated. He shook his head in disgust before lifting the radio to his lips. "He took out our eyes," he said. "We're blind here. Advise me as soon as you arrive."

"*Roger. No change in objective?*"

"No change," Szoke agreed. "Terminate all three targets."

"*Roger that.*"

He glanced at Carter. "Any objections? Because if you want back on the team, you need to be on board with the mission."

I don't have a choice, she thought. *In more ways than one.*

"If I say yes," she asked, "all is forgiven?"

Szoke smirked. "Sure. You only did what I planned for you to do, after all."

She didn't entirely like his answer. But, like it or not, she didn't have any other options.

"I'm on board," she said, and hated each and every word as she uttered them.

20

Sandy's hand found the door handle and turned it. To his relief, it twisted easily and the door swung open with a push.

The room was empty.

Sandy swept his gaze across the visible area, then strode toward the bathroom. The door knob didn't turn but he forced it open, snapping past the vanity lock.

Allison and Lita stood in the bathtub, holding onto each other. Concern was etched on Allison's face.

"I heard gunshots," she explained. Before Sandy could answer, her gaze dropped to the gun in his hand. She froze, except for her eyes, which shot back to Sandy's.

"We have to go," Sandy said. "Now. They're close."

"They shot at you?"

He shook his head. "It was a drone. I took it out. But they can't be far behind."

Allison stared back at him, her shocked expression frozen in place.

"We have to *go*," Sandy said urgently.

His words seemed to break through to her. Allison pulled at her daughter as she stepped out of the tub. The girl stood in place, resisting her mother's tug.

"Lita!" Allison said. "Come on. Quickly."

Lita eyed Sandy warily.

"Mom, no—"

"Let's go."

"No!" Lita's gaze snapped to her mother. "He shot Papá. He'll kill us, too."

"Now, *hija*!" Allison snapped.

Reluctantly, the girl stepped out of the tub and followed. She shot Sandy a dark, suspicious glared as the two adults led her back into the bedroom.

"Get your shoes on," Allison told her, grabbing a bag and shoving clothes into it. "We have to go."

Lita scowled. "We can't trust him."

"We have no choice right now. Come on."

Sandy turned away, cracking open the door and peering out. He listened for the approach of vehicles, but all he could hear was the rustling sounds behind him as the pair gathered their things. Alarms were going off inside him, telling him their window for escape was quickly closing.

"Leave the rest," he said over his shoulder. "And dump your phones, too."

Both mother and daughter stared at him, hesitating.

"Leave the phones," he repeated. "As soon as they ID you, those phones become a flashing neon tracker."

Allison scowled but took her phone from her purse and held it, hesitating.

Lita made no move to remove hers. "Mom, without our phones, we can't—"

"Leave them," Sandy barked. "Or don't come with me. Your choice."

Allison waited a second longer, then tossed her phone onto the bed. Reluctantly, Lita followed suit.

"Good," Sandy said. "Now, let's go."

"Wait!" Lita said. The teenager leapt across one of the beds toward the nightstand between the two queens.

Sandy narrowed his eyes but didn't move to stop her.

Lita grabbed something from the small table and turned to

Allison with it. Sandy saw it was a piece of silver jewelry. "Your bracelet, Mom."

Wordlessly, Allison took it from her hand and thrust it into her purse.

"Is that everything?" Sandy asked. "Because we're almost out of time."

Allison nodded to him. "We're ready."

Sandy swung open the door and waved to them with his free hand.

Both Allison and Lita approached.

"Down the stairs," Sandy said to Allison. "You lead us to your car. She follows. I've got the rear. Don't stop for anything or anyone."

"What if—?" Lita asked, but Sandy cut her off.

"Don't stop. If you stop, you're dead."

Lita's jaw clenched but she responded with a tight nod.

"Go," Sandy said.

Allison walked out of the room with a confidence that gave Sandy some hope that they might make it through this situation. Lita scurried after her. Sandy kept his gun at his side and followed. His ears strained for approaching vehicles or another drone but, for the moment, he heard nothing except the muted sounds of the city at night.

As Allison went down the stairs on the far corner of the motel, Sandy saw Greg standing at the window in the office, watching them. The clerk held a phone to his ear. Sandy realized he was likely calling local police but he didn't have time to worry about it. He reached the bottom of the stairs and followed Allison through the breezeway between the two sections of the complex.

"It's right here," she told Sandy, her hushed voice carrying in night air. She pointed a key fob and a green Subaru fifteen yards away chirped and emitted a flash of amber light.

"Hurry," Sandy urged.

A moment later, he heard the gravelly hiss of tires on concrete coming from the far side of the motel.

"Shit," he muttered.

Tires squealed with sudden turning and then screeched to a stop. Sandy heard the tramp of feet and the thudding of slammed doors immediately.

We have time. If they go to the room first, we have time.

At the car, Allison flung open the door and slid into the driver's seat. Lita opened the passenger front door, but Sandy grabbed her by the belt at the small of her back.

"Backseat," he said, his voice low. "And lay down."

Lita didn't argue, just did as she was told. Sandy dropped into the passenger seat as Allison fired up the engine.

"Keep the headlights off," Sandy directed her. "And go left at the arterial."

Allison put the car in gear and the Subaru lurched forward. She slowed but didn't stop at the intersection, ignoring the stop sign and turning left. Sandy gave her directions, sending her on a zig-zag path until they reached another arterial parallel to the one where the motel was located. He set her on a heading in the opposite direction they'd originally gone. He kept watch through the rear window, waiting for a small fleet's worth of SUV headlights to appear.

But there was nothing.

"Go ahead and turn on your headlights," he told Allison. "We don't want to get stopped by some beat cop."

"The cops are in on this?" Allison asked in disbelief.

"No. But the desk clerk was on the phone, probably with 911. I don't know how often reports of shots fired happen in this city but it has to raise the temperature for the local cops."

Allison flicked on the lights. "What now?" she asked.

"We get the hell out of El Paso."

"But where?"

"At the moment, out of El Paso is all that matters." He

pointed forward. "We're on the east side of the city, so keep heading east. Once we're clear, we'll figure out the rest."

Allison bit her lip but drove without protesting.

A few minutes later, Sandy gestured to one of the road signs. "Take I-10. Speed limit's higher. Drive five over."

She nodded.

The three of them sat in an eerie, tense silence. Sandy watched for intercepting vehicles while Allison seemed focused on the task of driving. Lita's silent resentment emanated from the back seat where she lay.

Ten minutes passed. Then thirty. Eventually, Sandy slid his gun back into its holster and allowed himself a deep breath. Allison glanced over at him.

"Do you think we're safe?"

"No," Sandy said. "But I think we slipped them for the moment."

"Then what the hell are we supposed to do now?"

Sandy noticed a sign for a rest stop one mile ahead. "Pull in there."

She squinted. "Why?"

"Just do it."

Allison's jaw set. The expression was immediately familiar to Sandy. He realized he'd seen Lita make the same face earlier. "Listen," Allison said, "we need to get something straight. You don't just tell us what to do like we're some kind of—"

"Everything I tell you to do is designed to keep you alive as long as possible," Sandy interrupted. "And time is usually a critical factor. That's just the way it is. You can live with it or take your chances on your own."

Allison's features remained fixed. "I still don't even know if I can trust you," she whispered, though Sandy wasn't entirely sure if she was talking to him or to herself.

"We can't," Lita muttered from the back seat.

Sandy chose not to reply to either of them.

The exit arrived and Allison took it. The rest stop was empty except for a truck with a camper at the far end. Allison pulled into a parking stall in front of the restrooms. She put the car into gear and looked over at Sandy. "Okay, now what?"

"We switch," he said. "I need to drive."

Allison hesitated, then she shrugged. "Fine."

She got out of the car and started around the front. Sandy did likewise. As Sandy reached the driver's side, he saw a flash of movement from the back seat. Lita reached for the door, but Sandy lifted the latch and pulled it open too quickly for her to engage the lock. The teenager glared sullenly at him, her arm outstretched.

"Don't do that," Sandy said flatly.

Lita didn't reply. Her only action was to retract her arm and lean back in the seat.

"Don't do what?" Allison asked as she settled into the passenger seat.

Lita crossed her arms and looked away.

"Sit up," Sandy lied. "She should stay lying flat."

"Why?"

Sandy sat down and pulled the door shut. "They're looking for three people. If they only see two, they might not immediately know it's us."

Allison smirked. "Is that really going to stop them from checking us out further?"

"No," Sandy admitted. "Probably not."

She shrugged and waved her hand. "Let her sit how she wants."

Sandy didn't answer. He put the car into reverse, pulled out, and drove.

For an hour, no one spoke.

Lita eventually leaned her head against the window and

seemed to doze off. Allison stared out at the passing desert. Sandy scanned the gauges.

"We're going to need gas," he finally said. The dashboard display showed the approximate range with their existing fuel. He did some quick math, then added, "We can refill once and still make Houston, but just barely."

Allison didn't answer him.

"Do you have cash?" he asked.

She lifted a shoulder slightly and let it drop. "A little."

Sandy stared out at the freeway ahead. Once Szoke identified Allison, he'd have his men monitoring her finances. If they used a credit card, Szoke would see that. It would reveal which direction they'd fled and narrow the search. With the access his computer gurus had, the net would tighten quickly.

Hell, it probably wasn't only the computer geeks that'd be helping him. Sandy had no doubt Carter would be on board, too, once she discovered what he'd done to Brian before he left.

Revenge was a luxury he probably should have forsaken, but Brian's betrayal went too deep. The idea the traitor might live a comfortable life, even if it was one of indentured servitude to the government, was too much for Sandy to bear. Brian getting caught and then flipping to the FBI is what set the entire series of events in motion that eventually led to Sandy's own captivity. That demanded a price be paid, and he was never going to get another opportunity to make sure it happened.

Still, having pushed Carter back into Szoke's camp may have been a mistake. She was smart. And she was tenacious. If she reacted to Brian's death the way Sandy expected, his actions had added another hound to the pack chasing them and probably the most dangerous one, at that. After all, she'd been the one who'd caught him once before.

Maybe they still don't know who Allison is, he thought. If that were the case, every hour that fact remained true kept them safe. By the time they figured out her identity, any cards they'd used for gas in Houston or wherever might be days old. If.

"We'll use what cash you have to refuel on the way to Houston," Sandy said. "Once we hit Houston, we fill up with gas and you hit an ATM. Take out the daily limit in cash. We might not be able to use cards again after that."

Allison nodded wearily. "When can we go back home?" she asked. Her voice cracked tiredly when she spoke.

"Never," Sandy said. "Your old life is over. You have to make a new one."

Allison swiveled her head to stare at him. "We have a life in El Paso. Lita has school. Friends. I volunteer. Our apartment—"

"The people after us now will not stop looking for you," Sandy said flatly. "Not ever. When they find you, they will kill you. Do you understand? The man in charge of this has nearly infinite resources if he wants them. The machine he can bring to bear is massive. You can't go home."

Allison stared at him while he drove. Sandy watched her in his peripheral vision, giving her the chance for his words to sink in. When she spoke, he could hear the despair in her voice.

"What are we supposed to do?"

"Create a new life, like I said."

"I... I don't know how to do that."

"Could you go to Héctor's people?"

"No."

The swiftness of her answer surprised Sandy. "Why not?"

She rubbed her eyes with the heels of her palms. "Lots of reasons."

"Such as?"

"He has a wife in Mexico, for starters. Two kids, both boys.

Lita and I are a dirty little secret."

He thought about that for a few moments, running the scenario through his mind. She knew the situation better than he did, but sometimes people who were close to a situation didn't see it as clearly. Yet, in this case, he was forced to admit he saw it the same as she did. If anything, the cartel might be as dangerous for her and Lita as Szoke and his crew. At best, she represented the kind of secret life Sandy knew was privately condoned but publicly condemned.

"They'd never accept you," Sandy said, voicing his agreement.

"No. They'd turn us away."

"Or disappear you."

Next to him, he sensed her tense up. "They'd have no reason to do that."

"Cartels aren't known for being reasonable. At worst, they'd worry about what you know about their operations from Héctor's pillow talk. Or they'd suspect you of being involved in the assassination plot."

"How can you be so cold about it?" Allison's voice broke when she asked the question.

Sandy hesitated. Then he said, "I've had a lot of years to get used to the idea."

"You're just as bad as they are."

Sandy didn't argue. She was right. Instead, he said, "Cartels also aren't big on leaving loose ends dangling. Even if Szoke gives up the chase, which he won't, there's a good chance the Cartel will be looking for you, too."

"Why?" Allison asked.

"I just told you why."

"No. I mean, why did you do it? You started all of this when you did what you did to Héctor. Tell me why."

Sandy drew in a breath and let it out heavily. "He was deemed a threat to national security."

She snorted. "By who? This guy you keep mentioning? Choke?"

"Szoke." He emphasized the *sh* sound in place of the *ch*. "He calls the shots."

"He's a moron."

"I don't disagree but that doesn't necessarily make him wrong about this. They had Héctor pegged as becoming the next boss in a few years. And a good one. The decision was made to stop that."

"And you just went along with it?"

Sandy could sense her hot glare burning toward him from the passenger seat. "I didn't have much of a choice in any of this."

"There's always a choice."

"You're right," he said, his tone turning brusque. "And I'm here now, so I guess I made my choice, didn't I?"

"But why?"

"It doesn't matter. Now, what about your family?"

Allison remained quiet for a few moments. Then she shook her head. "I don't really have any."

"Parents?"

"Both gone. No brothers and sisters either."

"Is there no one?"

Allison opened her mouth, then hesitated.

"What is it?" Sandy asked.

"I… have an aunt," she said. "In New Orleans."

"Do you trust her?"

"I barely know her anymore. She and my mom weren't terribly close. I haven't seen her since before Lita was born."

"She's still family, though. Would she take you in?"

Allison shrugged. "I don't know. But yeah, maybe."

Sandy thought about it for a moment, then said. "We'll head that way, then. New Orleans, it is."

21

Lori Carter stepped out of the motel office and lifted her phone. She had Szoke on speed dial, so she hit the button and waited.

He answered almost immediately. "What do you have?"

"Her name is Allison Delancey," Carter said.

"How'd you get that? She wasn't stupid enough to use her card to pay for the room, was she?"

"Sort of. She paid cash but the motel requires a card for security. The desk clerk, Greg, is a stickler for it."

Greg had also called the El Paso Police, but one of Szoke's gunmen had flashed a federal badge at the locals when they eventually arrived. The officers seemed more than willing to pass off the nuisance call to the feds. Carter wondered if they asked themselves why federal agents would be interested in a random shots fired call at a motel but assumed either apathy or laziness overshadowed their curiosity. Or maybe they had calls stacking up and welcomed taking one off the list.

"All right." Szoke's voice was muted as he spoke away from the phone mic. "Look up the address for Allison Delancey and send a team over."

"She won't be there," Carter said.

"I know, but I still have to check. And maybe they'll get something from poking around the house."

Carter shrugged. It was certainly possible. But, right now Allison and her daughter were almost certainly with Sandy

Banks, fleeing toward whatever passed for safety in their eyes.

"How about the room?" Szoke asked.

"Nothing. A few discarded items."

"Like what?"

"Generic stuff. Nothing identifiable, except for their phones."

"They dumped their phones?"

"Affirm."

"Shit," Szoke muttered.

That's about what we have, Carter thought.

"Get back here," Szoke ordered her.

"I will. But have Easton or Paulinus pull as much as they can on her before I arrive."

"Get back here," Szoke repeated, and broke the connection.

Carter lowered the phone, looking at it. Her lip curled and she thought about muttering what she thought of Szoke. But several members of his field team were within earshot, so she held her tongue. Instead, she motioned to the team leader.

The man was a shade under six feet, with a slender, athletic frame. An MP5 submachine gun hung from a shoulder strap. His left hand rested on the grip, though the weapon was pointed safely downward. At first glance, he looked to be in his thirties. However, the lines in his face told the story of at least a decade more than that in the profession.

At her gesture, he moved closer to her, but said nothing. He watched her expectantly.

"Your team didn't see anyone else besides the vehicle?"

He shook his head briefly. "I told you already."

"Just confirming. It was just the one car."

He nodded. "Headed west."

"Description?"

"Passenger car."

"Can you do better than that?"

"Red taillights."

Carter frowned at him.

The team leader returned her gaze, implacable. "It's the best I can do. I saw it from the motel room's bathroom window, already a block away, at least."

She sighed, but didn't argue. The team was ordered to secure the room and they had done so. It wasn't their fault Banks was no longer there.

She'd get Easton on traffic cams once she got back to the command post. Perhaps they'd turn up something. And Paulinus could access the Department of Motor Vehicles to find which cars were registered to Allison Delancey.

She paused, thinking.

Unless the car was registered to Maravilla. They'd need to check that, too.

"Anything else, Special Agent?"

"No." Carter turned away and headed back to where Atherton waited with the car.

She had work to do.

"Allison Delancey drives a green Subaru, two years old," Paulinus recited to her before she'd even settled into the seat at the conference table. "We've entered the plate as stolen."

"Good," Carter said, though she didn't know if that were entirely true. A stolen plate would attract any local law enforcement that came across Allison's vehicle. However, history had convinced her it wasn't necessarily good for those local officers to encounter Sandy Banks.

"It was the boss's idea," Paulinus said, casting a sycophantic glance toward Szoke to ensure he heard the praise. When Szoke continued to scroll on the tablet in front of him without giving any indication, Paulinus looked dejected. "Anyway," he added, "that should set a pretty good net to snare them in."

"What did the team find at the home?" Carter asked.

"I can answer that," said Szoke. He glanced up at her. "Almost nothing. They weren't there, of course. Sebastien found a few photos to help and Allison Delancey's laptop. He's breaking into it now."

"How far off is he from getting in?"

Szoke shrugged. "Three minutes. Three days. Who knows with computers?"

This was promising, despite the indeterminate timeline. "With the intel we gather from her computer, we should be able to figure out where she's heading."

"Unless Banks is calling the shots on their destination."

"I don't think he is."

Szoke scowled slightly. "Why do you say that?"

"What's he going to do? Run off with these two and live in a cabin in the woods somewhere, like it's a ready-made family?"

"Is that jealousy I hear?" Szoke gave her an acerbic smile.

She ignored the dig. "He's going to find a safe place for them before he goes to ground himself. That means it has to be someplace Allison views as safe. We need to check her family connections."

"I thought of that already. Easton is all over her socials."

"And?"

"Looks like it was just the two of them, mother and daughter. She didn't even post any photos of Maravilla."

Carter paused, thinking. The lack of Maravilla's public presence in Allison's life bothered her.

"What is it?" Szoke asked.

"Why did they meet in secret at the hotel?" she wondered.

"It's a moot point," Szoke said, waving his hand. "Stick to finding her."

"Fine," Carter said. "On Facebook, what did she put under

relationships?"

"Just the daughter. No other family. Only friends."

"Well, we'll have to dig harder, and elsewhere," said Carter. "Because, unless she has a bestie who is ride or die for her, it's going to be family."

"I agree. Easton is working on it."

"Where is he?"

"Next room over."

Carter stood to leave.

Szoke held up his hand to stop her. "He's got it handled. I need you to look at the friends she does have. Pick the ones that make the most sense and pay a visit. Brace them if you have to."

Carter's jaw tightened. "That's a waste of time."

"Until we find a better lead, it's time you've got to waste. So, go."

Carter debated arguing further but saw no profit in it. If there was a break in the research, Szoke would notify her immediately. She turned to go.

"Don't be shy on the bracing part," Szoke called after her.

22

Halfway to Houston, Sandy gassed up at a small gas station just off the freeway. Allison wordlessly handed him a wad of cash once the tank was full. He went inside and paid, keeping his contact with the tired clerk to a minimum.

An hour later, Lita roused from sleep. Sandy could sense her distrust from the back seat, though the teenager barely spoke. He was fine with the silence but as the driving wore on and he became tired, he knew he had to talk to remain alert and awake.

"Tell me something," he said. "Why the hotel?"

Allison didn't look his direction. "Why do you care?"

"I'm curious. You said you had a life in El Paso. I assume you had a home."

"Of course we did."

"Then why not meet there? What was the purpose of the hotel?"

Allison remained quiet for a long while. Sandy began to think she wouldn't answer. But finally, she spoke.

"Héctor isn't Lita's father," she said quietly.

"Yes, he *is*," Lita hissed at her from the back seat.

"*Mi hija*, you know what I mean."

"He doesn't need to know about us," she insisted.

Allison glanced sideways at Sandy. "Probably not," she agreed. "But we're committed now. He might as well know the truth."

Lita fumed in the back seat but didn't argue further.

Allison looked forward again, staring out of the windshield at the road ahead. "I met a boy name Ernesto in high school. He was sweet and we fell in love." She shrugged. "High school love, you know? We thought it would be forever, of course. And who knows, maybe it would've been. But after our sophomore year, Ernesto went back to Chihuahua."

"Why?" Sandy asked.

"His father's contract ended, so they returned home." She paused, and swallowed before continuing. "That summer, it didn't take long for me to realize I was pregnant with Lita. I should have written Ernesto right away, but after he left, he'd grown a little distant. I didn't know what to think. I worried that he'd think I was lying about the pregnancy. Trying to trap him."

A large bug splatted into the center of windshield. Sandy sprayed wiper fluid and let the wipers scrape frantically at the mess, which first smeared across the glass, then dissipated.

"I finally sent him an email when I was six months along. He didn't answer, so I actually sat down and wrote out an honest-to-goodness letter and mailed it. I didn't hear back for almost two months. When I finally did, it was Héctor who reached out to me."

She trailed off and looked out the passenger window. Sandy had an inkling where the story was going but he remained silent, letting her tell it how she chose.

Allison's voice was thicker when she spoke again, still staring out the passenger window. "Ernesto was Héctor's nephew. At least, that's how he described it, though I think Ernesto's father was actually a cousin of Héctor's. Either way, it was Héctor who contacted me."

"What happened?"

"Ernesto got caught up in some trouble while he was visiting Héctor. Wrong place, wrong time, with the wrong people. Some rival cartel members shot at the group. Ernesto was one of the casualties." She paused before continuing. "Héctor said Ernesto told him about me. He couldn't tell his parents about Lita and he didn't know what to do, so he'd asked his uncle for advice. Then he was killed."

Another victim, Sandy thought. The world seemed full of them.

"Héctor took it upon himself to take care of us. He did it for Ernesto."

"What about Ernesto's family?" Sandy asked.

"They never knew. Héctor said it was too dangerous. But I think there was more to it than that. Some shame, perhaps."

"But it was Héctor who bankrolled the two of you?"

"Yes. At first, I'm sure he did it out of duty, or guilt. But over time, it became something else. We grew close. He became a father to Lita. And a husband to me."

"You were married?"

"No, but… that's what he was to me."

Sandy considered what he'd heard. "Then the secrecy was to protect the two of you," he concluded.

She nodded. "He always said if anyone knew of our connection to him, it put us at risk. So I kept him invisible from our lives, at least to the outside world. He never came to the house. We always met at hotels or rental homes. Always in secret."

"That had to be hard."

"I suppose." Allison turned away from the darkened window to look forward again. "You get used to anything, though. Pretty soon, it just becomes your life."

"Not anymore," Lita muttered acidly.

"No," Allison agreed flatly. "Not anymore."

A Hard Favored Death

Sandy didn't answer. What was there for him to say? Instead, he drove deep into the night and well past dawn.

Once they reached Houston, Sandy headed downtown. He chose the largest parking garage he could find and entered.
"What are we doing?" Lita asked from the back seat.
Sandy glanced at her in the rearview mirror. Those words were among the first she'd spoken the entire drive, outside of murmuring one-word responses to her mother's queries about whether she was hungry or needed to use a restroom. Now, the dark-haired girl stared directly into Sandy's reflected eyes.
"Where are you taking us?" she asked.
"Gather your things," he told her. Turning to Allison, he added, "You, too. We need to change cars."
"Why?" Allison asked. "What's wrong with my car?"
"There's a good chance it's been reported as stolen."
Allison cocked her head. "But it's not."
Sandy didn't answer.
A moment later, Allison let out a muted "oh."
"Doing so multiplies their eyes by thousands," Sandy said. "So, we need to change cars. Be in something they're not looking for."
"Change?" Lita asked. "You mean steal."
Sandy met her gaze in the mirror. "If you want to survive, yes."
Lita scowled but didn't reply.
Sandy cruised through the levels of the garage until he found an older, blue and white Chevy Blazer. He parked in an open spot several stalls away. "Let's go."
He didn't wait for Allison and Lita to follow. Sandy walked quickly to the driver's side of the vehicle. He checked the door handle, just in case, but it was locked. Using the butt end of the knife Carter had given him, he delivered a single sharp

blow to the window. The safety glass shattered suddenly, popcorning into small pieces. Sandy reached through and unlocked the door. He swept aside glass and broke open the steering column.

The passenger doors swung open and the SUV rocked as Allison and Lita climbed in. Using the knife, Sandy bared the correct wires and crossed them.

The engine rumbled to life.

He checked to make sure both doors had been pulled closed. "Seatbelts," he said, and put the car in reverse.

The Chevy had half a tank of gas. Sandy took his time to find an independent gas station that didn't appear to have cameras.

"I need your credit card," he told Allison.

She hesitated, then dug a plastic card from her purse. She held it out to him reluctantly.

Sandy took it. "I'm going to fill up on gas. You're going to buy some food inside. If there's an ATM, you need to take out some more cash."

"How much?"

"Whatever the limit is. This will be the last time we use anything that can be traced to you."

Allison nodded her understanding. She motioned to Lita. "Come on, sweetie. Help me with the food."

"It's better if she doesn't," Sandy said. "If they put out an alert, the description will include mother and daughter. Go in alone so all the clerk sees is a single woman."

Allison thought for a brief moment, then dipped her chin. "All right."

Sandy ran the card through the gas pump, then removed the nozzle. He handed her back the credit card. "Any trouble, come straight back out here."

She took the card. "Got it."

Allison headed into the small convenience store. Sandy slid the nozzle into the gas tank and started the fuel. He looked up to see Lita staring at him through the window.

"Why'd you do it?" the teenager asked him, her tone dull and robotic.

"Do what?"

"Why'd you murder my father?"

The emotionless tone of her question surprised him. He'd expect her to be full of rage or grief, but the words came out flat.

She's still in shock, he told himself.

"That's a conversation for another day," he said.

"No. Now."

The two stared at each other. The chugging sound of gasoline filling the tank was the loudest noise Sandy could hear. Everything else faded into the background.

Finally, he said, "Your father wasn't who you thought he was."

"I know exactly who he was," Lita countered. "I know what he was."

"Yeah? And what's that?"

"He was a bad man. At least, to most of the world."

"Your mother tell you that?"

Lita scoffed. "My mother told me fairy tales. The internet told me the truth."

"Don't be so sure."

"There was plenty of information, once I knew how to find it. But that's not who he was to me. It's who he was to the rest of the world."

Sandy nodded slowly. "If you saw that, then you probably know why things happened like they did."

"I do," Lita said. "It's because you're a bad man, too."

Sandy kept his gaze locked on hers, surprised again, this time that her words cut him. "I suppose I am," he admitted.

"Then why are you helping us?" Lita demanded. "Or are you?"

"You know I am."

"Why, because you drove us away from those other people? People I never even saw? Do they even exist?"

"They do," Sandy said.

Lita scowled. "The only bad person I've seen so far is you. Maybe you're kidnapping us. Maybe that's why you had us throw away our phones back at the motel."

"Is that what you think?"

Lita glared at him for a few moments, then shrugged. "Maybe. I don't know."

Sandy glanced at the flicking numbers on the gas pump gauge. "If everything goes right, you won't ever have to find out."

"What kind of fucked up thing is that to say?" She leaned forward. "Even if you are actually helping us, do you think it'll make up for what you did? Because it won't. You'll still be a bad man."

"I know."

"Then why?"

Her tone reminded him of Allison's when she'd asked him the same question. Lita must have overheard that conversation, though he guessed she may have been sleeping. If she had been listening, though, she clearly wasn't satisfied with the answers he'd given her mother.

The gas hose jumped slightly as the fueling ended. Sandy reached for it, replacing it on the pump and closing up the gas tank on the SUV. When he finished, Lita was still staring at him. Her question hung in the air.

Sandy reached for the door handle and stopped. "You're right," he told her. "I've done a lot of bad things in my life. I've been a bad man. But the ones who are after you?" He pointed away from them. "They're worse."

Lita watched him blankly, taking in his words. Her expression did not soften.

Sandy held her gaze until Allison returned to the car. Then both he and Lita seemed to decide simultaneously to let the matter lie for now. She glanced away as her mother climbed into the passenger seat. Sandy got behind the wheel.

"I got five hundred dollars," Allison announced. She lifted a plastic bag laden with snacks. "And food."

"Good," Sandy grunted.

Allison looked back and forth between them. "What's going on here? I can feel the tension."

"Nothing," Sandy said. He started the vehicle.

Allison looked over her shoulder. "*Angelita?*"

"Nothing," the girl said sullenly.

Allison's eyes narrowed but she seemed to accept the reply.

Sandy pulled out of the lot and they continued east.

When they reached Beaumont, Sandy took the exit.

"Why are we stopping here?" Lita asked, leaning forward.

"Couple of reasons," Sandy answered.

Several long seconds went by in silence. Then Lita let out an exasperated sigh. "Like what?"

Sandy didn't reply. As he drove, Lita flopped back into her seat in frustration.

It took almost thirty minutes for him to find the same make and model in the same color scheme. He wasn't sure on the model year but the design was close enough. Sandy parked nearby, slipped out of the SUV, and made quick work out of switching the license plates.

Back in the vehicle, Lita said, "You could have just told me."

"Told you?"

"Before, when I asked what we were doing. You could have

just told me you were going to flop plates."

His eyes flicked up into the rearview mirror to meet hers. "Flop plates? Where'd you learn that?"

"Movies. I know why you did it, too."

"Why's that?"

Lita leaned back and crossed her arms with a smirk, saying nothing.

Fair enough, Sandy thought. He glanced at Allison. "You should call your aunt."

Allison lifted her hands. "I.. what am I supposed to say?"

"Just let her know you're coming. And listen to see if she sounds odd."

"Odd?"

"As in different. It's a long shot, but there's always a chance they've already connected all the dots and are waiting for us there."

"With Aunt Ophelia?" Allison shook her head. "No, I don't believe that. She'd never turn me in, even if I did something wrong."

"You might think that. So might she. But when armed men with badges show up on your doorstep, it's sometimes a different story."

"Not with Ophelia. She's always been… she's a resolute woman."

"I hope so. Even so, you should call her."

"Fine, but from what phone?"

"We'll find a payphone."

"They still have those?"

"A few."

It took nearly thirty minutes to find a payphone near a Pizza Hut. After Sandy parked, Allison remained in the passenger seat.

"What's wrong?" Sandy asked her.

"I don't have her number." She glanced at Sandy. "It's been

a long time."

"Call 4-1-1."

Allison nodded and got out of the car. Sandy watched her use the phone, speaking briefly before she returned to the car.

"No listing," she told him.

"Is that unusual?"

"I don't think so. She didn't have a phone when I visited her as a kid. I think the last time I was there I was fourteen or so and the lack of a phone drove me crazy at first."

"You said before you two weren't close."

"It's kinda weird. We're close but not close. Like, I only saw her every couple of years during the summer but, when I did, it was nice." She shrugged. "Kin, you know?"

"Well, your aunt will work as a temporary option for a few days, but you're going to need a master plan." Sandy turned away. He started the SUV and headed back toward the freeway.

They rode in silence for several blocks. Then Allison said, "So you're leaving us?"

"As soon as I get you to your aunt, yes."

Allison didn't reply.

From the backseat, Sandy heard Lita mutter, "Good."

He took the onramp and continued east.

23

"I told you everything I know."

The red-haired woman's gaze cut away from Lori Carter to the burly, expressionless man in dark tactical clothing beside her. The confusion and fear in her expression was palpable.

The disgust and shame in Carter's gut was, too.

Nonetheless, she forced herself to snap her fingers and bring the woman's attention back to her.

"Lucy, here."

Lucy met her gaze. Carter could see her lip tremble slightly.

"Why are you doing this?" Lucy whispered.

"I'm just asking questions," Carter assured her. "That's all."

Lucy flicked her eyes once more to the silent commando beside Carter. She opened her mouth to reply, thought better of it, and pressed her lips together.

Around them, the pleasant décor of Lucy's apartment seemed out of place to Carter. Given the tenor of their conversation, the antiseptic, bare walls of an interrogation room would have been more appropriate. Instead of sitting in a suspect's chair in custody, Lucy Belmont huddled in her own pale blue Pamplona, looking shell-shocked.

"You said Allison didn't have many friends," Carter continued. "Why not?"

Lucy swallowed. "She was just a private person, I guess. I mean, we were *barely* friends. An occasional drink or wine night at her place once in a while."

"What'd you two talk about?"

"Reality shows. Work. Girl stuff."

"How about her family?"

"Aside from Lita, I didn't know of any."

"Boyfriends?"

Lucy hesitated, then shrugged. "One. She never said much about him. He supposedly traveled a lot for business. Never came to the house. I thought he might have been one of you, if you want the truth."

"One of us?"

"Government people. The secret kind. CIA or whatever."

"You thought he was a spy?"

She shrugged again. "I wasn't sure. It was just something I wondered."

"What about other family?"

"No." Lucy's tone sounded doubtful.

Carter paused. She turned her head slightly toward the man at her side. He inched forward slightly. Lucy shrank back into her chair involuntarily, staring up at him. Then she looked back to Carter.

"Okay, maybe," she said.

"Maybe what?"

"Maybe she had some relative in New Orleans she might have mentioned once or twice."

"What's her name?"

"I don't think they were very close."

"What is her name?" Carter repeated forcefully.

"I don't know."

Carter sighed. She turned her head, this time meeting the eyes of the man beside her. "I'm going outside for a smoke. I'll be back in three minutes."

The man grunted and turned his flat gaze back to Lucy. Then he shifted forward a half step, seemingly straining like a greyhound in the chute.

Carter turned to walk away. When she reached the door, Lucy called out to her.

"Wait."

Carter didn't stop. She dropped her hand onto the door knob.

"*Wait!*" Lucy pleaded.

Carter paused. She looked over her shoulder at Lucy. "What's her name, Lucy? Last chance."

Lucy blinked rapidly and swallowed. She cast a sideways glance at the man in black, then back to Carter.

"Ophelia," she said. "Ophelia Reed."

"I've got a name for you to check," Carter told Paulinus as she strode into the command center. "Ophelia Reed."

Paulinus's fingers rested on the keyboard. However, he didn't type. Instead, he said, "We got a hit on Allison's debit card."

"What? Why didn't you call me?"

Paulinus didn't respond. Carter turned her attention to Szoke who sat at the head of the conference table. A closed laptop, along with a pen and notepad, sat untouched on table in front of him.

"There was no pressing need to inform you," Szoke said. "I instructed him to hold the intel until we reassembled here."

His self-important tone grated on her nerves. More and more, Szoke's attitudes and mannerisms reminded her of Danforth. It had been years since she'd seen the shadowy figure. She assumed he only met with Szoke, whether in person or via messages, to relay his directives. Despite his physical absence, his presence loomed large over the team. She wondered if the slow shift in Szoke's behavior came from his interactions with Danforth.

Better him than me.

She suppressed her irritation. "Fine. What's the hit?"

Szoke waved for Paulinus to continue.

The analyst cleared his throat. "She withdrew cash from an ATM at a convenience store in Houston."

"Was it definitely her?"

"I got the ATM camera footage," Paulinus said smugly. "It's confirmed."

Carter nodded slowly. "Houston makes sense," she said.

"Why's that?" Szoke asked.

"We know Allison has barely any family. But she does have an aunt on her mother's side. I think that's where she's headed."

"Where'd this intel come from?" Szoke asked her.

"Lucy Belmont."

"The friend? So, she was cooperative, then."

It was a statement, not a question. Carter didn't reply. She suspected Szoke already knew the information. The men who'd accompanied her no doubt called in the details as soon as she was out of earshot. The fact didn't surprise her. The only real surprise was Szoke retained the façade of trusting her. She wondered how much longer that nicety would last.

"Reed is a sixty-one-year-old white woman." Paulinus said, interrupting her thoughts. He recited information from the screen in front of him. "She lives in a lower middle class neighborhood in New Orleans." He paused, then added, "Louisiana."

"I know where New Orleans is," Carter snapped. She twirled her finger. "Just give me the address."

Paulinus read off the street and numbers, unfazed by her tone.

"Can you text that to me?" she asked, standing to leave.

Paulinus struck several keys. A moment later her phone buzzed. She didn't bother to view the message. "Call the airport," she instructed Paulinus. "I'll need a flight. Get me something, even if it's small—"

"That won't be necessary," Szoke informed her.

Carter paused. "Have you got something else more pressing?"

"Not at present."

"Then this is our best lead. We know she has an aunt in New Orleans. She withdrew money in Houston. They're headed in the right direction."

"You're correct."

"Then I'll be on my way. If we can get a charter—"

"I've already arranged it," Szoke said. "We'll head to the airport in an hour and a half."

Carter frowned. She turned back to Paulinus. "When was the ATM withdrawal?"

"Fourteen eleven hours," the analyst said.

She glanced at her watch. "Almost two hours ago. What's the drive from Houston to New Orleans? Five hours?"

"Five hours and twenty minutes," Paulinus corrected her.

Carter ignored him, directing her efforts toward Szoke now. "Time is burning, Mark. They have a huge head start. With all the assets in place here, you couldn't get us on a plane any sooner?"

Szoke smirked. "You're right about time being of the essence and the need to put assets in place. That's why we're taking the later flight."

It only took a moment for her to grasp his meaning. "You sent the team directly to the airport from Lucy Belmont's."

"I did."

"Then why keep up pretenses that I'm in charge?"

"That's finished," Szoke agreed. He turned over his hands. "As you point out, there wasn't much time. Certainly not enough to entertain your ego."

"*My* ego?"

"You're still hanging on to this image of yourself as the fearless FBI special agent. For a long while, I've allowed you to cling to that illusion. But as useful as it's been over time, mission necessity outweighed your fragile ego needs here. In fact, the mission trumps *all* the lies we need to tell ourselves."

Carter gaped at him. "And which ones do *you* tell *your*self? I'd think it'd take a monumental batch of rationalizations just for you to get up in the morning."

"I used to lie to myself," Szoke admitted, his smooth tone continuing. "But that only causes psychological dissonance. Stress. It gets in the way of the mission. Besides, once you accept who you are now, life gets significantly easier."

Carter was surprised at the burst of honesty from him, even if the philosophy he spouted didn't sit right with her. "What if what we are is monsters, Mark? How do you accept that?"

"We're all monsters. Every single one of us is a monster to someone. When we eradicate a man or woman who is a direct threat to safety of this country—a monster to us—we are, no doubt, a monster to them. Then we also become a monster to whatever misguided souls loved that person." He shrugged benignly. "It's all perspective."

"Sounds like moral relativism to me."

"Call it what you will."

"That *is* what it's called, and it's straight out of a freshman philosophy class. I didn't buy it then and I don't buy it now."

"I'm not selling it. I don't have to. This shit sells itself. You know why?"

"Because it's another massive rationalization?"

"No. Because it's true. And I'm tired of letting you pretend otherwise, Lori. So I'm not going to any longer. You're not in the FBI. Newsflash—you don't even work for the CIA anymore."

Carter blinked and cocked her head. "Come again?"

"Danforth deep-sheeted our files years ago. We're on the other side of the black curtain now." He smiled humorlessly. "All illusions swept away yet? You know who you are?"

Carter remained silent while the information seeped in. *I'm just like Banks now. An invisible, throwaway tool. Another cog in a killing machine.*

"Lori? Are we clear?"

She nodded slowly.

"Good," said Szoke, "because there's something else I need to tell you about Ophelia Reed."

24

Cities were like people, Sandy mused. Some had personality, others were bland. He'd been in plenty of towns that could have been lifted wholesale and plopped down anywhere in the country without missing a beat. Vanilla towns, he considered them.

Not New Orleans.

The city had a distinct personality. Even away from the tourist zones, the streets spoke to Sandy in a strange way. It had all the mystery of an old friend you never quite really knew, resulting in a wave of nostalgia, comfort, and unease, all at once.

That's the road weariness, he told himself. The adrenaline dump, followed by long hours of driving and no sleep. Men start to hallucinate after a while. Gray ghosts they called them when he was in the Army. Streaking movement at the edge of vision. Sandy figured it was the brain's way of tricking the body into spiking adrenaline to keep itself awake.

But the mind drifted, too. Odd thoughts and memories forced their way in. An hour outside of the city, he'd found himself reliving a day on the sandy banks of Sugar Creek with Janet. The absolute innocence of those moments seemed long distant to him now, detached, like a foreign film in a language he couldn't identify with no subtitles.

Had that been him once? Someone who loved and dreamt? Sandy could remember he'd felt that way but, for the life of him, he couldn't dredge up the emotional memory of *how* that felt. The capacity to feel love, even heartbreak, seemed lost to him. Only bitterness and rage seemed real. He could touch those, remind himself how those corrosive emotions felt. Even that took effort, though.

Coldness was the easiest. Detached weariness. That was who he had become. The boy who kissed the girl at Sugar Creek was as gone as the soldier who carried a dead man through the Central American jungle or the ex-cop who exacted penance on the worst criminals who had somehow managed to elude justice.

Now, cruising through the streets of New Orleans with its unique blend of history, architecture, joy, danger, and poverty, Sandy tried desperately to feel something. Anything.

All he could muster was icy regret.

"There it is," Allison said, leaning forward in the passenger seat and pointing. "The church with the tree growing up inside it."

Sandy slowed to peer at the curiosity. The simple white church sat on the corner of the street. It was made of the same clapboard siding he'd seen on many houses in this part of town. There was nothing extraordinary about it except a thick-trunked tree extended out of the roof on the street side. Stark, leafless branches darted out in all directions, like splayed fingers. The image spoke more of danger than religious comfort.

"Cool," Lita murmured from the backseat.

"Auntie Ophelia lives three streets that way." Allison pointed east. "Take a left when we get there."

Sandy followed her directions. As he drove away from the church, he stole a few final glances in the rearview mirror. He wondered what the parishioners thought of the tree. Did they see it as something special? A monstrosity? Or did they even see it all anymore?

"Here," said Allison. "You'll miss the turn."

Sandy hooked a left. He kept his speed slow, scanning the street ahead for any signs of Szoke's team. It was a safe assumption they'd managed to identify Allison by now. How long would it take to figure out her possible destinations? He hoped it was days instead of hours, at least for the sake of her and the girl.

"That's it." Allison gestured toward a dark green bungalow mid-block.

Sandy rolled to a stop. Allison pulled her purse strap over her head, wearing the strap cross-body. She reached for the door, but he touched her shoulder to stop her.

"Wait," he said.

He could sense her wanting to ask why, but she held her tongue.

Sandy swept his gaze over the quiet neighborhood. It was mostly quiet in the last light of the dying day. No porch lights were yet burning, but the sun had dipped below the roof line, casting faint shadows that slashed across the tiny lawns. At a few homes, figures sat comfortably on the porches, seeming without a care.

He took the time to examine each of them. None had the telltale appearance he'd come to recognize in an undercover operative—that vibe of trying very hard not to seem to be trying at anything at all.

"Okay," he finally said. "Let's go."

"You mean you're not just going to drop us off?" Lita's sarcasm was plain as she kicked open the rear door.

Sandy ignored the dig, instead looking at Allison. "But slowly, yeah?"

The woman nodded.

Absently, Sandy touched the butt of the handgun in the holster on his belt. Reassured, he pushed open the door. The heat and thick humidity pressed in on his skin as soon as he left the SUV.

Allison was already halfway around the front of the car. She stopped at the end of the short walkway and waited for him.

"She's painted it since I was here last. It used to be yellow." Allison shrugged and started toward the door.

Sandy followed, angling his approach opposite the hinge side of the door. When she arrived and raised her hand to knock, he stood with the best view of where the door opening would occur. He put his hands on his hips so the gun under his light jacket was mere inches from his right hand.

There was a long pause after Allison knocked. She raised her hand to knock again when there was the jangling rattle of a lock. A black woman around forty pulled open the door. She eyed Allison with a mixture of surprise and suspicion.

"Yes?"

Allison glanced at the house numbers. "I'm looking for Ophelia."

The woman shook her head. "Ain't no Ophelia here."

Allison appeared momentarily confused. Then she asked, "Are you sure?"

The woman cocked her head. "What are you talking about, am I sure? Who *are* you?"

Allison glanced over at Sandy. "I know this is the place. This is my aunt's house."

"This is *my* house," the woman corrected her.

"Ma'am," Sandy interjected, "you mind if I ask how long you've lived here?"

The woman crossed her arms. "Going on seven years. Bought it from a man named Griffin." She looked back and forth between the two of them. "What's this about?"

"I'm sorry," Allison said, rallying. "My aunt used to live here. I was… we wanted to surprise her with a visit."

"Well, sorry to say she don't live here no more. Like I said, I've been here seven years. I think Mr. Griffin only had the place for a couple of years 'fore he moved to Baton Rouge." She peered more closely at Allison. "You ain't seen your auntie in almost ten years, child? That's a shame."

Allison nodded. "I know."

"You wouldn't know where Ophelia Reed moved to, would you?" Sandy asked the woman.

She shook her head. "First I've heard of the name. Some one of the neighbors might know. Hell, they always sticking their noses in other people's business anyway."

Allison took a deep breath and let it out. "All right. Thank you. Sorry for bothering you."

"Ain't no kind of thing." The woman uncrossed her arms and touched Allison lightly on the shoulder, just briefly. "Good luck finding your auntie, child."

"Thanks."

The woman closed the door.

Allison trudged down the porch steps. Halfway down the walk, she turned to Sandy. "I need to get a smart phone. A burner or something. If I can get on the 'net, I can find her." She glanced at Lita. "Or she can."

"Not yet," Sandy said. He didn't bother telling her that once Szoke identified Ophelia Reed, he'd have computer intelligence scouring the web for any searches on the name. It wasn't a guarantee, but the risk of them getting a hit on Allison's search and tracking it back to her phone, burner or not, was too great. Besides, he had another, more analog idea.

"Where are you going?" Allison asked.

Sandy continued down the sidewalk until he was two houses down from where they'd parked. Behind him, he heard Allison and Lita scurry to catch up.

"Not every answer has to come from Google," Sandy told her as he turned up a walkway. He wiped the sleeve of his jacket across his forehead, which was already streaming with sweat.

A trio sat on the porch in front of the pale blue house. Two women and a man. They watched Sandy with skeptic curiosity. Halfway up the walk, he raised a hand in greeting. The man lifted his chin while the two women remained impassive.

When he drew close, one woman spoke. She wore a casual summer dress of deep orange patterned with flowers in bold, dark colors. "Whatever you were selling her, we don't want it, neither."

Sandy didn't bother trying to force a smile onto his face. Any lack of authenticity would only cause these three to throw up further defenses. Instead, he motioned toward Allison. "My friend is looking for her aunt who used to live over there. I was hoping you might know her?"

The woman in the orange dress drifted her gaze to Allison as she reached Sandy's side. "Who's your auntie?"

"Ophelia Reed," Allison answered.

The two women on the porch exchanged a glance. Sandy caught the meaning behind it and felt himself sag slightly. Then the first woman returned her attention to Allison. She looked her up and down. "Ophelia was your auntie?"

"She is. I haven't seen her in a long time. She moved and we're trying to figure out where."

Sandy glanced at the ground, waiting for realization to kick in for Allison. When he looked up again, Allison was still watching the woman in the orange dress, waiting for an answer.

The woman finished her examination of Allison. She asked the other woman, "What you think?"

The second woman shrugged. "Could be, sure."

The first woman pursed her lips. "I think so, too." She drew in a breath and faced Allison. "So you'd be little Alli, then?"

Allison smiled. It was the first time since he'd met her Sandy had seen any genuine joy on her face.

"Yes, I am. You remember me?"

"Can't say as I entirely do. Just saw you coming and going a few times when you was younger. But we sure heard about you often enough."

"Uh-huh," agreed the other woman. "Sure did."

"That Ophelia, she was proud of you."

Allison's smile broadened. Her eyes glistened. "That's nice to hear."

The woman in orange smiled slightly. "It's nice, but hearing it about a thousand times over, near every day? Maybe not so much."

"Did you keep in touch after she moved?" Allison asked. "Do you know where she is now?"

The two women on the porch exchanged glances again, saying nothing.

It took a moment longer before the penny finally dropped for Allison. Her smile faltered. "No…" she said.

The woman in orange nodded sympathetically. "I'm afraid so, child. She passed on, must be ten, eleven years ago now."

The tears of joy in Allison's eyes spilled out now, heavy drops of sadness instead. "I didn't know."

Neither woman said anything but looked on in sympathy.

"What happened?" Allison asked, her words sound wet.

"Stroke, I believe. Ambulance man said she went quick. No pain." She shrugged. "Like to think he knows his business, but who can say?"

Allison stood stock-still, tears streaming down her cheeks. Lita stepped up and wrapped her arms around her from behind, squeezing. Allison reached up and clasped her daughter's hands.

"Our condolences on your loss," the woman in orange said. "Ophelia was a fine person."

"She was," the other woman agreed. Next to her, the man nodded his head in vigorous agreement.

Sandy waited a few moments to give Allison a chance to process the news. She'd said she wasn't close with her aunt, but he supposed the combination of Ophelia being wrapped up in childhood memories and the overwhelming nature of recent events supercharged the woman's emotional state. He'd give her a minute before they needed to leave and Allison asked him about their next move.

Instead, Allison surprised him with her next question, and it wasn't directed at him. She swallowed and asked the woman in orange, "Do you know where she's buried?"

"We don't have time for this," Sandy told her.

"Just keep driving," Allison insisted.

"We need to figure out a plan."

"The plan is I'm going to pay my respects to my aunt." She pointed at an upcoming sign. "Turn right there."

Sandy did as she requested. "Sentimentality isn't something you can afford right now."

"What do you care?" Lita snapped from the back seat. "You were just going to dump us off at her house anyway."

Sandy opened his mouth to reply but Allison cut him off. "These people you worked for, did they know my name?"

Sandy shook his head. "Not when I left. But they probably do by now."

"Do they know the car we're driving? Or are they still looking for my Subaru?"

"I can't say. But, even if they haven't put us in this rig, it's still most likely been reported stolen."

"That's why you switched the plates in Beaumont, though, right? *That* person probably hasn't even noticed the difference yet."

"Maybe not," Sandy allowed. "But, if the original set of plates are hot, which they probably are, then a cop may have spotted them on the switched truck and stopped the unsuspecting driver. It won't take more than a few minutes before they figure out he's not involved, only the victim of a plate flop." He glanced up in the rearview mirror to meet Lita's gaze. The girl tried to smirk, but a little bit of a smile slipped through her expression. "They'll run the VIN on that rig and get the plate assigned to it—the one that's currently on this rig. Then this will be listed stolen as well." He gave Allison a meaningful look. "All of this may have already happened."

Allison was undeterred. "*Or*," she argued, "they could still be trying to figure out who the mystery woman and daughter were in that hotel room."

"Unlikely. They know. And every moment we're driving around is a risk."

"I need to say goodbye to her," Allison said.

"It's a waste of valuable time."

"A *waste?*" Her tone sounded vicious.

"A luxury we don't have," Sandy amended.

Allison turned her gaze forward, her tone resolute. "You can drop us off at the cemetery if you want."

Sandy said nothing. He kept driving.

Lafourche Cemetery was everything Sandy expected it to be.

The entrance to the remote cemetery was a simple iron-wrought black archway with the name across the breadth of it. Sandy parked nearby, backing the SUV into the parking stall. Neither Allison nor Lita said anything about this, though he felt the young girl's eyes on him when he swung his arm onto Allison's seat and looked over his shoulder while backing.

Once out of the car, they made their way under the entrance arch. Allison consulted a posted index map on a sign hanging to the right of the entrance, unseen from the outside. Sandy swept his gaze across the many tombstones, markers and tiny crypts. Lafourche held none of the garish mausoleums Sandy had seen pictures of in more famous cemeteries, but that tracked for him. Ophelia's home had been nice but modest. It made sense her final resting place would be the same.

Allison returned from the map. "It's this way," she said, her tone subdued.

She started walking. Lita stepped forward and took her hand. Sandy trailed several yards behind the pair, continuing to scan the environment. The multitude of weathered, white monuments provided a slew of possible hiding places for any attackers. Yet, aside from the stray visitor here and there, he saw no suspicious movement.

After a few minutes of slow, purposeful walking, Allison turned down a narrow row of crypts. Sandy followed. The right side of the passageway was a wall lined with memorial plaques. The image reminded Sandy of a series of oversized, ramshackle mailboxes at a central post office. Two thirds of the way down, Allison stopped in front of a small square. He slowed then held up a respectful distance away.

Allison put her arm around Lita and drew her close. With her free hand, she reached out to touch the stone in front of her. Sandy heard her whispering. He strained to hear her but whatever she said died in the hot, humid air between them. Tears streaked down her cheeks.

He noticed Lita was not crying.

She's a tough one. Or good at faking it.

Then again, the teenager never knew Ophelia, so the impact might not be there for her.

Sandy tried to remain still as he waited. The line of large crypts that stood opposite the more modest sepulchers provided shade but even so, sweat ran down his temples and the sides of his body. His eyes darted around continually, watching for movement. He saw none.

Seeing no threats, and surrounded by the dead, Sandy's thoughts unerringly drifted to his own losses.

His mother, taken violently and too soon. The revenge he exacted from the man responsible sealed his own destiny, hadn't it? Started him down that path that led him to this cemetery?

Then there was Evan Lloyd, the wounded comrade Sandy carried through the jungle on his back only to find he'd died during the journey. Except his name wasn't Sandy then, was it? It was Keegan, and even that wasn't his real name.

Lies upon lies, dating back to the beginning.

Once he became Sandy Banks—another lie—and tried to break free of that cycle, there was Yvonne Lewis, the battered wife he'd failed. His struggle to cope with the massive guilt over that event was what cued Lieutenant Cal Ridley to believe he'd be a perfect addition to the Four Horsemen. Vigilante justice for the worst of criminals who slipped through the system. It sounded like a cop's dream but it had ended in a nightmare for Sandy.

Enter Kelly Merchant, the innocent woman he'd been tricked into murdering. Another mother, no less. Dead because of her piece of shit husband.

No. Dead because of me. I pulled the trigger.

It was my fault.

Not the last death that was his fault, either. Cousin Mayford made his last stand in the woods of Tennessee to provide Sandy time to escape. Regardless of how the man might have relished the manner of his exit from this world, one truth remained immutable: his death was Sandy's fault.

And then there was Janet. At least her passing wasn't on him. She'd made a life for herself. A good and decent life, full of love and purpose. He'd done what he had to do to ensure she kept it for as long as fate allowed.

Watching Allison and Lita stare quietly at the hard, silent

stone in front of them, Sandy wondered briefly who would mourn him when he shuffled off this mortal coil. No one, he realized. Perhaps Brophy, though the old soldier might already have beaten Sandy into the afterlife. The same could be said of Hank, the only remaining Horseman aside from Sandy. Even if one of them were still alive, they'd never hear about Sandy's death when it came. The most either man might do is wonder about him. Maybe feel a vague sense of bittersweet sadness. Perhaps lift a glass in a silent toast. That was the most he could hope for, wasn't it?

It would have to be enough.

It was certainly more than he deserved.

Allison and Lita stood in front of the marker for a long while. Finally, Allison wiped at her eyes and gave Lita a final squeeze. The two walked toward Sandy.

"Thanks," Allison said, her voice thick with tears and holding little of the earlier recrimination for him. "I needed to do that. Not just for Ophelia, but…" She paused, her eyes locking with Sandy's. He read the mixture of grief, hate, and gratitude in her gaze. After a moment, she said, "Not just for her."

He nodded. Wordlessly, he motioned for them to head back to the SUV at the front of the cemetery.

It was time to move on.

For both of them.

25

He spotted the first of the mercenaries as soon as he rounded the corner behind Allison and Lita.

These two weren't even trying to hide. The men stood in the path ahead, near carbon copies of each other. Both wore khaki tactical pants and long-sleeved military style shirts, stained with sweat. Wraparound sunglasses adorned the faces of both men. They awaited the trio, hands dangling like gunfighters above the drop-down holsters strapped to their thighs.

Sandy saw two others trotting up from behind, still at a distance, but angling along the sides of the path, carrying submachine guns.

"Down!" he shouted automatically, reaching for his pistol.

Both men on the pathway drew.

Sandy ripped the gun from his holster with one hand. With the other, he pushed Lita toward a nearby crypt. The girl collapsed behind the stone monument just as the first shots rang out. In reaction, Allison crouched to the ground.

Bullets whizzed past Sandy, chipping at the stone crypt behind him. Sandy returned fire with a three-round burst. One of the men in the pathway clutched his gut and crumpled to the ground. The other strode directly toward Sandy, shooting rapidly. Hot pain sliced into Sandy's outer thigh and he buckled. Sandy went with the motion, dropping to his opposite knee and returning fire.

Just as the slide locked to the rear, one of Sandy's rounds caught the advancing soldier in the forehead. He toppled over backward.

"Come on!" Sandy yelled at Allison. He grabbed her by the arm and pulled her to Lita's position. The two men further away opened fire and several rounds chased Sandy and Allison, biting into the ground as they made it behind the small crypt.

As soon as they reached cover, Sandy dropped the empty magazine and slammed in another, his mind assessing the tactical situation. He had only one remaining mag. There were at least two soldiers still attacking, armed with superior weaponry and considerably more ammo. They might be the extent of the element, since four-man teams had been the standard throughout Sandy's tenure in the unit. But more could be on the way.

"You're bleeding," Lita said.

Sandy glanced down at his leg. A hole was torn in his pants near his left quadriceps and the material around the entrance wound was already soaked with blood. He could feel the sensation of pain hovering there but adrenaline kept it momentarily at bay.

"No time for that," he said. "We have to move."

Several bullets smacked into the stone crypt, sending up a spray of debris.

"We can't!" Allison said. "It's too dangerous."

"If we stay here, one of them will circle around and flank us," Sandy said. He peered around the edge of the crypt, only to be met with another burst of gunfire.

"See?" Allison said. "We're trapped."

Sandy motioned in the opposite direction. "Run to the next crypt," he said, pointing to one in the next row. "That one."

Allison's gaze cut to his wounded leg.

"I'll be fine," he told her. "Go. Stay low. I'll cover you."

"But—"

"Do it now!" Sandy barked.

Without waiting for her reaction, Sandy leaned outside of cover and fired several shots. One of the attackers ducked behind a large gravestone, but Sandy was unable to spot the second man.

He pulled back behind cover and glanced to his right. He was relieved to find himself alone. When faced with critical stress, some people froze. Others fled. Fewer fought. Right now, all he needed was for neither Allison nor Lita to freeze.

Sandy forced himself to his feet, slouching to stay below the top of cover. He tested his wounded leg. It couldn't hold his full weight but he was able to limp the several steps to the far side of the stone monument.

Allison and Lita were crouched behind the next crypt, pressed against the stone. Both bore expressions of fear but he saw no panic there.

Not yet, at least.

Sandy dashed across the short open space in an awkward, limping gait. No sooner had he ducked behind the stone when a pair of shots ricocheted past. One knocked out a chunk of stone, which brushed Sandy's shoulder as it fell.

He crouched down, grimacing slightly. Allison looked at him expectantly.

"We're going to keep doing this," he told her and Lita. "Leapfrogging from cover to cover." He used his open hand to signal the direction of the SUV. "We'll work our way all the way back to the SUV. Do you understand?"

Both of them nodded. Allison's gaze dropped to his leg. "What about that?"

Sandy looked down. The bloodstain had spread past his knee. The pain remained a distant threat but the dull throb he felt told him it was coming as soon as the adrenaline dump wore off.

"Shit," he muttered.

Sandy leaned around the corner of the crypt and snapped off a quick shot. He caught the soldier he'd previously seen duck behind a gravestone moving in the open space between cover, so he fired twice more. The man scrambled behind another stone monument, seemingly unharmed.

Next to him, Sandy heard a tearing sound. He whipped the pistol around in that direction only to see Allison had taken off her shirt, leaving her clad in the tank top she wore beneath. She tore at one of the sleeves, ripping it free.

More shots plinked into the stone near Sandy. He pointed toward the next crypt. "That one," he said. "Now."

"Just a second."

"Now!"

Allison didn't obey his command. Sandy felt a stab of frustration. She didn't understand. These men were professional warriors. There was no room for—

"Here," Allison thrusted the ragged remains of her sleeve toward him.

Sandy took the item without thinking, handing her the gun in return. "You know how to use that?" he asked.

"Theoretically."

"Then just point and shoot at anything that moves."

Allison held the gun uneasily, her expression queasy.

Sandy put his back to the stone and let himself slide down into a sitting position. Then he wrapped the sleeve around his thigh and wrenched down on the makeshift bandage, making the knot as tight as he could. The pain finally broke through the adrenaline, vividly lancing up and down his leg. He gritted his teeth and finished the knot, then reached out for the gun.

Allison returned the weapon, looking relieved to be rid of it.

"The next crypt," Sandy ordered. "Go."

He leaned out to fire at the crouching soldier. As soon as he did, rounds spit at him, forcing him to duck back behind cover. Nonetheless, Allison and Lita had already dashed to the next location. Sandy forced himself to stand, feeling his leg stiffening with every step.

This time, bullets chased him from the first move from cover, biting into the turf near his feet as he scrambled toward the next crypt. One bullet sailed past his head. The buzz of the sonic pressure told him it was a near miss.

"We'll never get to the SUV like this," Allison said.

"Yes, we will. Just keep moving." He pointed then wheeled out to provide covering fire.

The soldier had been moving as well and dove behind a nearby gravestone. He slid on the grass, skidding past the marker. Sandy fired several more shots and was rewarded with a cry of pain from the man. The soldier was still able to drag himself behind cover, however.

Wounded but not out of the fight, he thought. *Like me.*

But where was the other one?

Sandy kept his head on a swivel, searching for the second combatant. Shots struck nearby. From the angle, those had to be coming from the wounded man.

"Which one next?" Allison asked.

Sandy shuffled to his right and peered around the crypt. Forty yards away, he could see the SUV. He'd half-expected it to be hemmed in by another vehicle, so he was pleasantly surprised to see the way was clear.

The SUV meant escape.

If only they could get to it.

His gaze swept the ground in between their location and the vehicle. Then he dropped the mag and checked his round count. Four more plus one in the pipe. After that, he was down to one final magazine.

Allison was right. At this rate, he'd run out of ammo before they reached their destination. When that happened, the soldiers would take their time in the approach, but it would be inexorable. Once Sandy's group was flanked, they'd be virtually helpless. It was pretty clear what that meant. This was no capture mission. It was an execution.

"We're going to have to take some risks," Sandy said, pointing to a larger mausoleum about halfway to the parking lot. "See the one with the small French flag next to the door? That's where we go next."

Allison squinted. "That far?"

Sandy nodded, sliding back to his original position. "It's our only chance."

Allison glanced at Lita. "You ready?"

The girl was staring at her mother. She bobbed her head once.

"Go!" Sandy said.

He didn't wait to see if they did as he bade. Instead, he leaned around the corner of the crypt and sought out a target. Due to the angle, he could see a tiny bit of khaki behind the same gravestone as before. He snapped off two shots. One went wide but the other splashed into the stone, causing the soldier to recoil.

Still alive. Still dangerous.

Sandy limped to the other end of the crypt and glanced to see if the way was clear. Allison and Lita were crossing the last few yards to the other mausoleum. He was relieved to see they continued around the corner, putting the bulk of the small shrine between them and the known attacker.

Slipping around the corner, Sandy steeled himself for the same run the women had just accomplished. Automatic gunfire erupted from the other side of the crypt, splatting against the stone. Sandy eased up to the corner and sent two more rounds toward the soldier crouching behind the gravestone.

Then he ran.

His limping stride was already more exaggerated than before as he surged forward. Sandy worried his leg might give way entirely, causing him to collapse to the grassy ground.

If he fell, he was dead.

If he stopped running, he was dead.

Gunshots rang out. Another slicing pain raked across his scapula.

Sandy kept moving. His leg was pounding with pain now. Every breath was ragged. He could taste blood in his mouth along with the tang of gunpowder in the air.

More shots dotted the ground in front of him, kicking up tufts of sod and dirt.

Sandy zig-zagged briefly to throw off the man's aim. Another burst of rounds struck the mausoleum wall just above his left shoulder. Sandy ducked around the corner to join Allison and Lita.

Mother and daughter were crouched with their backs against the mausoleum wall, holding hands. Sandy dropped the magazine from the pistol and slammed in the last one remaining. While he did this, he took a moment to examine Allison and Lita. Fear ran high on their faces, he could see. That was to be expected. But, now that the initial shock of the attack had subsided, he also saw steel emerging in their demeanor. Both of them held some fire in their eyes, a grim resolve to survive.

Good. We're going to need that.

Allison peeked around the corner. "The SUV is too far away."

Sandy grimaced as his leg throbbed loudly. He slid closer to them, sensing the wetness his back left along the dull white stone. "We're almost out of time and ammo," he said. "We have to get to the vehicle."

A pair of shots pinged against the far side of the mausoleum.

Why is he wasting ammo?

"There's another crypt, not far from the lot," she reported. "Just past that tree." She glanced over her shoulder at him. "One more lily pad to hop."

Sandy felt a slight wave of dizziness. He shook his head to clear it.

Allison's eyes narrowed. "We can make that crypt," she urged. "Then the rig, like you said."

Reluctantly, Sandy nodded. Something seemed off. He realized it was his injuries taking their toll. How much blood had he lost? It didn't seem like much, but he hadn't been monitoring his wounds that closely. He glanced over his own shoulder at the dull smear he'd left on the mausoleum wall.

Not too much blood there. The back injury might be more than a graze, but nothing too serious. He turned his attention to his leg. His clothing was soaked near the wound but the wet stain didn't appear to have grown since he put the makeshift bandage on it.

"Ready?" Allison asked.

"Ready," Sandy answered without hesitation.

Allison took Lita's hand and dashed around the crypt. Sandy swung around the opposite corner and leveled three quick shots to where the soldier had last been hiding. Then he turned and followed in Allison's footsteps.

It took only a couple of seconds for more bullets to chase them along their way. Several zinged past, ricocheting off nearby grave markers. As they approached the gangly tree with its gnarled limbs branching out, Lita tripped over a root and hit the ground hard. Before Sandy could react, Allison was pulling the girl to her feet and urging her on. Sandy ducked under a tree limb just as a round struck the wood and shook loose some dirty, leafy debris. He slowed, turned, and shot twice. He was rewarded with the sight of the soldier hunching down behind another tombstone.

A Hard Favored Death

Sandy resumed running. He reached the crypt just a few strides behind the pair. A bullet tore a chunk out of the mausoleum wall just as they arrived.

"To cover!" Sandy yelled. "Around the corner!"

Another burst of shots rattled toward them. Allison let out a cry as a bullet tore into her upper arm. She fell to a knee, reaching for the wound with her free hand.

This time, it was Lita who grabbed onto her mother and pulled her to feet. Together, they moved forward, around the corner of the mausoleum.

Sandy followed.

Another shot rang out as he hooked around to safety. It immediately registered that this one was louder than the previous. In that same moment, Allison collapsed heavily to the ground, leaving Lita standing above her lifeless form, her face splattered in blood.

Sandy surged forward, knocking Lita to the ground just as another shot was fired. He felt a buzzing heat pass near his midsection. Shattered chunks of stone bit into the small of his back.

The other soldier stood in a classic Weaver stance, his handgun leveled toward Sandy. An MP5 dangled from its straps, slung from his shoulders. He stood behind a grave marker, giving him cover from the waist down.

Sandy crouched low and whipped the gun toward his target, firing rapidly. The first three shots missed wildly, but caused the soldier to flinch before returning fire. Sandy steadied his aim and squeezed off four more in quick succession.

The soldier jerked suddenly, backward and to the left. Then his head snapped in the same direction and he fell to the ground.

"No!" The shriek that came from Lita's throat was preternatural, stronger and more horrific than a young woman should be capable of mustering.

She had risen from where Sandy had knocked her down, crawling on her hands and knees to her mother's side. When Sandy turned away from his fallen target, Lita was in the midst of rolling Allison's still form onto its back.

The next scream that passed her lips was unintelligible. Even so, the sound was laced with horror and grief.

A significant portion of Allison's skull had been blasted away. Her flat, fixed gaze stared up at the sky without comprehension, already glazing over in death. Lita shook her mother by the shoulders, screaming at her to get up.

Allison's body rocked lifelessly in response.

Sandy's hand shot out, taking Lita by the arm and jerking her back.

"No!" the girl shouted, slapping frantically at him, but keeping her eyes glued to her mother. "Let me go! I have to help her!"

Sandy gave her two seconds—two precious seconds—then pulled her sharply to him.

"She is *gone*," he told her, his voice low and resolute.

"Noooo-ho-oh!" Lita wailed. She stopped clawing at Sandy and reached out toward Allison.

"We have to go or we're dead, too."

Lita continued to sob, her arms extended.

Sandy didn't wait any longer. Gun in his right hand and Lita's arm still grasped in his left, he forced himself into a standing position with a grimace. Then he dragged Lita around to the far side of the crypt.

"We can't leave her!" Lita screamed at him.

"We can't help her," Sandy said. He shoved her slightly so she was near the wall. "There's still one more soldier out there and who knows how many more on the way." He pointed to the SUV. "When I say go, we run for it. You don't stop until you're inside the back seat. Lie down on the floor and don't get up until I say. You got it?"

Lita cast a glance over toward where her mother lay on the ground.

"Hey!" Sandy barked, and Lita's head snapped back toward him. "Do you understand?"

Lita gave him a quivering nod.

"Then let's do it." Sandy let go of her and started to peek around the corner to provide covering fire.

Lita darted back the way they'd come, surprising him.

"Goddamnit." Sandy hobbled after her.

He found the girl struggling to lift her mother from the ground. Allison's dead weight made it impossible. Lita pulled at her arm, straining without success.

Sandy put his hand on Lita's shoulder but the girl shrugged it off. "I'm not leaving her."

Sandy grabbed onto her and jerked her close again, this time putting his face near hers. "She is fucking *gone!*" he snarled at her. "She died to make sure you make it. If you don't get away, then she died for nothing. Is that what you want?"

Lita stared at him dumbly for a moment. Then she shook her head.

"Then get your shit together," Sandy snapped. "And let's get out of here."

She swallowed then nodded.

"Listen, then." Sandy took a deep breath. "When I break cover, you follow me. But don't stay with me. You're faster, so keep running to the truck. Get in like I said."

"Wait," Lita said urgently. She reached toward her mother's still body. Sandy thought about restraining her but hesitated. Lita slipped the strap of the leather purse from her mother's shoulders and hung it from her own.

"Go cross-wise with it," Sandy told her.

Lita obeyed wordlessly, lifting the strap over her head to rest on the opposite shoulder.

Sandy waited until the strap was in place before continuing. "One change in plans. Can you start the engine? Do you know how to do that?"

"I think so."

"Just put your foot on the brake and touch the two bare wires hanging from below the dash until the motor starts. Can you do that?"

Her head bobbed frantically. "Yeah. Yeah, I can do it."

"Good. Start it up, then climb into another seat and get on the floor. I'll be right behind you."

"What about—"

"I'll be right behind you," he repeated.

Lita hesitated, then nodded again. "Okay."

Sandy didn't waste any more time. For misdirection, he took a few steps back and peered around the way they'd come. He could see the slightest bit of khaki extending past one of the grave markers. He fired twice, both rounds pinging off the stone. Then he reversed direction and headed toward the SUV.

Lita trailed behind him as he left cover.

As soon as he was in the open, Sandy slowed and pointed his gun toward the last remaining soldier. When the man peeked up from behind the gravestone, Sandy fired, causing the soldier to hunker back down.

He saw a flash of movement in his peripheral vision as Lita sprinted past him toward the SUV. He kept his focus on the threat. When the soldier didn't make a move, he snapped off two more rounds to keep him pinned down. Sandy's leg pounded with every step. His arms ached from holding the weapon outward. Sweat suffused his entire body, streaming down his sides and dripping from his brow.

He forced himself to keep moving.

In times like these, his hearing was fine-tuned. That's how he heard the door to the SUV open a few moments later.

He fired another shot toward the tombstone the soldier huddled behind.

A few moments later, he was rewarded with the sound of the engine rumbling to life.

He fired twice more.

As soon as he finished shooting, the man popped up from behind the marker and sent a burst of automatic fire in his direction. Sandy didn't react as the bullets slapped into the ground nearby or whizzed past him. He returned fire, forcing the man to drop back behind cover.

Lita had left the driver's door open for him. As he reached it, Sandy sent a final volley toward the soldier, emptying the magazine. He tossed the gun into the cab of the SUV, grasped the steering wheel and hauled himself inside. Without bothering to close the door, he jammed the transmission into drive and scorched the tires, thankful he had backed into the space earlier.

The vehicle leapt forward. The driver's door slammed shut as they rocketed out of the lot. Sandy kept his foot flattening the pedal to the floor until they burst out of the cemetery grounds and onto the main street again.

Sandy scanned traffic, looking for pursuit, but saw none. He forced himself to slow to normal speed. He definitely didn't need to attract attention from local cops who might already be on the way to the cemetery due to the shots fired. If they were detained by NOPD, Szoke would hear about it and find a way to intervene. He might have another team in New Orleans—almost certainly had, he realized—so Sandy didn't want to make it easy for him to find them.

As he drove, he glanced to his right. The empty handgun rested on the passenger seat, slide still locked to the rear. Huddled on the floor in front of that, was Lita. The girl's arms were wrapped around her knees, which were drawn to her chest. She stared straight ahead, focused on nothing.

Sandy noticed she was no longer crying.

26

Agent Lori Carter stood under the archway to Lafourche Cemetery, staring at the scene in front of her.

Several black SUVs and a forensics van were lined up nearby blocking access to the cemetery. Next to her was Mark Szoke, the team leader having made a rare foray out into the field. Usually, he directed activity from the safety of his chair in the operations center. She was actually surprised he was willing to come out to the site of this mess, since the op had been his call in the first place. Showing up was a tacit admission of his responsibility. Responsibility was another role Szoke didn't tend to accept.

Still, she had to admit she was glad for his presence when it came to brushing off the local police. NOPD had a reputation in the profession for corruption and laziness, but she saw no sign of either when a patrol captain argued ferociously with Szoke regarding the jurisdiction of this shooting. In the end, however, Szoke out-maneuvered the man and sent him and his team packing.

Carter didn't know how he accomplished the feat. She'd been standing over Allison Delancey's body. The woman's jagged head wound left no doubt as the cause of her demise. Carter had stared down at the crumpled form, suffused with a sense of failure. Setting Banks loose was supposed to have prevented this death.

By the time Szoke broke free of the New Orleans PD captain, Delancey's body had already been hurriedly photographed, bagged, and loaded into the back of one of the vehicles now behind the pair. Carter had moved to the entrance near the archway and watched the forensics team—more of a clean-up crew—do their work swiftly and efficiently.

Next to her, Szoke shifted impatiently from foot-to-foot.

"Casualties?" he asked her.

Carter had already briefed him on this. That made his question more for dramatic purposes than anything useful. "Allison Delancey, for starters," she reported icily. "Which should make you pretty happy."

Szoke frowned at her. "I asked for facts, not commentary."

Carter relented. Giving him what he wanted had proven the path of least resistance. Or, minimally, the least amount of pain. "Beyond that, three dead and one wounded."

"And Banks was alone?"

"Except for the mother and daughter, yes."

"Neither of them was armed?"

"Not according to Ricardo."

"Who the fuck is Ricardo?"

She turned her head sideways to look at him, not sure if what she was feeling was wholly surprise or disgust. "The surviving soldier."

Szoke turned and spat. "Shouldn't have sent the fucking B-Team."

Carter wasn't certain this was the B-Team. If it was, why had Szoke chosen them over the other squad? He'd stopped sharing his thought process with her early on in this journey, slowly relegating her from project lead to just another piece on his chessboard.

"These were good men," she said. "Soldiers."

Szoke sniffed. "Please. They haven't been soldiers for a

long time. These men were mercenaries, Lori. And, apparently, fucking scrubs at that." He shook his head. "One old man with a Sig Sauer. How do they mess that up?"

She'd seen this before. Men tended to trivialize their enemies to diminish their standing. It was an ego-driven practice and counter-productive. "Banks isn't old. He's a veteran."

"Semantics."

"And you know what his skills are."

"Yeah, Lori, I fucking do. But you'd think four mercenaries armed with assault rifles would be enough to overcome those skills."

"MP5s aren't assault rifles."

"Jesus, give me a break. It was an expression." He scowled at her. "You're getting to be habitually pedantic."

And you're consistently an officious prick.

"You want to know why Banks won this battle?" Carter asked.

"What, are you suddenly the Sandy Banks Whisperer now?"

"Suddenly?" Carter cocked her head. "You might not remember, but I conducted a manhunt for him way back when. Part of any manhunt is getting to know the man you're chasing. After *I* found him, you and your boss swooped in and took control. As a result, I've been forced to work with him for the past decade. So forgive me if I think I've managed to gain some insight into the man through all of that."

"Enough to decide to help him escape?" Szoke finally turned to meet her gaze. "Don't think I've forgotten your transgression, Lori."

"I don't think you forget anything," she said. "Especially the petty stuff."

"Treason is petty to you?"

She smiled humorlessly. "Don't play the high road card with me. Not after your little speech about accepting who we are."

A bigger man might have smiled back and offered her a reluctant touché. Szoke, however, would never allow his own ego to let him admit even a small defeat. Instead, he said, "I don't think Banks *is* knowable. Rather, I think everything we need to know is right there on the surface."

"You're wrong."

"How do you know?"

"Because that's not true of hardly anyone in this world." Her flat smile returned. "Except maybe you."

"Who's being petty now?"

Carter didn't answer. She turned her gaze back to the cemetery and waited while the cleaners masked as a forensics team carefully combed the grounds for evidence. She often wondered which kind of evidence was prioritized more—the kind that helped solve a mystery or the kind they needed to remove to protect the operation itself?

Szoke lasted almost a minute before he finally grunted, "Why?"

She turned to him. "Why what?"

"Don't be a bitch."

Carter remained silent. If he wanted petty, she could do petty.

Szoke sighed. "You have a theory on why Banks won this fight."

"You're surprised he was able to."

"Is that a question?"

"Did it sound like one? You're surprised because the odds were stacked well against him. Four shooters to one. Facing superior firepower. Plus the additional task of protecting the non-combatants. Odds makers would have made him a severe underdog. Yet he prevailed."

"He didn't prevail. He escaped."

"Three men are dead and one wounded. *And* he escaped. I

think he prevailed here."

"Semantics again. Cut with the shit and give me your theory. You know you're dying to rub it in my face. Let's see if there's any actual value to your armchair psychological profiling."

Carter didn't rush, giving Szoke a taste of his own medicine. "You have to remember Banks has been an underdog most of his life. He's used to long odds. They don't frighten him."

"They should. Everyone eventually craps out if they keep rolling the dice."

"Sure." Szoke had actually stumbled upon her point without realizing it. "And he did, when I caught up to him in Nashville over a decade ago. The result of losing that roll has been his indentured servitude all these years since. One could argue that is one long loss."

Szoke scoffed. "You're being overly dramatic again. Get to the point."

"You ever hear the story about the legendary samurai who fought with a wooden sword?"

"*What?*" Szoke shook his head and waved a hand at her. "You know what, forget I asked."

Carter ignored his protest and continued. "This samurai—I forget his name—took on all comers, without exception. One day, the greatest swordsman in all the land arrived to challenge him. Before they fought, the samurai recognized the man's superior skill. He also acknowledged a fine metal blade was better than a wooden practice sword. He knew the odds were severely stacked against him." She cocked her head. "Sound familiar?"

"No," Szoke said, but she could hear through the cold insolence in his tone. He was tracking her.

"The two men fought. Despite the superior skill and weaponry of the sword master, this samurai defeated him. Battered and beaten, the challenger finally surrendered. Afterward, the two warriors spoke. The sword master asked the samurai how he had defeated him when he had greater skill and finer weaponry." She paused for a moment, eying Szoke meaningfully. "The samurai told him, 'You were determined to win, but I was resolved to die if I lost.'"

Szoke smirked. "Is that real history?"

"Does it matter? It tells me exactly why Banks drove that girl out of here and left behind this mess." She motioned toward the cemetery where the cleaners were finishing up. "It's also why we shouldn't underestimate him."

Szoke didn't answer for a long while. The former CIA agent had changed a lot in the decade since he was drafted into this program right along with her and Banks. To Carter's mind, most of those changes were for the worse. And, while his arrogance occasionally clouded his judgment, one thing was certain.

Szoke wasn't stupid.

"So, he's desperate. I already knew that. Why the samurai shit? You could have just as easily told me some tale about a cornered animal."

"I could have," she agreed. "But the story I told you was more appropriate."

"Why?"

"Because the first time I heard it was from Banks, years ago." She smiled grimly. "And because the only thing worse than chasing a desperate man is chasing one resolved to die rather than lose."

27

Sandy drove almost to Gulfport. The entire way, his leg throbbed. The graze across his back burned. His muscles stiffened. Worse yet, he experienced the same dizziness he'd faced in the cemetery, causing him to shake his head several times to ward it off.

He realized he must have lost more blood than he thought.

I need to find a safe place to rest before I collapse.

Despite these distractions, he endured it all and kept the SUV on the road.

Lita remained huddled on the floorboard of the passenger side, hugging her knees to her chest. Sandy didn't bother trying to coax her out of her grief. He'd learned everyone had to deal with it in their own way. If someone had asked him a week ago if a thirteen-year-old suburban girl could handle seeing both her father and her mother shot dead in front of her in the space of two days, his answer would have been a categorical no.

Now, he wasn't so sure.

Lita was subdued but not catatonic. She hadn't resumed crying since that initial moment in the cemetery. Sandy wanted to chalk that up to resilience but he suspected it was simply shock. Or the girl was pushing her grief down.

Given the situation they faced, he preferred the latter. Post-traumatic stress was no joke, but having to face it eventually also meant she was still alive. That was his only purpose now.

Sandy took secondary roads as he worked his way eastward. When he stopped at a roadside gas station, Lita showed the first signs of life since their escape. She roused herself and followed him to the outdoor restrooms, where they took turns cleaning up as best they could. Sandy left the bandage intact, opting to wait for a better opportunity to doctor himself. Once they'd finished, Lita waited in the SUV while Sandy gassed up.

While the fuel was pumping, Sandy opened the door and pointed to Allison's purse. "Hand me that," he said.

"No!" Lita cried. She clutched the purse protectively to her chest. "Don't touch it."

Sandy held up his hands placatingly. "Fine. You hold onto it."

Lita glared at him, keeping the purse tight to her body.

"There's some cash in there, though," Sandy said. "I need it to pay for the gas."

Lita hesitated. Reluctantly, she unsnapped the purse and opened the flap. After rummaging briefly, she withdrew a wad of money and held it out to him.

Sandy took it. "Thanks."

He left her in the SUV and went inside the ramshackle store. He limped around the store briefly until he found the small shelf with first aid items. He gathered what he needed before grabbing some water and several protein bars as well. He made his way to the counter, where a man with the look of hard living eyed him warily. He could have been anywhere from thirty-five to sixty-five but one thing was certain—his gaze was discerning.

The man's eyes flicked down to Sandy's bloody pants. "Cut yourself?" His accent came out thick.

Sandy forced a grin. "Knife slipped while I was gutting a fish."

"Like could bleed out from that."

"It wasn't deep. Just bled like it."

The man grunted.

Sandy put the water and bars on the counter and motioned toward the fuel tanks out front. "I've got the gas, too."

He rang up Sandy's items. "That all?"

Sandy glanced around the store. "I didn't see any needle nose pliers on the shelves. You sell those?"

"Nope."

"Have you got any? Maybe in a toolbox or something?" Sandy peeled a bill off the wad of cash in his hand and held it up.

The man paused, eyeing the money. Then he reached below the counter and lifted a tool kit. A moment later, he removed a small pair of red-handled needle nose pliers. "These do?"

Sandy handed him the bill, then paid for the rest of the gas and groceries. "Thank you," he said.

The man nodded to him.

Back in the SUV, Lita was seated in the passenger seat, her mother's purse tucked to her hip. Then he noticed the silver bracelet hanging from her wrist. He remembered her grabbing it from the nightstand when they were preparing to flee the motel room in El Paso.

Her mother's.

Sandy didn't acknowledge the jewelry. Instead, he resumed driving eastward. His mind wrestled with his next move. Traveling with Lita made him exponentially more identifiable than traveling alone. Every identifier added to the puzzle. Single, white male in his fifties was generic enough. Add in a known vehicle and the situation became more dangerous, but he could always swap out the vehicle.

But a single, white male in his fifties traveling with a thirteen-year-old girl?

That stood out.

This fact was part of the reason he'd chosen the remote gas

station to refuel instead of something within the city. The city represented more camouflage, more people to try to blend with, but a rural sensibility about people not prying into the business of others seemed a better bet in this part of the country. His assessment could turn out wrong, but at least there were no cameras at the roadside store.

"What's next?"

Lita's voice broke the silence of the cab. He glanced over at the girl. Her hard expression glared back at him.

"We hole up for the night," he said. "And we figure out exactly that."

He chose the broken-down motel for the same reasons as the gas station earlier. The single strip of dirty, white bungalows was out of the way and looked like the kind of place where people minded their own business.

Sandy asked for the cabin at the end. He paid cash for the room, handing the desk clerk an additional pair of twenties.

"For incidentals," he said.

The skinny woman tucked away the extra cash without a word and handed him the room key.

He parked the SUV around the corner and behind the building, tucking it in so they could slip out the rear bathroom window and drive away if needed. Then he and Lita went into the room.

Sandy knew how the scene might look to an onlooker. A middle-aged man leading an underage girl into a no-tell motel, neither one carrying any luggage. The scene had illicit written all over it. Him slipping the clerk the extra money only added to the perception. He had to hope no one was watching and the woman at the front desk appreciated the windfall enough to ignore what she saw.

Sleeping in the SUV would have been smarter, he knew.

But he needed to take care of something and it required both light and running water.

The two narrow twin beds took up most of the small cabin. Sandy dropped the remaining food and first aid supplies on the bed nearest the door. He kicked off his boots and headed toward the bathroom.

"What are you doing?" Lita asked. She'd sat on the edge of the other bad, her mother's purse over her shoulder, absently fingering the silver bracelet at her wrist.

"Cleaning up," Sandy said.

He took the first aid supplies into the bathroom, closing the door. There, he slowly peeled off his shirt. Sharp needles of pain pricked at him as he did so and the material stuck to the dried blood. Once he had removed the shirt and dropped it into the tub, he craned his neck to look over his shoulder into the mirror.

A long, shallow furrow ran across both scapula. The wound was heavily scabbed already, though bits of scabbing had broken away when he pulled off his shirt. Sandy moved his arms forward and back, testing his range of motion. He was rewarded with light stinging but no structural inhibition. It seemed this injury would be slightly painful and inconvenient, nothing more.

Sandy lowered himself onto the closed toilet and unwrapped the makeshift bandage. Then he slid out of his pants so he could examine his injured leg more closely. The entrance wound looked deceptively small. He saw no signs of infection, but it was early yet. With the bandage removed, there was no further bleeding for which he was grateful.

He continued his examination. When first injured, he hadn't felt an exit wound and he confirmed this fact now. Sandy frowned. That meant the bullet remained inside his leg.

It had to come out.

Sandy tipped the travel-size bottle of hydrogen peroxide,

splashing some into the wound. The substance hissed and bubbled with white foam. Sandy gritted his teeth. He held the needle-nose pliers under the faucet and ran some hot water over them. He followed up by pouring hydrogen peroxide over the tool. Once he was satisfied the pliers were as clean as they could get, he turned back to his leg.

Carefully, he prodded the hole with the tip of the pliers. Even the gentlest touch of the metal against the wound caused him to wince. He clenched his jaw and kept exploring. Eventually, the metal tip of the tool tapped against the bullet still inside.

Sandy took a deep breath, steeling himself. Then he spread the jaws and pressed downward, trying to get a grip on the bullet with the pliers. Pain lanced up and down his leg like hot fire. His vision blurred, so he closed his eyes. When light-headedness kicked in, he stopped. He spent a few moments catching his breath, preparing to try again.

The second time hurt worse than the first. The pain forced him to stop again. It was simply too much for him to concentrate through.

Sandy was soaked in sweat. He grasped the sink and pulled himself to his feet. Turning on the faucet, he sipped the lukewarm water then splashed some on his face. Then he pushed open the door.

Lita hadn't moved from the edge of the bed, still staring down and lightly touching the bracelet on her wrist. She looked up at him expectantly.

"I need your help," he said.

She remained seated.

Sandy met her stare. "I need your help or this is going to go septic on me. I'll die."

"So?" she said flatly.

"So, wherever we decide you need to go, I'm no good to you if I can't get you there."

Lita considered briefly. Then she set down her mother's purse and came into the bathroom. "What do I do?" she asked.

Sandy explained it to her. When he'd finished, he added, "Once you grab onto the bullet, work it out. Don't stop, even if I pass out."

Something flashed in Lita's eyes, but it was gone before Sandy could identify what it was.

"Grab my belt from my pants," he told her.

Lita reached down to the floor and slid the leather belt out of the loops. Then she handed it to him.

Sandy folded it over and put it between his teeth. Then he braced himself against the wall and the sink with both arms and nodded to her.

Lita poured some more peroxide on the pliers. Then she crouched in front of him and splashed the last of it onto the wound. Sandy winced and took a deep breath, steadying himself for what was to come next.

The pain started cold this time when the metal first touched his injury. Almost immediately, though, it flashed hot again. A white wall slammed across his vision while every nerve in his leg felt like it was raging with fire. His arms tensed against the bracings. He drew shuddering breaths in and out through his nose, closing his eyes against the pain as Lita rooted around with the pliers.

She managed to get the jaws around the bullet and pulled. The pliers slipped free, eliciting a sharp, muted cry from Sandy. Sweat poured down his body while Lita silently tried again.

The second time, she got a better grip. Each time she worked the bullet left or right, waves of nausea rose up in Sandy. The flash of white crossed his vision again and for a moment, he thought he might pass out as predicted.

Then, all of the sudden, the pain diminished, going from a thundering inferno to a deep, dull throb.

Sandy heard the sharp *plink* of metal on porcelain. He opened his eyes. Lita still held the pliers. When he glanced at the sink, he saw the slightly malformed bullet resting next to the drain stop, a bloody smear trailing behind it.

He pulled the belt from his mouth and dropped it to the ground. The bullet wound was trickling with blood again, but he'd expected that. If the bullet had been pinching shut an artery, he'd be facing a much different problem now.

Sandy reached for one of the dark brown towels hanging from the rack and pressed it to the wound. When he glanced up at Lita, she was watching him coldly.

"Is that all?" she asked.

"That's it," he said. "I can bandage it myself. Then we'll figure out our next move."

She nodded slowly. Then she said, "You didn't pass out."

"Almost. But no."

"It hurt a lot, though?"

"Yeah," Sandy said. "A lot."

She nodded again, this time with greater satisfaction. "Good," she said. "You deserve it."

Sandy sniffed because he didn't have the energy to laugh. "You're right about that."

"I know." She stood up and looked down at him. "I hate you, just so you know."

"I do know."

"Good," she said again, and left the bathroom.

Sandy kept direct pressure on the bullet entry point until the bleeding stopped. Then he did his best to re-bandage the injury. The process took some time and he used the opportunity to sort out his thoughts. An idea had struck him during the drive and he examined it further as he dressed his wound.

Short of taking Lita underground with him, he didn't see a

lot of options. Keeping her at his side only increased the danger to her. The sooner the two of them separated, the safer she'd be and the more difficult it would be for Szoke to find either of them.

The trick was, he had to leave her somewhere she'd be safe. She was only thirteen. She had to be protected. There weren't many people he knew who could do that. The few who might take on the task were well known to Szoke which eliminated them as possibilities.

All except one.

He rolled the idea around in his head. Did he even have a favor to call in with this man? Sandy thought so, but the other man might not see it that way. If he did, however…

It might work. A longshot, true, but still a chance.

Once finished, he hobbled back into the motel room. Lita sat on one bed, her back to the wall and her knees drawn to her chest. The silver bracelet dangled from her wrist. Her pose reminded Sandy of how she'd looked on the passenger seat floor, immediately after the shooting.

He eased himself onto the edge of the bed opposite her, sitting with his injured leg extended. Lita's eyes flicked from the bandages to his face, her hard scowl unrelenting.

So much anger, he thought. *Who does that remind you of?*

"I'm going to talk to you like you're an adult," Sandy said. "Not only because of what you've been through, but also because the situation you're faced with is serious. It requires a hard decision that will affect the rest of your life. I figure you deserve to hear it like a grown woman. You okay with that?"

Lita dipped her chin slightly in response.

"Good," said Sandy. "The problem is simple: where can I take you that you'll be safe?"

Lita watched him silently.

Sandy raised a brow. "Any ideas?"

She shook her head slowly.

"You speak Spanish?" he asked.

Her eyes narrowed in confusion. "*Bastante*," she said. "But Mom said—"

"I know. Your mother didn't seem to think your father's people were an option. But that was before..." He hesitated, then continued. "That was before. She's not in the picture now. Does that change anything?"

"I don't know."

"Do you think Ernesto's family might be an option? They might have a different view now, given the situation."

"I never met any of my father's family," Lita said. She paused, then added, "Either father."

"Héctor never talked about—"

"He kept his Mexico life separate from us." She swallowed and glanced away, her eyes shining with tears. "He said it was for our own safety, but I think maybe he was ashamed of us."

Sandy didn't know how to reply to that. He waited a beat before continuing. "So Mexico's probably not an option. Any other relatives your mother didn't tell me about?"

"No," Lita said. "It was just us."

Sandy frowned, thinking. His longshot idea might be all he had.

"Even if we did, I wouldn't tell you," Lita said.

Sandy cocked his head. "Why not?"

"Those men who found us at the cemetery. If Aunt Ophelia was still alive, what would they have done to her?"

Sandy looked her straight in the eye. "If she didn't cooperate? Terrible things."

"That's what I thought." She shook her head. "I couldn't do that to someone else."

"I could help them," Sandy said. "If there is other family—"

"There's no one." Lita's tone was final. "And I'm glad there isn't. I wouldn't be safe with them and they wouldn't be safe with me."

"You're not safe now," Sandy told her.

Lita shrugged, glancing at his shot leg. "Maybe not, but at least I don't care if *you* die."

The corner of Sandy's mouth twitched as he suppressed a grim smile. This girl was made of sterner stuff than he'd imagined.

"Our best option is for me to get you somewhere safe that has no known connection to either of us," he said. "And soon. Right now, they're looking for the two of us together. We're easier to spot as a pair. Once I get you squared away, I'll go my own way. I'll make some noise to get their attention. As long as you don't poke your head up after that, you should be safe."

"Take me back to Texas," Lita said.

"Too dangerous."

"Arizona, then. Or New Mexico. Drop me at an orphanage and fuck off. Go back to killing people or whatever it is you do."

He considered the southwestern states she mentioned. His first take was they were too far away and back through territory Szoke would be watching. Then again, maybe he wouldn't expect them to backtrack.

The truth was the man was watching for them everywhere. How widely he shared information was unknown but, at the very least, he'd make sure the SUV was bulletined out as stolen. Who knew what other tools or agencies he might bring to bear. Szoke liked to keep things as quiet as possible, involving as few parties as necessary to accomplish the mission. Even when he brought in outside agencies, there were layers of lies and cover stories to obscure what was really happening.

At the moment, Szoke's desire for as much secrecy as he could maintain worked in their favor. How long that desire would last before the need to catch him and Lita outweighed it, Sandy didn't know.

Even so, he rejected the idea of turning west, if for no other reason than there was no purpose for that destination. He didn't have any assets in place there that could help them. And while Lita's orphanage idea wasn't entirely crazy, it was even more of Hail Mary than his own long shot idea.

"Let's put a pin in that one," he said.

Lita shrugged again. "Then I'm out of ideas." She gave him another hard look. "You caused this. You fix it."

"Fair enough," Sandy said. He leaned to his right and struggled to his feet. He limped into the bathroom and grabbed his bloody pants from the floor. With some difficulty, he put his feet through the legs and worked the material over his wound and finally up to his waist.

"What are you doing?" Lita asked.

Sandy returned bedside and reached for his boots. "I need to make a call."

The desk clerk directed him to a pay phone a quarter mile up the road, outside a small grocery and fish tackle shop.

Sandy gave her another bill and thanked her. Then he limped stiffly down the road to the shop. Although the pain didn't slacken at any point, his leg limbered as it warmed up. Despite his weariness, Sandy welcomed the sensation of movement. It felt purposeful.

The pay phone hung on the wall outside the business. He would have preferred the privacy of a booth but took solace in the low traffic in the area.

He dropped coins into the slot and dialed the number from memory.

Jellik answered on the third ring. "Who is this?"

"Jelly," Sandy said. "It's Keegan."

There was a long silence. Then Jellik asked, "Keegan who?"

Sandy heard the suspicion in the man's voice. That was to be expected—it was part and parcel to his trade over the long haul. From the time they'd first met during their shared military operations, when Sandy was called Keegan Fuller, Jellik was already piloting missions the Army wouldn't have confirmed if questioned. Since getting out, Jellik had turned to other, more lucrative types of transport.

Calling Jellik was a risk. Szoke knew about him. On Sandy's recommendation, he'd contracted for Jellik's services on a mission. Neither the mission nor Jellik's role in transporting them was overly memorable, so Sandy hoped Szoke wouldn't think of Jellik. Or, if he did, that the man would be further down whatever list Szoke or Carter compiled.

More than that, he was counting on Jellik's loyalty, always a dicey proposition where smugglers were concerned.

"We both have the same uncle," Sandy said. "We vacationed with him down south back when we were kids. Got us some jungle tacos."

There was another silence, this one shorter. Then Jellik muttered, "Shit."

"Sorry to call."

"Me, too."

"What's the sit-rep?"

"Helter Skelter," Sandy told him, using an old code word for a blown operation. "They've got me labeled for a black, zippered bag, my friend."

"Shit," Jellik repeated. Then he asked, "What do you need?"

28

Lori Carter watched Paulinus work the computer search for Banks and the girl. Nearby, Easton scoured traffic cameras for a hit on the license plate. She knew, if he got one or even saw a vehicle that suspiciously resembled the SUV, he would search for and access any other cameras in the area to augment the hunt for the pair. It didn't matter if he had legal access to them or not. As long as the camera was connected to the internet, Easton had the software to commandeer it.

The world we live in, Carter mused darkly. Privacy, it seemed, was becoming as antiquated as buggy whips and passenger pigeons.

To anyone watching, she might have appeared to be a micro-managing supervisor overseeing the real workers. But Carter's mind was buzzing as she strove to figure out the best approach to finding Banks. Paulinus and Easton represented the technology approach to a manhunt. She was all in favor of utilizing those methods. At the same time, she knew other, more traditional, means might be called for if this one was going to be successful.

The door to the trailer opened and Szoke strode in. He took in the two men working and Carter standing nearby and frowned.

"Update?" he asked her.

"There isn't one. Easton has the SUV leaving New Orleans, headed north."

"Destination?"

"Unknown. Outside of the city, the traffic cameras all but disappear. He could have turned any direction from there. As long as he sticks to less traveled roads, we're unlikely to catch him on camera."

Szoke's frown deepened. He glanced over at Easton. "Are you using the AI package we installed for you?"

Easton nodded without looking away from the screen. "It's got a learning curve, though."

"You're a professional. How hard is it for you to master a piece of software?"

Easton's fingers faltered then resumed typing. "Not me," he said. "The AI has a learning curve. It's clunky, so I have to double check the hits manually. There've been a lot of false positives."

"What's a lot?"

"All of them so far," said Easton. "Since they left New Orleans, anyway."

Szoke grunted. "Well, keep at it. They'll have to show up somewhere."

"Yes, sir."

Szoke didn't bother asking Paulinus for an update. Carter figured the man didn't want to hear a second time how they had nothing. Instead, he beckoned for Carter to follow him. Without waiting for her to comply, he turned and left the trailer.

She suppressed a sigh, pushed herself away from the wall, and went outside. The trailer that served as a mobile command center was pulled by a semi tractor. Carter wondered if the driver had any idea who he actually worked for.

Szoke stood near one of the oversized tires, smoking a cigarette.

Carter approached him. "When did you start with that?"

He blew out smoke. "I quit sixteen years ago," he admitted. "Started again last week."

She didn't have to ask why. Losing Banks and having two loose ends out in the world wouldn't please Danforth. Carter wondered when the elusive director would make an appearance or if he would at all. Either way, Szoke was facing dire consequences if this operation failed.

So am I, she realized.

Szoke may have forgiven her role in Banks's escape, especially since he masterminded it. She doubted Danforth would share his sentiment on the matter. Based on his lack of physical presence in the unit, it might appear he took a hands-off approach to the missions and team management. However, she knew the missions themselves came directly from the shadowy figure. How much he micromanaged Szoke's leadership or made the smaller decisions was up for debate but, if she were a betting woman, she'd lean toward more fingers in the pie rather than less.

"Give me one of those," she said.

Szoke raised a brow but said nothing. He shook loose a cigarette and extended it to her. Carter took it and leaned forward for a light. Szoke used his pen lighter to ignite the cigarette.

The harsh smoke bit her lungs. She'd smoked as a teenager but quit when she decided to join the FBI. The habit had reemerged briefly when she was drafted—hell, it was more like an impressment—into this unit, but good sense had driven her to stop smoking a second time. She'd told herself all of the reasons to quit and they made sense at the time. Now, however, she couldn't think of a single good reason to quit.

"If he stays off the main freeways, it will take weeks before the boy genius in there gets a camera hit," she told Szoke. "Even with AI." Her own opinion was the AI was more of a hindrance than a help at this stage but that ship had sailed so she didn't bother arguing the point.

"It won't be weeks," Szoke argued.

"Days, then. Either way, it gives Banks too much of a head start. And if he changes vehicles again, which he'll definitely do, then it *will* be weeks."

"What do you suggest?"

Carter drew in deeply on the cigarette, considering. "Right now," she said, letting the smoke billow out, "we're running quiet. The only public aspect of this search is the stolen status on the plates of the SUV he was driving in New Orleans. That search is largely passive. All we're doing is stealing other people's eyes—in this case, state and local law enforcement."

"Your point?"

"You're trying to keep this search as invisible as possible. I get that. But a quiet search like this is also a weak one."

"What Paulinus and Easton are doing isn't weak."

"No, but outside of their efforts, all we've got is the stolen plate. And that has the potential to be noisy in its own right, depending on what happens when it's spotted."

"Like I said, what's your point?"

"Look," Carter said, "when I was FBI, we were trained to always consider the impact of our ops on local law enforcement. We had to find the balance between operational security and the potential danger to those officers." She took another drag from the cigarette and blew it out. "We both saw what Banks did in that cemetery. That was against four trained soldiers, well-armed and prepared for what they were walking into."

"He's not invincible," Szoke said sourly. "We caught him once; we can catch him again."

I caught him, not you, she wanted to say, but she was too weary to dredge up the energy to argue the point. More importantly, Carter wasn't so sure Szoke was right. Last time, she'd had a significant card to play—the woman Banks had loved since childhood. Now, though? She imagined he was more like that samurai, willing to die if he didn't win.

"Maybe we can catch him," she conceded, "but the point is, what chance does an unsuspecting local cop have if he stumbles across a stolen vehicle containing a desperate man with the skills Banks has?"

"Local cops aren't idiots," Szoke said. "Most of them, anyway. They have protocols for approaching stolen cars."

"Sure," she said, "but are those sufficient for what they'd actually be facing?"

Szoke stubbed out his cigarette and immediately lit another. "That's your point?"

"No. My point is I think we're risking noise if the stolen gets a hit or if we manage to find him otherwise. So why run silent now? We need to go loud and increase our options."

"That's not our M.O. We keep things quiet."

"Really? Because that cemetery in New Orleans made a lot of noise. We're lucky as hell the location was remote and bordered a not-so-great part of the city. Otherwise, commandeering that scene would have been much more difficult. It may have blown up the entire operation."

"I'm the reason we kept that scene secure," Szoke said testily. "My political acumen is what did the trick. At any rate, you're making a case against your own point."

"Not really. Right now, by limiting our search methods, our net isn't wide enough and the strands of the mesh are too weak. If Banks isn't already outside our range, he'll find a way to slip past or break through."

Szoke considered. "How loud do you mean?"

"Call it a kidnapping. Issue an Amber Alert."

"Are you kidding me?"

"No. Turn this from a secret fugitive hunt to a very public search for a heinous killer."

His eyes narrowed with interest. "Go on."

"We paint Banks as a man who kidnapped a woman and her daughter, then murdered the mother. He kept the child for unnatural purposes. No telling what he's doing to her now or when he might choose to kill her, too. Time is of the essence." She finished off the cigarette and lifted her heel to scrape the last of the embers. "We get the public engaged this way. And state and local law enforcement is on high alert. Hell, with the kidnapping angle, you'll get assistance from the FBI."

"Not bad," Szoke said. "Very utilitarian. Not weighed down by your usual moral objections, Lori."

She smiled thinly. *Don't remind me.*

"I learned from the best," she said acidly.

Szoke sniffed outward, expelling a puff of smoke from his nose. "Always the ball buster." He pondered her plan for a moment then said, "There's a problem with what you propose."

"I know. It's loud."

"Not only that. If it gets us Banks and the girl, the noise is worth it. And with state and local authorities, taking custody of both isn't a problem. But, if the FBI gets involved?" He shook his head. "Bureau types have never had a taste for the nuance it takes to make the hard decisions in this world, Lori. All we need is some crusader, someone like you used to be…" He turned over his hands. "You see the problem."

"Call Danforth."

Szoke frowned.

"What?" she asked. "Are you telling me Darth Vader can't fix an inter-agency conflict?"

"Don't call him that."

"You're right. He's more of the Emperor, isn't he?"

"You have no idea about the bigger picture," Szoke said, "so don't talk about it. You only look ignorant."

She glanced around. "To who?"

"Me."

Carter scoffed. "I care what you think of me?"

"You should. You're on thin ice here."

"Oh? I thought all was forgiven."

"Forgiven," Szoke agreed, "but not forgotten." He took a deep drag on the cigarette and blew out the smoke. "Your idea has some merits. I'll think about it."

"Don't think too long or Banks will be gone."

"Let me worry about that."

"I thought that's what you were paying me to do."

"I'm paying you for ideas, like the one you just gave me."

"Well, I'll keep them coming, then." Carter motioned toward his cigarette. "Another," she said.

Wordlessly, he shook one out for her and they went through the lighting ritual again. Once she'd finished the first inhale, she said, "I think we need to start tracking Banks's contacts."

"What contacts? He's been with us for a decade. All his old running buddies are dead or retired."

"The retired ones might be convinced to help out," Carter said. "Besides, he's worked with people while in this unit, too."

"You think we've got a traitor?"

"Not exactly. But I think we should go back through our old missions and list out anyone we contracted with no matter how small the service or if they were witting or unwitting operatives."

"To what end? Finding some secret ally?"

"Not a secret one exactly but anyone who had a connection to Banks or seemed to establish one during the op itself."

Szoke shook his head doubtfully. "I stick with professionals. I don't see one of them betraying us."

"I'll focus on the ones who are… less professional," Carter said. "Somone he might risk reaching out to for help."

"That'd be quite the risk on his part."

"True, but he's desperate."

"All right," Szoke said. "Put Paulinus on it."

"I'll do it," Carter said. "I have a better idea of what I'm looking for than he does."

"Suit yourself." He smoked some more, then asked, "Say he finds someone to help him. Or even if he doesn't... where's he going to run to, do you think? Out of the country?"

"Almost certainly, if he can manage it."

"To where, though?"

"That's the real question, isn't it? Instead of chasing him, we should be trying to figure out where he's headed and beat him there. That's how we almost caught him in New Orleans."

Szoke frowned at the mention of the bungled capture attempt. "You're saying we need to find her mother's remaining relatives?"

"I don't think so," Carter said. "At this point, the girl's family tree is a stump. There's no one else."

"Are we sure of that?"

"Pretty certain. I had Paulinus run some genealogy on the mother. Allison Delancey was an only child, born to parents in their forties. Her father was an only child as well. He died almost twenty years ago. Allison's mother, who has also passed on, was a late-in-life baby and the youngest of several sisters, all of whom were closer to their mother's age than hers. Those sisters are gone, too. Ophelia Reed was the last one." Carter lifted her hands. "No surviving relatives on her mother's side."

"Were any of those sisters married?"

"All of them. And each of their husbands beat their wives to the grave."

"How about cousins? Or divorces? Is there an errant ex-uncle out there that she could turn to?"

Carter shook her head, though she grudgingly admired Szoke's thinking. "All passed. Aunt Ophelia was it."

"Shit." Szoke drew in smoke. "What about her father's side?"

"As near as we can tell, Héctor Maravilla kept Allison and his daughter a secret."

"How secret?"

"No way to know for sure. Why?"

Szoke glanced upward, thinking. "Mexican culture is different than ours. Patriarchal, sure, but there are certain instances in which women exert considerable power and authority." He met her gaze. "Especially over children."

"You're thinking Banks might try to get the girl to Maravilla's family?"

"It's possible."

"To who? His *wife?* How does that look?" She shook her head. "Lita Delancey is a secret bastard child. I don't see Maravilla's widow welcoming her with open arms."

"You might be surprised. But even if it wasn't the wife, what about a sister? Or Maravilla's mother, the girl's grandmother?"

"They don't even know her."

"She's blood," Szoke argued. "That might be all that matters."

It was Carter's turn to consider. Finally, she shrugged. "I don't know. It seems like a long shot."

"Look into it," Szoke said. "Long shots are all Banks has left."

29

"How did you get this number?"

"That's not important," the voice on the other end of the line told him. "What I need you to focus on is the debt you owe."

Alexandros Dimitrakos frowned. He glanced around his library as if an answer rested upon the shelves like one of his books. A warm, salty breeze drifted in off the water through the open doors that led to the balcony. He'd been sitting there, enjoying a glass of Skouras when his business phone rang. It didn't ring often anymore but he still knew to always answer it when it did.

"What debt?" he asked, legitimately unsure what the caller was referring to.

"Ten years ago," the man said. "A boy that was spared."

Despite the warmth in the library, a chill passed across Dimitrakos's shoulders.

"Do you remember?" the man asked.

Dimitrakos did. The assassination of Bogdan Marković had occurred in this very home. That death had been part of the reason Dimitrakos scaled back on his activities as an underground haven.

"Who are you?" he asked.

Marković had been an activist. Some called him a terrorist. As a result, he consorted with people of a dark nature. Had one of them somehow worked out that Andrej wasn't killed along with his father?

He didn't think so. The voice didn't sound Balkan to him. It sounded more like an American.

"My name doesn't matter," the man said. "Do you remember?"

"I remember a man was killed," Dimitrakos said carefully.

"And a boy was spared," the caller stated unequivocally. "My friend said you might not remember, since neither you nor the boy were ever there."

The caller paused while Dimitrakos considered. He recalled the short conversation he'd had with the American assassin. This was the point he'd stressed with Dimitrakos.

You were never here.

He'd forced Dimitrakos to repeat those words back to him to ensure he'd understood. And Dimitrakos had understood. Afterward, he'd shuttled Andrej to Italy. The boy had grown into a man near Naples, married, and became a draftsman, all under a different name. The last report Dimitrakos had was his wife was with child. They led good lives. Lives made possible because of another man's mercy.

"I remember," he said.

"Do you acknowledge the debt?"

"I do. I owe him."

"Good. Then, this is what he needs."

Dimitrakos listened. When the man had finished, Dimitrakos told him how it could best be accomplished. They discussed logistics briefly before the man agreed, said he'd relay the message, and hung up.

Alexandros Dimitrakos put down his phone. He left the library and went to his bedroom to pack.

30

Branches and leaves scraped against the sides of the SUV as Sandy guided the vehicle down the narrow, overgrown dirt road. Next to him, Lita stared out the window dubiously.

"Your friend lives *here?*"

"He's not a friend exactly," Sandy answered, "but yeah."

He'd been forced to slow to a near crawl, nudging the SUV forward in tiny bursts and trying to keep it centered along the roadway. *More like a pathway,* he thought. Tall weeds sprouted up in the center and brushed against the undercarriage. Sandy had an image of the hot engine igniting the straw-like vegetation, causing a forest fire they'd be right in the middle of.

Thank God for humidity, he thought.

After a quarter-mile, the road opened into a small clearing. Jellik's battered trailer sat on the far side, mid-way up a slight hill. Sandy took care to remain on the rudimentary road as he approached. He wanted to think Jellik wasn't crazy enough to mine the field but knew better.

He drove to within ten yards of the trailer before stopping. Once he shut off the engine, he rested both hands on the steering wheel. Then he sat for a few moments, scanning the rust-spattered home for any signs of movement.

"What are you waiting for?" Lita asked.

"Him to say it's okay to come in."

"Why not just knock on the door?"

"Most of the people I know don't like that approach."

"Most people you know must be weirdos, then."

"No argument," Sandy said. He squinted as a momentary red splash of color seemed to wink at him from the windshield.

"Wait, what's that?" Lita pointed at his chest.

Sandy glanced down. A red dot hovered just below his throat, quivering there like a nervous firefly.

"Stay still," he told Lita calmly.

"Is it them?" she asked in a frantic, hushed voice.

"No." He didn't add, if it had been one of Szoke's snipers, they'd both be dead already.

Instead, slowly, he reached out for the truck door. He popped the latch and pushed the door open with his foot. Keeping his hands up at shoulder level, he swung out of the seat and walked around the open door toward the trailer. The red dot continued to dance across his chest.

"Far enough," a voice bellowed. It sounded like Jellik.

Sandy stopped. He clocked the sound as coming from the second window on the left, through the slight part in the curtains. The position corresponded to the angle of the laser sight.

"Who didn't come back?" Jellik called.

Sandy's mind snapped to a Honduran jungle, decades ago. The humidity and the smell of vegetation here wasn't exactly the same but similar enough. He could almost feel the dead weight of another man across his shoulders.

"Evan," he shouted back.

"And who did?" Jellik's voice remained hard.

"Brophy," Sandy answered. "Barely."

The red dot disappeared. Jellik pushed aside the curtain and peered more closely at Sandy.

"Jesus," he said, his tone softening. "You got old, man."

Sandy lowered his arms. "It happens."

"Door's unlocked," Jellik told him.

Sandy turned and waved to Lita. The girl joined him. At the front door, Sandy tested the round of firewood serving as the front step before realizing Jellik had secured it in the ground. He opened the door and went inside.

The interior of the trailer surprised him. He'd expected the same utilitarian, low-cost furnishings the exterior hinted at. Instead, the home was nice. Not luxurious, but something that wouldn't be out of place in most middle-class suburban homes.

Jellik greeted them in the living room, extending his hand in welcome.

"Long time, Keegan," he said.

"Long time," Sandy agreed.

"I thought I might get another contract or two out of your group after that transport to…" He trailed off, then shrugged. "After that last job."

"My experience, they don't use outside contractors more than once," Sandy told him. "Don't take it personally."

"I didn't," said Jellik. "Anyway, it opened up my time for some more lucrative work. Can I get you a beer?"

Sandy shook his head.

Jellik's eyes cut to Lita. "How about you? I've got some Coke in the fridge. Ginger ale, too."

Lita nodded appreciatively. "Coke's good."

Jellik brushed past them on the way to kitchen. "Have a seat," he said, sweeping his hand. "Anywhere you want."

Sandy moved a tablet from the chair facing the door and eased himself into it. Lita perched on the edge of the nearby couch.

Jellik returned and handed a can to Lita. He also held a bottle of water, which he offered to Sandy.

"Thanks," Sandy said, taking it. On the couch, Lita cracked open the can of Coke.

"I noticed you're limping pretty badly." Jellik gave him an appraising look. "Bloody trousers, too."

"I took a round in New Orleans." Sandy twisted the cap off the bottle.

"You need medical at all?"

"A fresh dressing is all. It can wait, though."

"Through and through?"

Sandy shook his head while he drank.

Jellik squinted in concern. "Bullet still in there, then?"

Sandy lowered the bottle. "No. We got it out."

"*We?*" Jellik glanced over at Lita. "She played medic?"

"Yeah."

"No shit?" He sounded impressed. "Nice work," he told her.

Lita didn't seem to know how to respond. She smiled falteringly, then looked away and sipped her Coke. "Nice place," she said.

Jellik looked around, as if appraising it himself. "It's comfortable. And it's low-profile." He grinned. "And the rust spots on the outside are painted on for effect. She's a solid HQ." He turned his attention back to Sandy. "It's good you called when you did. Six more months, and I hit my number. Retirement, baby."

"Let me guess: a beach somewhere."

"You got it. Sun, tons of Mai Tais, and beautiful women in skimpy…" He caught himself, glancing side-eye toward Lita. He cleared his throat. "And nice women. To talk with."

Sandy nodded. It was a common dream among mercenaries and smugglers, one rarely achieved. Jellik seemed on the brink of making it happen. His remote location and simple living spoke to him putting away most of his profits. Ostentatious living and big spending contributed to the failure of most people who didn't make it out of the drug business to retirement. That, and the murderous nature of the cartels.

"I wish it all for you, my friend," Sandy said. "Now, did you talk to the Greek?"

"Ah, straight to business. Sure." Jellik sat on the opposite end of the couch and leaned forward. "I did. Your number worked."

"He'll help?"

"Surprised the shit out of me, but yeah, he's on board."

"What's the plan?"

"Cuba," Jellik said. "If you can get there, he can get you both out. Back to the islands."

"Cuba, huh?" Sandy thought about it. Getting into the island country as an American was a risk, but it made good sense. The nation was only ninety miles off the U.S. coast and there was no extradition treaty. He'd already considered the destination as a potential endgame for them both. The Greek's cooperation only added another layer of security for Lita.

"When?"

"He's already on his way," Jellik said. "Said he'd register at the Hotel Louvre in Mantanzas. It's in the Plaza de La Vigia, not far from the beach."

"Not Havana?" Sandy admired the decision. Mantanzas was about an hour and a half away from the capital. Close enough to do business there but still removed from the kind of prying eyes that could lead to whispers Sandy couldn't afford.

"He said he has people there. They can help with the paperwork for legit travel back to Greece under new cover."

"Great," Sandy said. "When can you fly us there?"

"Wait," Lita interrupted. "Don't talk about this like I'm not here."

Jellik met Sandy's gaze and raised a brow.

Sandy turned his attention to Lita. "Okay. What do you want to say?"

"What if I don't want to go to Cuba?"

"You said you spoke enough Spanish for Mexico, right?"
She nodded.

"Then you'll be fine in Cuba while we're there."

"It's not about the language," Lita said. "You're making choices for me, about my life. *I* should be choosing."

"You're a—"

"Don't you dare say I'm a kid," Lita snapped. Her sharp tone surprised Sandy. "Where we go is making a choice that will affect the rest of my life. Isn't that so?"

Sandy nodded.

"Then *I* should choose."

"She's right," Jellik agreed.

"Shut up," Sandy told him. He turned back to Lita. "There aren't a lot of options here. You know what we're up against. You saw it for yourself."

A shadow passed over Lita's face. Her lip quivered briefly. She swallowed and pressed them together defiantly. "I want to choose."

Sandy saw the resolve in her expression. He knew he could force the issue, take her to the destination under duress, but that raised the risk factor significantly. If Szoke didn't eventually enlist outside help and spin the story to declare him a kidnapper of some sort, he would do so soon. If Lita were uncooperative when that happened, it would be seen as proof of the false narrative.

"Part of being an adult is making hard choices," he began, but she cut him off.

"Don't talk to me like that," she snarled. "You said in the motel you'd treat me like a grown up because these are grown up decisions. Don't be full of shit now."

Sandy raised his hands in surrender. "Fine. Here's the reality of the situation. There is almost nowhere to run that Szoke won't eventually find you. Time is not on our side, either. We have only a few options and all of them are risky.

Cuba, then Greece, that's the best of them, as far as I can see. Unless you want to live on the steppes of Mongolia or something like that."

He glanced over at Jellik, who tilted his head and nodded to her. "It's what I'd do. Mongolia sucks."

Lita ignored Jellik and stared at Sandy, unrelenting.

"Look," Sandy said, "if we get to Cuba and you want to stay there instead, we can figure something out. It's dangerous but better than staying here in the States. Greece is half a world away, though. Much safer. The man that's coming to help is accustomed to sheltering people. Or he used to be, anyway."

Lita watched him as he spoke. He could see her mind whirring behind her eyes. He waited, letting her process the information. Finally, she asked, "Is it nice?" She glanced at Jellik. "Greece, I mean?"

"It's beautiful," the pilot told her.

"And I'll be safe there?"

Jellik didn't answer. Instead, he glanced at Sandy.

"You'll be as safe as you can be," Sandy said.

Her eyes returned to his. "Are you coming?"

Sandy shook his head. "I'll get you as far as Cuba. It's better if I don't go all the way to Greece."

Lita was silent for a few moments before bobbing her head slightly. "Good," she said.

"It's settled then?"

"Yes," said Lita. "But, if we get to Cuba and I don't like this Greek guy, I'm staying."

Sandy shrugged. "That's your call." He turned back to Jellik. "When can you fly us to Mantanzas?"

Jellik frowned. "I can't, man. At least, not for a week."

"A *week?*" Sandy's eyes narrowed. "We don't have a week. The people chasing us have too many resources. Sooner or later, they'll come across a camera that picked us up. Then they'll link to historical satellite data and whatever else Szoke can commandeer. They'll track us quickly after that." He set his jaw. "We need to be out of the country in a day. Two, max."

"I hear you, brother." Jellik's expression was pained. "But I can't do it. I'm flying a load for some important people tomorrow afternoon."

Sandy put his hands on the armrests and pushed himself up. "Then let's go tonight."

"Whoa," Jellik said, pumping his palms toward Sandy. "Sit down, man. Rest up. That's not happening, either."

"Why not?"

"My girl's already prepped for the upcoming run. She's in the hangar, ready to go."

Sandy remained standing. "Good."

"Yeah," said Jellik. "Good. Good for tomorrow's flight. Man, the false tail numbers have already been painted. She's in full camouflage mode."

"So much the better."

"You don't understand. I can't risk burning those reg numbers. Besides, the interior has been stripped for max payload. There's no seats for passengers."

"We'll sit on the floor."

Jellik sighed. He gestured to the chair behind Sandy. "Will you sit down, man? Let me explain?"

Reluctantly, Sandy eased himself back into the chair. He looked at Jellik expectantly.

The smuggler cast a side-eye glance at Lita before continuing. "The people I fly for are particular. Are you hearing me? *Very* particular. Any deviations from the plan…" He lifted an index finger and drew it shortly across his throat. "I'm too close, Keegan. Too close to retirement to risk pissing these guys off. They don't mess around."

Sandy frowned, looking Jellik dead in the eye. The two men were bound by a shared history, by battle, and by worldview. There was a code, unwritten but inviolate. Even so,

Sandy knew Jellik had more than met his obligations to that creed, simply by giving them shelter tonight. Flying them to Cuba at the risk of getting killed by drug lords was too much to ask.

"I understand," he told Jellik.

"Not entirely." Jellik grinned. "I knew this was going to be a problem for you, so I made another call, called in a favor. I've got a guy. His name's Dufresne. He runs a go-fast boat out of Key West. You get to him and he'll run you both into Cuba."

"Along with a load?"

Jellik shook his head. "No. Passengers only. Just the two of you."

"He knows what he's up against? Who I'm running from?"

"Dufey doesn't give a fuck. All he cares about is getting paid." Jellik's grin broadened. "And I already took care of that part for you."

Sandy thought it over. There were a hundred things that could go wrong between Mobile and Key West, but it was still their best chance. He glanced over at Lita and lifted his eyebrows questioningly.

The girl nodded.

"All right," Sandy said. "We go to Key West."

"Wait till morning," Jellik said. "Dufey won't be available until eight o'clock tomorrow night, at the earliest. You leave here by eight in the morning, you'll be at his slip by ten that same night. Now, he will wait for you until midnight but, after that, no guarantees. That gives you a two-hour buffer on the drive down, so don't dick around, all right?"

"No intention of it," Sandy said.

"Good." Jellik clapped his hands together. "Now, let me make you something to eat. Then you can get cleaned up and grab some sleep. In the meantime, I'll see what I can do about swapping out your rig."

The delay bothered Sandy but he knew the smuggler was

right. Their newly arranged passage to Cuba wouldn't be available for more than twenty-four hours. Besides, he couldn't continue to drive without some sleep. They both needed a good meal. Most of all, a different vehicle gave them better odds of making it to Key West.

"Okay," he relented.

Jellik pointed to the far end of the trailer, past the kitchen. "Guest room for you, little lady. And Keegan, my bedroom's down the hall."

"Couch is fine for me," Sandy said.

"I've got the couch tonight," said Jellik. "I'll be coming and going a bit, anyway." He stood up and headed into the kitchen. "How's steak and eggs sound?"

Sandy's stomach growled. "That sounds great," he said.

From the couch, Lita echoed his words. "Yeah, sounds great."

Sandy leaned back in the chair while Jellik rattled pans in the kitchen. He closed his eyes, intending to rest while the smuggler cooked but he fell asleep long before the meat even began to sizzle.

31

"Any progress?"

Szoke leaned over Carter's shoulder, his cheek uncomfortably close to hers. She could smell his aftershave, a pleasant, woody fragrance. She could also smell his harsh, smoky breath and the sour stench of sweat.

I don't imagine I smell like a pretty flower, either.

"I'm working through possible contacts then tracking them. It's slow."

"Any hits?"

"I would have told you." She rubbed her eyes. "But eliminating suspects is a form of progress."

Szoke grunted and stood again. He didn't move from behind her, though.

Carter pushed her chair back, forcing him to adjust his position. "I've been thinking some more about his destination."

"Do tell."

"So far, he's been traveling east along the seaboard. Now, at first, that was to get to New Orleans, right? That didn't work for them, so what's the next move?"

"Isn't that what we're trying to figure out?"

"How long could they hide here in the U.S.?"

"A while," Szoke admitted.

"But not forever. If we keep looking, we're going to find them stateside. Once they get out of the country, it gets harder on us. Harder yet if they split up." She waited a beat, then added, "Which is why we should put out the Amber Alert."

"I'm still considering that option."

Consider faster, she thought, *or he'll be gone.*

"If getting out of the country is the goal—and I think it has to be—then the question becomes, which country?"

"You have an answer?"

"No. But I have an idea or two."

Szoke twirled his finger. "Let's pretend this is a briefing instead of making me interrogate you to get any information, huh?"

A prick to the end, she thought.

"He's not going to attempt to drive all the way to Canada," she said. "Mexico is a bad choice for the girl and Banks will have figured that out. Given their last known location, somewhere in the Caribbean makes the most sense, though perhaps only as a weigh station before South America."

"That's sound," Szoke said. "Colombia? Peru?"

"Brazil or Argentina, I'd guess." She drummed her fingers on the tabletop, thinking.

"What is it?"

"I mean, that whole stretch of islands is right there. Cuba, the DR, and all of the vacation heavy isles, all off the coast of Florida. He gets to Miami, how hard is it to make it to the Bahamas?"

"We're pretty friendly with the Bahamians. It wouldn't take much to put them on alert, or to get a quiet extradition. Our tourist and banking dollars—"

"If I'm him, Cuba is the better choice," said Carter. "Moderately unfriendly government, no extradition. Ninety miles off the coast. It's a strong option."

"But we don't know for sure."

"No way to know until he shows up at a marina which he is certain to. Unless he can arrange a flight somehow." Her eyes narrowed suddenly.

Szoke noticed. "You got something?"

"Just another thought." She slid her chair forward. "I need to keep looking. I should've been looking more specifically at this angle before."

"What angle, exactly?"

"Pilots," she said.

32

In one sense, Sandy Banks felt like a new man.

The previous night, Jellik had roused him from his impromptu nap in the living room chair for his first good meal in days. The juicy steak tasted better than any he could remember. The eggs were soggy and under-done to his taste, but he wolfed them down so fast, it didn't matter.

Afterward, he cleaned up in the bathroom. A hot shower was tempting, but with the creased wound across his back and the hole in his leg, he decided it wasn't worth the risk. Instead, he sponged off as best he could before collapsing into Jellik's king-sized bed for a deep sleep.

In the morning, the smuggler had outfitted him in some of his own clothes—baggy cargo shorts, a light green T-shirt, and a subdued, dark blue Hawaiian shirt. A pair of new athletic shoes rounded out the ensemble. All that remained from Sandy's original attire were his belt, socks, and underwear. The latter two had been washed during the night.

When Sandy walked into the living room, Jellik was already cooking breakfast. The smell of bacon whetted Sandy's appetite.

"Morning," Jellik greeted him.

Sandy held up the shoes. "You just happened to have brand new tennis shoes in my size lying around?"

Jellik grinned while he flipped the bacon. "I made a run into town last night while you two were sleeping."

"For *shoes?*"

"Shoe size matters. You're close enough to my size that my clothes will work. A little big on you, but barely. Shoes, though, that has to be exact." He glanced toward the opposite bedroom and lowered his voice. "Besides, the lady friend I see sometimes only stays the night once in a while. So, what little feminine attire I have around here is too big for the girl in there. And not exactly age-appropriate, if you follow me."

"Got it. You're saying you like to wear women's clothing now."

"Fuck you, Keegan." There was no animosity in Jellik's tone and the insult was almost like music to Sandy's ears, reminding him of better friends in better days.

"You're not my type," Sandy shot back dryly. "Though, if you offer to fly us to Havana, I might reconsider."

"Life is full of lost opportunities," Jellik said. "Asshole."

"Don't make the eggs so soggy this time, huh?"

Jellik held up the spatula and fired him the middle finger.

In that moment, the bedroom door opened and Lita shuffled into the kitchen, yawning. She wore a T-shirt that hung to her knees that bore the logo of the Crimson Tide. Her hair was askew.

Jellik greeted her with a chipper "good morning." Lita smiled distractedly.

"Smells good," she said.

"Almost done," Jellik said. He shot Sandy a sideways glance. "Just have to scramble the eggs."

Lita nodded absently and plopped onto a chair at the small kitchen table. She stared off into space then rubbed her eyes.

"You sleep good?" Jellik asked her.

"Hard," Lita said. "Like I thought I might never sleep again."

He waved the spatula at a plastic bag on the chair opposite her. "There's some clean stuff in there for you. I guessed at the sizes, so hopefully I wasn't too far off."

Lita reached out for the bag and sorted through the items, a slight smile on her face. To Sandy, she looked like an older kid at Christmas, excited but trying to be cool.

Jellik finished the eggs and they ate. While they did so, the pilot told Sandy, "I took your rig to a guy I know who does vehicle work. He traded me for a sedan."

Sandy's fork stopped halfway to his mouth. "You know both the plate and VIN on that are bad, right?"

"He doesn't care. It'll get parted out anyway." He reached into his pocket and pulled out an oversized key fob. "There's a couple grand in the center console."

Sandy put down his fork. "Jellik, you don't need to—"

"I don't want to hear it," the pilot said. "After what we've been through..." He trailed off.

Sandy glanced down, a hundred images flashing through his mind. M-16s, the jungle, blood. Surreptitious flights to places he and his men weren't supposed to be. Lives lost on both sides. He imagined Jellik had his own horrific slideshow he couldn't shake. The pilot had done far worse than merely transport soldiers, Sandy knew.

When he looked up, Jellik was watching him. His expression was one that made Sandy wonder if he'd heard his thoughts. Finally, Jellik cleared his throat, and said, "Evan was my brother, too. So eat your goddamn eggs—which I made to your specifications, by the way—and then get rolling before a swarm of black clad feds start stumbling across my traps out there, making a mess and scaring off the squirrels."

Sandy stared at Jellik for a few moments before nodding. "Thanks," he mumbled.

"Nothing to thank me for. After all, you were never here. Neither was Terry Spencer."

Sandy's eyes narrowed in confusion. "Who's Terry Spencer?"

"He's the registered owner of the car. He's got an Alabama license and is a downright handsome son of a bitch." Jellik smiled mischievously. "On that last count, you might not be able to pass if someone has direct access to the DMV database, but the other physicals are close enough if you get stopped."

"Jesus," Sandy groaned. "Don't say that. You'll jinx us."

Jellik's grin broadened. "Hell, I thought pilots were the only ones so superstitious."

"Why tempt fate?" Sandy said. He thought for a moment. "I appreciate the cover, but it's pretty flimsy since I don't have any ID."

"No," Jellik said. "And hopefully you won't need it. But, lucky for you, Alabama doesn't play nice with other states. Accessing the department of licensing for anything other than driving status and physical description takes some effort. Most entities outside Alabama, cops included, won't be able to pull up a photo, at least not easily. You remember the date of birth and the fact you're supposed to be an inch taller and ten pounds heavier and that ought to satisfy anyone not looking hard at you."

Sandy picked up his fork again and resumed eating. He didn't have to ask what would happen if someone did look hard. The ruse wouldn't hold and his options would narrow.

After breakfast, Lita spent a half hour in the bathroom. Sandy wanted to leave quickly, but he didn't argue or rush her. He figured it might be the last bit of peace she would encounter for a while.

Jellik took the opportunity to give him one last gift.

"I don't have any extra mags for what you were carrying," he said, "so here's the next best thing." He presented Sandy with a Colt 1911 .45 caliber in a shoulder harness. The rig held two extra magazines on the off side. Jellik handed him a third. "Slip that one in your cargo pocket," he said.

Sand accepted the bundle.

"Four mags," Jellik recited. "That equals twenty-eight rounds. Plus one in the chamber." He lifted a shoulder and let it drop. "I figure, if you need more ammo than that, it's the Alamo and you're pretty much fucked, right?"

"We're probably fucked anyway," Sandy said, but he hefted the holstered weapon gratefully. "Thanks for this, though. I'll leave the Sig in trade."

"Shitty trade," Jellik said, "but I'll make an exception for old times' sake."

Sandy slipped on the shoulder harness, adjusted it, and put the Hawaiian shirt on over the top, leaving it unbuttoned. The fact the clothing was slightly too large for him worked in favor of disguising the weapon. He held out his arms to the side for Jellik's appraisal.

"Sonny fucking Crockett," Jellik said.

A short time later, Lita appeared from the bathroom, dressed and ready. They said their goodbyes. Hers to Jellik seemed genuinely heartfelt. When he handed her a grocery bag with jerky, chips, and water, she even smiled.

Sandy held out his hand and Jellik clasped it warmly. Neither man spoke but Jellik pulled him forward in a short, tight embrace. The pilot slapped Sandy on the back, causing him to wince sharply as Jellik struck his injury.

Jellik didn't bother to apologize. He pulled back, gave Sandy another clap on both arms with his open palms, and nodded.

Sandy nodded back, and they left.

As they crept out down the overgrown road to the county two-lane, Lita said, "I like him. He's nice."

Sandy grinned slightly but said nothing.

They headed east to Florida.

Sandy accessed the map feature in the car, then turned it

off once he'd memorized the route to Key West. He drove without a word. Thanks to the rest, the meal, and cleaning up, he felt almost human again. Even so, his body felt battered and sore. The dull throb from his leg was a constant reminder he wouldn't be whole for a while yet. He popped some Tylenol from the care package Jellik had provided Lita, and drove.

Lita matched his silence. For a while, she fiddled with the radio but was seemingly unable to find a station she liked. She settled for staring out the window at the passing scenery.

In another world, Sandy mused, the drive could have been a strained father and daughter road trip, a pair struggling with emotional distance. His - confused and generational; hers - sullen and aloof.

As they neared Tallahassee, the serene quiet was broken. Not by noise, but the flashing blue and red lights behind him.

Unbelievable, he thought. *Goddamn Jellik jinx in action.*

"Shit," Sandy grunted.

Lita glanced around. "What is it?"

Sandy slowed, looking for a place to pull to the side while he mulled over whether or not to do so. If the local cop knew who he was, his best move was to punch it and try to lose the patrol car behind him before others joined in the chase. But, if this was just happenstance, he might be able to get through it with his cover intact. Worst case, he might initiate his escape from a better position, catching the cop out of his vehicle.

Or...

Sandy didn't want to think about the last possibility. He knew it could happen. He knew the choice he'd make if it did. But he used to wear a uniform like the man behind him. Any good cop out there would say Sandy betrayed his badge, at least at some point down the line. Sandy knew that sentiment was probably right. His choices didn't mean this cop deserved to die, though. Hell, in Sandy's estimation, it meant more the opposite.

He chose his path, pulling to the side of the road. As soon as he put the car in park, he motioned to the glove box.

"There's some paperwork in there," he said to Lita. "Hand it to me."

While the girl popped open the door, Sandy reached under his arm and broke the snap on the holster there.

Just in case.

"Don't forget," Sandy told her. "We're headed to Disney World. You're excited."

"I know." She handed him two slips of paper.

Sandy took them and waited for the officer to approach. The tan uniform and broad campaign hat told him it was Florida State Patrol. He clenched and unclenched his jaw. Would a statie have better access to a neighboring state's DMV than a local? He imagined so.

The trooper was black, tall and fit. He radiated professional confidence as he walked forward. Sandy noticed his eyes darting over the vehicle and then lighting on him and Lita. He kept one hand on the wheel, holding the paperwork, and rolled down the window with the other.

"Afternoon, officer," Sandy greeted him as he stopped just before the driver's window. "Is there a problem?"

"Can you turn off the vehicle, sir?" the trooper asked him. The request had a firmness to it Sandy knew from his own days on the job.

Even so, he hesitated. "The air conditioning won't work," he protested, keeping the challenge out of his voice.

"I know," the trooper said. "I'm sorry for that. But we'll only be a few minutes."

Sandy didn't argue further. He shifted the paperwork to his left hand and turned off the engine with his right.

If he asks me to remove the keys, then he knows.

"Thank you," said the trooper. "License, registration, and insurance, please."

Sandy held out the paperwork. "Pretty sure I wasn't speeding, officer."

"It's trooper." He took the items from Sandy's hand and glanced at them, then looked up. "Your license?"

"Sorry," Sandy said, correcting himself. "Trooper. And I don't have my license on me."

"You're not required to carry a license in Alabama?" the trooper asked. There was no sarcasm in his voice but definite suspicion.

"I believe so, yes." Sandy gave him a chagrined smile. "I left my wallet on the counter when we left home, though. Didn't realize it till we stopped for gas in Pensacola."

"Where are you headed?"

"Disney World." He motioned toward Lita. "She's never been."

"How're you planning to pay for that without a wallet?"

"Cash," Sandy said. "I carry my cash in my pocket. My wallet's actually one of those Ridge models. You know, the metal squares? You've seen 'em?"

The trooper eyed him for a moment then dipped his chin. "Don't those have clip for cash?"

"They do, but I like to carry mine separate in my pocket."

The trooper considered him for another few seconds. Then he removed a pen from his breast pocket without taking his gaze off Sandy. "Date of birth?"

Sandy rattled off the birth date he'd memorized.

The trooper jotted it onto the paperwork. Then he lowered his stance and bent forward slightly to address Lita.

"What's your name, hon?"

"Angela," Lita said.

"How old are you?"

"Thirteen."

"You excited for Disney World?"

"Sure."

The trooper's gaze flicked from her to Sandy and back again. "And who's this man?" he asked.

Lita gave him a genuinely confused look, cocking her head. "My dad," she said, drawing out the word and injecting a tone that suggested the question was ludicrous.

The trooper didn't react. He watched them both for a little longer. Then he said, "All right, wait here for a couple minutes. I'm going to check a couple of details and get you on your way. Okay?"

"Okay," Sandy said.

The trooper turned to go, walking forward but keeping his eyes on the vehicle.

"Trooper?" Sandy said.

The trooper stopped, giving him a questioning look.

"You never said why you stopped me."

"It's fifty-five through here."

"I thought it was seventy."

"Only on the interstate," the trooper said. "I'm guessing you got off I-10 at exit 192. This is State Highway 90. Fifty-five miles an hour."

Sandy appeared crestfallen. "Damn," he said. "I... I honestly didn't know."

"All right," said the trooper. "Anything else?"

"No, sir."

The trooper continued retreating to his vehicle. Sandy saw nothing in his demeanor beyond the typical measures of officer safety with which he was familiar. But, if the trooper was good at his job, he wouldn't let on he knew something was amiss.

"Are we going to be all right?" Lita asked. Sandy could hear the slightest tremor in her tone. "Does he know?"

"I don't think so. But we'll find out in the next minute or two."

The seconds crawled by. Sandy avoided staring into the

rearview or door-side mirrors. Undue vigilance like that would send another warning sign to the trooper. Instead, he kept his glances into either mirror as casual as he could, and waited.

A typical traffic stop without issuing a citation took less than five minutes, maybe as little as three. If the trooper chose to cite him, that might take slightly longer, though he imagined the computer auto-populated many of the entries done by hand in Sandy's day. As two minutes stretched into three and then four, Sandy ran alternatives through his mind. How long did he wait before making a dash southward? Outrunning a patrol car wasn't a simple task and outrunning a radio was more difficult yet. Still, that was a better option than waiting for a second vehicle to show up and for the reinforced duo to call him out of the sedan at gunpoint.

Two more minutes, he thought. That or if backup arrived. If either of those things occurred, he would start the car and the chase would begin. It was a bad plan, he knew, but it beat the alternative.

Another minute ticked by. Sandy alternated the focus of his peripheral vision between both mirrors and the digital clock on the dash. He waited for the block number three to roll over to a four. Sweat tricked down from his temple.

Almost time.

Next to him, Lita remained silent. He imagined she could sense the tension in the air. Thankfully, she had the sense to be quiet.

The three on the dash clock morphed into a four. A small, slow burst of adrenaline seemed to open up in Sandy's core and seep warmly out to his extremities. He reached for the key.

Behind him, he spotted movement. The trooper's door swung open. The man exited the patrol car and walked toward them. Sandy lowered his hand, instinctively resting it on his lap, palm up. If he had to reach for his gun, he was prepared.

Nothing in the trooper's stride indicated anything was

amiss. He stopped in the same position as before, just prior to the B pillar. He held out a slip of paper that looked like an oversized receipt, which he gave to Sandy.

"Mr. Spencer," the trooper said, in a practiced tone, "I'm issuing you an infraction for speeding this morning. Also for failing to carry your driver's license while operating a motor vehicle."

Relief washed over him. The sensation was almost the reverse of the adrenaline shot a few moments prior—comfortably cool instead of warm, and from his shoulders down his body to his feet.

"Aw, man, really?" Sandy asked, looking at the ticket and trying to inject disappointment into his voice.

"Yes, sir. At fifteen over, I could have cited you for negligent driving, so consider this a bit of a break."

Sandy sighed. "All right. Thanks for that."

The trooper returned his paperwork. "If you get stopped again, show that infraction to whoever it is. I can't promise they won't write you up again for the no operator's license on person, but most cops won't."

"Okay."

"That's not a free pass to speed, though."

"I understand."

"Good. Now, do you have any questions for me, sir?"

Sandy shook his head.

"Drive safely, then." The trooper broke contact retreating to his car in the same safe manner he had done so before.

Sandy waited until the man reached his patrol car. Then he started the sedan, signaled, and pulled back into traffic. The trooper vehicle remained still but the flashing lights cut out.

Next to him, Lita let out a long sigh of relief. "That was close," she said.

"At this point," Sandy muttered, "everything we do will be

close. But we got lucky."

Lita was quiet for almost a minute before she answered him. "I don't feel so lucky," she said. The flatness in her voice had returned, along with the sullen anger around its edges. In his peripheral vision, he spotted her touching the silver bracelet at her wrist.

"No, I don't suppose you do," Sandy agreed. "Not in the grand scheme of things. But you have to recognize luck wherever it shows up."

"You mean, lucky that cop didn't figure out who we were?"

Sandy had meant that, but something more, too. Lita Delancey was much luckier than she could possibly comprehend, despite their situation.

Lucky it was him Szoke sent and not someone else.

Lucky Jellik picked up his phone and agreed to help them.

Lucky the Greek remembered his debt.

In the end, he thought, *she's lucky to still be alive at all. Does she realize that?*

Sandy thought maybe she did. She may not truly know the enormous odds she'd beaten, but he believed she had an overall sense of it. He also believed she shouldn't have to be reminded of it constantly.

So he answered, "Yes. That's what I mean."

And he drove.

33

Carter nearly ran over Szoke as she exited the trailer of the command post.

Szoke stumbled back a step, then eyed her with irritation. "What the hell?"

"Sorry," she said. "I have to catch a flight."

Szoke tilted his head. "To where?"

"Mobile. I chartered with a local flight club." She lifted a finger to the nearby driver, who had exited the transport car to stand in the doorway, waiting. "I should be there in about an hour."

"When were you going to tell me this?"

"In the car, on my way to the airfield."

"Lori, do you want to tell me—"

"I ran through any and all of the contacts I could find for Banks," she interrupted. "I eliminated most of them on various grounds, but there were a few that looked good to me. Problem is, most of them are hard to find without arousing suspicion."

"How so?"

"They're off the grid, either due to false identities or literally living somewhere self-sufficient and without outside connections."

"Like Cousin Mayford," Szoke mused.

An image of the cabin in the Tennessee woods sprang to Carter's mind. The old man had sheltered Banks during her pursuit of him. When she finally arrived and surrounded the place with a tactical team, Banks was already gone. But Cousin Mayford took the opportunity to go out in a blaze of glory. She didn't want a repeat of that debacle.

"Something like that," she told Szoke. "Usually difficult to track. But one of them just stuck his head up—Abel Jellik."

Szoke squinted. "Pilot, right?"

"That's right. We used him for transport on an op years ago. Very smooth, very low key, and we never contracted with him again. But the original contact was suggested by Banks. He vouched for him. Said they served together."

"Must have been a while ago, if Banks made the suggestion," Szoke said. "Back when he was still resigned to his situation. You said this pilot stuck his head up?"

She nodded. "I flagged him for detention through the FAA. An alert tower supervisor saw it and recognized the name. It's a small airfield where Jellik has a plane. The supervisor called it in and I had the local sheriff's office swoop in. Jellik was at the hangar, prepping for a flight. They're holding onto him now."

"At the police station?"

"No, still in the hangar."

Szoke's face brightened. "Don't tell me he was their ride?"

"I thought he could be. But the deputies confirmed there wasn't anyone else there. And his plane was prepped to carry cargo."

"Cargo? What kind?"

"The unmarked kind, I'm sure," she said. "My guess, he's going to fly somewhere south and bring back a shitload of drugs."

Szoke's expression returned its usual sour state. "I don't care about drugs."

"No, but plenty of other people do. It gives me some leverage when I talk to him."

"Except the locals are involved," said Szoke. "They've probably already torn the plane apart, found nothing, and called a press conference anyway."

"Nope. I told them to stand down and only detain him. No arrest, no further search, no interrogation." She tapped her chest. "Until I get there."

Szoke dipped his chin in reluctant appreciation. "Well, nice work, Lori." He motioned toward the car. "I'll let you get to it, then."

Carter started past him, but Szoke grabbed her wrist lightly. She looked down at his hand in surprise, then back up to his face.

"You should know," he said. "We're issuing the Amber Alert."

She tilted her head. "Why now?"

"You were right," Szoke said. "We're running out of time. And I can't afford for Banks to escape. Or the girl, but especially him." He shook his head slowly. "Can you imagine this guy sitting down in front of Congress and testifying about us? He'd make Oliver North look bush league in comparison."

Carter didn't answer. A few days ago, she might have welcomed a little sunshine on this dark operation, despite her own culpability. Now, all she wanted to do was catch Banks and even the scales as best she could.

What difference a few days makes.

"None of us would survive it if he went public," Szoke told her. "So you know what's at stake here, right?"

She shook her wrist free. "I've always known."

She turned away from him and headed to the car.

Eighty minutes later, Carter was speaking with the county sergeant outside the hangar doors. He looked like a grizzled veteran and his no-nonsense approach aligned with her initial assessment of him.

"You cleared the hangar?"

"Yes, ma'am," the sergeant said. "No one else is in that plane or the hangar."

"What *is* in the plane?"

"It's like I told you on the phone. It's empty. Looks like he's rigged to fly in a drug load, clear as day." He peered at her. "You DEA?"

"We'll take it from here, sergeant." She motioned to one of the two men she'd brought along with her. "Give my associate your name and your deputies' and we'll be sure to send a formal thank you to the sheriff."

The sergeant frowned but didn't argue.

Carter headed to the hangar with one soldier in tow. Inside, Abel Jellik sat on a metal folding chair about twenty feet from the Cessna he'd been intending to take off in about a couple hours earlier. He wore khaki 511 trousers and a long-sleeved shirt of the same color and brand. His wavy hair extended from the back of his ball cap down below his collar. He had the look of a man who was usually easygoing but she could see his queasy discomfort riding below the surface.

Two deputies stood guard nearby. "Thank you for the assist, gentlemen," she said. "You are relieved. Your sergeant is waiting outside."

The pair exchanged a glance before they headed toward the door. Carter heard one of them mutter something but she couldn't make out the exact words. Experience told her it was most likely a gripe about federal jurisdiction.

If he only knew.

Once the deputies were gone, she turned to the pilot.

"Where are you headed today, Mr. Jellik?"

Jellik peered closely at her. "Who the hell are you?"

"I'm either your lucky day or your nightmare," Carter said

smoothly. "Which one is entirely up to you."

"Great. A fucking fed."

"Why do you say that?"

"Only feds talk like that."

"Like what?"

He waved his hands. "All grandiose and shit, man."

Carter grunted noncommittally. Then she repeated her question. "You were getting ready to fly out when the deputies detained you. What's your destination?"

Jellik shifted in his seat. "Houston. Check my flight plan with the tower. It's all there."

"I'm sure it is. But you weren't going to Houston, were you?"

"What are you talking about? Of course I was."

"No," Carter said. "You were headed elsewhere." She glanced at the nearby Cessna. "Did the deputies look in the plane?"

"I guess. They said they were looking for someone else."

"They were. And you know who it is."

"I don't know shit, man."

"Only they didn't find Banks or the girl in the plane. Instead, they found a whole lot of empty space."

Jellik swallowed and looked away. "What do you want? If you're going to bust me for having an empty plane, take me in, charge me, whatever. But I want my lawyer."

"One supplied by the cartel?" she asked.

"What's a cartel?"

"Funny." Carter didn't laugh. "I'm impressed. I don't know if I'd be able to make jokes if I were in your shoes."

"Lawyer," Jellik repeated.

"Yeah, I heard you. But now you need to hear me, Abel. Because we are off-book here. As in *un*official." She swept her hand toward the door. "Official just left sixty seconds ago with your friends in uniform."

"The hell's that supposed to mean?"

"It means no lawyer, for starters. It means I know you may not be late yet for your rendezvous, but the clock is ticking. I know you'll be in deep shit with your employers if you don't show on time to pick up their product. And I doubt they're the kind of people who reschedule. Or take disappointment easily."

Jellik tried to smirk but the expression seemed forced to her.

"Now, I don't much care where you fly or what you transport, so I'm more than willing to walk away from this hangar and let you get on with your business. *That's* where I'm your lucky day." She lifted her left hand and looked at it, then slowly lifted her right, turning to watch it rise until it was equal to the left. "Then there's how I can be your nightmare. You want to hear about that?"

"No," Jellik said. "I want my lawyer."

"No lawyers," Carter said dismissively. She clapped her hands together. "Here's something you don't know, Abel—we've worked together before. You flew an op down to Monterrey about seven years ago. Transported a man there and back. You remember that?"

"I fly a lot," Jellik said. "I'd have to check my records."

"You remember," Carter said confidently. "And I doubt there are any records of the flight. Your passenger was a man you knew as Keegan Fuller. An old Army buddy. He goes by Sandy Banks these days."

Jellik shifted in his seat. "Yeah, okay. So I flew a charter a long time ago for an old friend. So what?"

"The so what is he's been working with me for the past ten years. Doing not-so-nice stuff. And now he's hiding from us, along with a thirteen-year-old girl he's kidnapped."

"Keegan?" Jellik looked doubtful. "That doesn't sound like him."

"I'm not here to argue with you about it," Carter said. She gave Jellik her most confident stare and played her bluff. "He's on the run and he reached out to you for help. You're going to tell me where he is or where he's going to be."

"Even if that were true—and it's not—I wouldn't tell you a damn thing, lady. I knew Keegan. I've never even heard of you. I still don't know who you are."

The hangar man-door opened and the second soldier slipped through.

"Are they gone?" Carter asked him.

He nodded.

"Good." Carter pulled her gun from her holster and covered the distance between her and Jellik in two long strides. She pressed the barrel of the gun to his forehead. "Who am I? Let me clue you into the facts of life, Abel. Fact one, and you probably already know this one, but here it is anyway: your pal Keegan and I don't work for an official agency. We operate in the dark. So you're not getting a lawyer and I can do pretty much anything I want." She pressed the barrel forward against his head, pushing him back in his chair. "Say you understand."

Jellik was trying desperately not to cower. "I understand," he croaked, lifting his hands in surrender. "Easy, man."

"Fuck easy. I don't have time for easy." She pushed the muzzle even harder against his skull. "Fact two: if you don't tell me what I need to know, I will blow your fucking brains out right here in this hangar. Say you understand."

Jellik turned his face away. "No way, man. You're bluffing."

"I know you'd like to believe that, but think about it for a second. Who's going to miss you? Some little slut from a trailer park somewhere? A dog? Your friends down south sure won't. They'll find another monkey with a toy plane in no time to mule for them and keep on without skipping a beat."

"Those cops—"

"Are bought and paid for," Carter lied. "And how hard do you think they need to investigate to make this look good? A cartel drug smuggler gets iced. So what? Those people kill each other off all the time."

"Bullshit," Jellik said, but she could hear his resolve weakening.

Carter pulled the gun away from his head and held it in front of his face. "Let me tell you about this gun. It's a Beretta-92FS, nine millimeter. Unregistered. Never been used outside the firing range. After I shoot you in the head with it, this weapon will go into a furnace at a steel plant ten miles away. Bowdry Steel. You know the place?"

Jellik nodded reluctantly.

"So it's a simple choice, Abel. You get lucky, which means you're on that plane and on schedule." She pointed to his plane. "You avoid a nasty problem with your nasty friends down south. Or…"

She drew back the hammer.

"Well, the *or* doesn't really matter to you after I paint the side of your Cessna red, does it?"

Jellik let out a wavering breath as he stared into her eyes. She knew he was weighing out the scenario, gauging his own loyalty, and trying like hell to decide if she was bluffing or not.

Am I?

She honestly didn't know and the fact scared her.

Carter pressed the tip of the gun forward.

It turned out, Jellik didn't know if she was bluffing, either. And, more importantly, it scared him, too.

"It's Miami," Carter told Szoke over the secure phone. "Banks has a contact there who will ferry them to the Bahamas."

"Who's the contact there?" Szoke asked.

"Banks didn't tell him."

"Did you push him?"

Carter thought back to the muzzle of her gun pressed hard into Jellik's temple. "Pretty hard," she said. "He asked Jellik to fly them. When he said he couldn't, Banks made other arrangements. Jellik gave them a safe haven for the night. They left early this morning."

"In the SUV?"

"Supposedly. But Jellik said he thought Banks would swap that out in Mobile."

"He did, apparently."

"What?"

"We got a hit about forty minutes after the Amber Alert went out," Szoke told her. "A Florida state trooper reported having stopped them in a silver sedan outside of Tallahassee. Obviously, this was before the alert, so he had no reason to detain. But he remembered them perfectly and ID'd Banks off the photo in the bulletin."

"Did he get any intel off the encounter?" Carter asked.

"Not much. Banks said they were headed to Disney World."

"Did he have ID?"

"No, but the name he used checked out, at least for a run-of-the-mill traffic stop."

Carter thought about it. "If he was in Tallahassee a few hours ago, that checks out. It's on the way to Miami."

"We updated the alert with the vehicle info," Szoke said. "But you know how many silver sedans are running around out there?"

"Someone will spot the plate. Or a camera will pick it up."

"Probably."

"This is solid progress. Why do you sound so disappointed?"

"Because I've already got an FBI Agent up my ass to liaise with me over this. He's claiming jurisdiction over the case due to the kidnapping. He's also asking a lot of questions."

"What'd you tell him?"

"That we've got it handled."

"No, I mean about who we are. Why we are holding onto the case."

"I said we're associated with Homeland Security. But that'll only work if he doesn't do any digging."

"Keep him focused on the manhunt, then," said Carter. "This is good, Mark. The Bureau can bring more assets to bear on this. We'll catch him."

"Maybe. But our entire operation might get caught up in the same web."

"Tomorrow's problem," she said. "Today's is finding Banks."

"We're moving the command post to Miami," he told her. "Meet us at Mobile's main airport. You and I will fly to Miami and meet with this prick."

"What's his name? I might know who it is."

"Maw," Szoke said. "Special-Agent-in-Charge Edward Maw. You know him?"

In spite of everything, Carter smiled. "I do, actually."

34

Sandy drove silently, his gaze flicking to the rearview every few seconds.

The signs for Tampa had become more plentiful and the upcoming exits would lead him into the city if he chose to take them. He'd gassed up outside of Gainesville and some quick math told him they'd make it into Key West on their existing fuel.

Darkness wouldn't fall for hours yet. The cushion surrounding their arrival time remained intact as long as he kept pace with minimal stops. The route through Tampa was actually slightly longer than if he'd taken the Orlando route, eventually going via Miami. But, after telling the trooper about their fictional trip to Disney World, he decided the extra twenty minutes of drive time was worth the cover the route change provided.

He glanced in the rear-view mirror again.

"You do that a lot," Lita said.

"Do what?" Sandy asked evenly, not looking at her.

"Look in the mirror. Are we being followed again?"

"No."

"Then what are you doing?"

"Making sure of it."

"Oh."

She fell silent again.

The girl had been quiet since the traffic stop, but Sandy

noticed her seeming more and more antsy with every passing mile. Her fingers toyed with the silver bracelet absently. He wondered if the reality of her situation and all that had occurred were starting to finally settle in on her. He hoped not. As tragic as it was, the trauma was better dealt with from the safety and comfort of a Greek island than during the last hours of their escape.

"We'll make it," he told her.

She didn't reply immediately. Then she turned to look at him. "Don't talk to me like I'm a kid."

"You are a kid."

"Not anymore. Not thanks to you."

Sandy absorbed the barb. She was right, after all. "I'll get you out of here," he said. "I'll make sure you're safe."

"You can't promise that."

"How's this, then? I'll do my very best."

She turned to face forward again. "Whatever." Lita adjusted her position in her seat. "How many people are chasing us, anyway?"

"I don't know."

"It's your people, isn't it?"

"The kind of operation I was in, I didn't know all of the people involved. It was very compartmentalized."

"What's that mean?"

He thought about it then said, "The different groups don't know what the other groups were doing. Or even that they exist, actually."

She considered his answer. "So it could be hundreds?"

He shrugged. "Could be. I don't know."

"Will they get help from others, too? Like that trooper or the Army or something?"

"Maybe. I don't think they have yet, though."

"But you don't know?"

"I don't." He drove in silence for another mile. "Look, this is the last stretch. That much I can promise. Another seven hours or so and we'll be at the marina."

"There's still a long boat ride after that," she said.

"Not a long one, actually. They don't call them go-fast boats for nothing. It'll only take a couple of hours. Maybe less." He glanced over at her. "But you'll get windburn."

She didn't smile.

"Trust me," Sandy said. "Once you're to Cuba, it becomes a milk run."

"Milk run? The hell is that?"

"An easy mission. An uneventful trip."

"Why's it called a milk run?"

"I have no idea."

"You don't know much of anything," Lita said acidly. "Do you?"

"No," he admitted. "Except this: if we get through this last bit, it'll be over for you. You'll be safe. Just this last piece and then you'll have all the sunshine you can take."

Lita sat quietly for a while then lifted her shoulder in a bare shrug. "That sounds nice, I guess. If it happens."

"Just a few more hours."

"I know. You said that." She fidgeted again with the bracelet, then pulled away her hand and turned to look out the passenger window. "I still hate you, you know."

"I know."

He drove.

35

This is surreal.

Ex-Special Agent Lori Carter stood next to a man in a custom fit suit inside an empty office building in a Miami strip mall that had been quickly set up as a temporary command post. Somewhere on I-95, the semi-truck pulling their mobile CP still lumbered southward, but Carter didn't hold out hope it would arrive before this entire affair ended.

Working on laptops and paper maps instead of surrounded by large screens wasn't the surreal part. Rather, it was standing next to Special-Agent-in-Charge Edward Maw. Her former boss, who she pegged as being one of the biggest climbers in the Bureau back when she'd been on the job.

Part of the odd dynamic was how quickly they fell back into their old roles. He, the officious, dismissive boss whose confidence often outkicked the coverage of his common sense. She, the expert field operative with outsized contempt for bureaucratic climbers like him.

As if to emphasize the nature of the reunion, both stood watching the room, not speaking. Carter added to the coolness by crossing her arms and not looking at Maw, taking him in strictly through her peripheral vision.

He'd aged, she saw. He was thinner and had more gray in his hair. His shoulders had rounded slightly, giving him the hint of a stooped posture. A loose wattle of skin was beginning to form under his chin, making her think of him as a skinny turkey.

And he was still a Special-Agent-in-Charge (SAC). No "director" in his job title. The Spokane debacle must have stunted his career, she realized. For him to still be a SAC meant his upward mobility had been blocked, since she knew the man would never voluntarily remain at that rank.

Checking up on her former colleagues had never occurred to her during her stint on Szoke's dark squad. Scott McNichol, her old partner, was her only connection to the Bureau, and he'd long since retired in the aftermath of the Banks incident.

Retired due to his injuries, she recalled. *Because Banks shot him.*

The way her long past emotions flared up again when she relived those moments added to the strangeness of this moment.

She stood quietly, watching Szoke take a considerably more proactive approach to directing activity than he usually did. This was theater, she knew. Designed for Maw's benefit and to pre-empt any intent the FBI man might have to take over Szoke's operation.

Without looking at her, Maw said quietly, "Tell me something—how is the CIA directing an op on US soil?"

"We're with Homeland," she answered, matching his low tone. "Not CIA."

"Since when?"

She shrugged. "Not my area."

"Nor mine," said Maw. "But I've made a few calls over to Homeland. No one seems to be aware of exactly where your unit falls on the organizational chart."

"Special dispensation, I guess."

"It's irregular."

"Szoke says it's necessary."

"It's irregular," Maw repeated. "And irregular usually

means a front for the Company. That sounds like something someone should look into."

Someone? Like a SAC trying to repair his career, perhaps?

Carter resisted the urge to frown. If Maw spearheaded an investigation into this operation, she knew it wouldn't stand up to scrutiny. The unit would fold and go into damage control mode. Depending on the outcome, Szoke or Danforth might be able to re-form a new version down the road but with different operatives.

Not her, though.

She'd be out.

What might that mean? Probably not retirement to a condo in Arizona, she knew. Maybe it even meant testifying before Congress and finding herself in a federal jail cell somewhere. Was that preferable to this life?

The fact that she didn't have an immediate answer told her all she needed to know.

"We're in the middle of a manhunt here," she said, knowing Maw expected her to defend her new boss. Hell, the Poindexter likely relished the interplay, probably thrived on it. "Not the time for splitting bureaucratic hairs."

"I'm aware. A search for a man who is supposed to have been captured over a decade ago. Or killed? Which was it? I forget. The official memo was vague on that point."

"He wasn't killed."

"Clearly, or you wouldn't be chasing him now. But all of it begs a question. Many questions, actually, but one of them is paramount." He actually deigned to turn his head to face her. "Would you like to know what that question is?"

Carter recalled Jellik's comment about feds being grandiose and decided the pilot might've been right on that point. She feigned disinterest, not meeting Maw's gaze. "Do I have a choice?"

"Actually, I suppose you do. You don't work for me anymore, so you can simply walk away. Stand on the other side of the room. Not much I could do about."

She didn't move. After a few moments, she said, "What's this so-called paramount question?"

Maw smiled tightly, as if he'd won a victory. "The question is, what's Sandy Banks been up to for the last decade?"

"Pickleball?" she deadpanned.

Maw's smile didn't diminish. "I'd wager a bit more than that. I'd go so far as to hypothesize his activities are bound up in yours… and Mr. Szoke's." He tipped his head toward the show-boating supervisor.

Carter didn't answer. Secretly, she hoped this was a bone Maw had no intention of relinquishing. If his inquiries ended this hellish existence for her, one way or another, it would be a relief.

"We're in the middle of a manhunt," she repeated, making her point to him quite clear.

First we catch Banks, then you do what you want. Maybe I'll even be a witness for you.

But first, Banks. If, after finally bringing him to justice, she had to face a justice of her own, so be it. She felt resigned to the inevitability. Secrets never lasted, even if they took time before coming to light. Hell, the Spokane vigilante group lasted for over a decade, just like this unit had managed to do.

"Boss?" Paulinus interrupted, his tone urgent.

Szoke stopped speaking mid-order, and turned to the analyst. "What is it?"

"I've got him. On traffic cams."

"Where? Is it live?"

"No, it was over two hours ago, but not on I-95," Paulinus said. "I've got him on 75 eastbound."

"Seventy-five?" Szoke narrowed his eyes, scanning a map on the table in front of him. "He must have gone down the other side of the panhandle."

Smart, Carter thought. Banks was adapting, being careful to account for the lie he told the trooper.

"Where is he now?" Szoke demanded.

"I don't know," Paulinus replied. "I'm tracking via camera history now."

"Track faster."

Paulinus focused on the screen and typed furiously.

"Wherever he's headed in Miami," Maw said to her, still keeping his voice low, "we'll catch him. I've got a ready response team on standby. He's not getting away."

Carter wanted to feel good about that, but she didn't. She figured some of it was the maelstrom of mixed emotions she had regarding Banks and this entire operation. But the sensation that rose out of that mess as the strongest one was something else entirely.

Doubt.

"What if he's not going to Miami?" she murmured.

"What?" Maw asked.

Carter stepped forward and looked over the maps spread out across the long table down the center of the room. She ran her finger over the laminated paper, thinking.

Maw joined her, once again falling into old routines. Despite his arrogant, dismissive nature, she'd always known him to be smart enough to know how to capitalize on her abilities. Outthinking criminals might be the one and only true talent she brought into this world, but it was one that sometimes mattered a lot.

"What do you have?" Maw asked her.

"Nothing certain," she said thoughtfully, still examining the roadways south of Miami. "But if he skips Miami…"

"Why would he do that?"

"I don't know."

"Didn't your informant say—"

"Informants lie."

"So bring him back in. Be sure."

"He's almost certainly somewhere in Mexico at the moment."

"You let him go?" Maw asked, astonished.

"That was the deal I made."

Maw didn't answer, but pressed his lips together, a clear sign of his disapproval. The small gesture gave her a sense of déjà vu.

"Update," Szoke demanded loudly. He drifted closer to Carter, eyeing her and Maw with suspicion.

"He took the 27 exit, southbound," Paulinus reported. "Then I lost him."

"Well, *find* him." Szoke moved to stand directly across from Carter. "What are you doing?"

Carter looked up. "Jellik may have lied to us. If Banks stays on 27 South, he's not going to Miami at all."

Szoke's jaw tightened. "And let me guess—your pilot is also in the wind."

"He's wherever he wants to be," Carter said. "I let him go after he gave up Banks. That was the deal."

"You said you were *sure*." The accusation in Szoke's tone was sharp. "Now you're not?"

Carter returned her gaze to the map. "I focus on facts, not on my ego. I thought I broke him. Maybe I did and Banks changed his plans. Or maybe he held out or changed enough information to misdirect us. We'll know in a few minutes." She traced a finger southward on the map. "If not Miami, then Key Largo is our best bet. That's if his destination is truly the Bahamas, like Jellik told me. If that was bullshit, too…" Carter ran her finger down Highway 1. "Then it's likely Key West and Cuba."

"I'll get our flight assets on standby," Szoke said. "If he goes to Key Largo, we'll chopper down. Key West, it's under

A Hard Favored Death

an hour by plane."

Carter glanced at her watch, hoping they could beat the clock.

"Highway 1," Paulinus announced. "Southbound."

"Time?"

"Seventy-six minutes ago." Paulinus kept typing. "The AI is quicker than me at tracking a single camera system, so…" He hit a few keys then waited. Carter stared at him, along with everyone else in the room. Tension hung in the humid air like a wet curtain ready to fall. "There!" Paulinus said excitedly. "Still headed south, passing Key Largo as of fifty-eight minutes ago."

"It's Key West then," said Carter, "with Cuba as the likely end point."

"Shit," Szoke muttered. "Cuba."

Maw drew himself up. "I'll alert the Coast Guard, and—"

"I'll alert the Coasties," Szoke interrupted. "You focus on scrambling your tactical team. Paulinus will catch up to him in real time and keep you updated. When Banks rolls up to whatever marina he thinks is his route out of this country, we're all going to be waiting for him."

Maw's pinched expression told Carter he didn't like taking direction from Szoke. Officially however, the FBI was there in support of the operation. Szoke still retained operational control and Maw knew it.

The SAC dipped his chin once, spun on his heel, and headed out of the room.

"What a dick," Szoke muttered after him. "You worked for him for how long?"

"Too long," Carter said, though she didn't entirely feel the sentiment. When she was working for Maw and the FBI, she never questioned the legitimacy of her mission. She glanced at her watch again. "We're not going to make it. We should call in local law enforcement."

"We will," Szoke said. "When we know where he's going."

Carter turned to him, tilting her head in surprise. "He's going to Key West."

"I meant which specific marina. Do you know how many marinas there are in that town?"

"What does it matter? Get the locals and state to watch for him. Hell, there might still be time to blockade the highway outside of—"

"No!" Szoke spoke with low vehemence. "I want him."

"You'll get him."

"I want him *dead*. Not in some state trooper's handcuffs. He's too dangerous alive."

"What if he surrenders?"

"He won't."

"Something I've learned about this man, from chasing him and then working with him, is he doesn't always do what you expect."

"That's exactly why he won't surrender."

She shook her head. "You're not making sense."

"I am." He tapped a finger on the table. "Banks knows we're looking for an unexpected move from him. Therefore, the unexpected move, in this instance, is the chalk one."

"You're grasping."

"No, I'm right." He leaned forward. "But so are you. If we set up a roadblock or get the locals to start a pursuit with him, it might very well end in his surrender. Maybe he has no choice, gets knocked unconscious or something. Or maybe he decides to do it to save the girl. In any event, I'm not willing to risk it."

"Then you're risking his actual escape."

"That's not happening."

"What if he gets to whichever marina he's headed to first? You know that's the most likely outcome, right?"

"If he gets there first, we'll still be right behind him. Instead of an ambush, we'll have to go in guns blazing. Either way, it'll be us who stops him. Not locals. And there'll be no arrest. Just a body."

Carter didn't share his optimism, but she knew it was his call. Even so, she saw another problem with his logic. "Maw's team is not going to shoot him unless he starts the gunfight. They'll have strict rules of engagement and they'll adhere to them."

"His team won't be the only ones in the element, though, will they? My A Squad knows what they need to do. One way or another, the threat of Banks surrendering and running his mouth about what he knows is terminated."

"So you have one of your guys snipe Banks, regardless of what he does. Fine." She leaned forward earnestly. "What about the girl? One of them is just going to take her out, too?"

"No," Szoke said, managing to sound almost disappointed. "At this point, with the cover story we've put in place, she's an innocent victim. All she can really say is Banks murdered her parents and kidnapped her. Whatever story he told her is just that—a crazy story from a traumatized child." He shrugged. "She can live."

"Is that a promise?"

"Sure," he said. "Now let's mobilize."

How noble of you.

"All right," she said, not entirely satisfied. "I'll notify the Coast Guard and we'll move out."

"Hold off on that, too," Szoke said.

Carter pulled her head back and looked at him in confusion. "I'm sorry, do you *want* him to get away?"

"Of course not. I also don't want to spook him at the marina. He needs to get out of the car. Once he's on foot, his mobility is limited and we'll have him."

"Unless he makes it to the boat that's waiting for him," she pointed out.

"In which case we'll call in the Coast Guard. You do realize how heavily patrolled the Florida coastline is, don't you?"

"I literally have no idea."

"That's why I'm in charge," said Szoke.

"They'd still be better off if they were prepared. I'm sure the patrol boats could remain well away from Key West and still be ready."

"Very true. But there's another issue you're not seeing."

"Which is?"

"Op-Sec. Or more specifically, Com-Sec."

"You're worried people are going to hear about this?" she asked, incredulous. "Are you forgetting we put out an Amber Alert? Banks might get stopped by law enforcement before reaching Key West just based on that alone."

"I canceled the alert."

"What? When?"

"After the trooper reported in." He met her gaze flatly. "It served its purpose. Now, if you don't mind, let's stop arguing and get on a plane to Key West."

Carter shook her head. Her goal was to catch Banks. She now realized Szoke's was much more specific—to kill Banks, as quietly as possible and likely the girl as well, and to do so under a precise set of controlled circumstances.

"I don't like it," she told him. "Doing this your way, he's going to escape."

"You don't have to like it. Besides, your job description on this op just changed."

"To what, exactly?"

"Running interference with that Bureau dick. He looks way too nosy for any of our good."

She almost answered he didn't know the half of it, but held her tongue. Instead, she glanced at her watch again and shook her head.

A Hard Favored Death

"We're not going to make it," she said again.

36

Sandy pulled into the lot for the marina. Before he turned off the engine, he swept a careful gaze over the area, looking for anything suspicious.

Despite his weariness, he experienced a burst of energy now that they'd reached the marina. It wasn't elation but rather a spike in uneasy readiness, that sense that he was entering the most dangerous stage of a mission—when success was so close he could almost touch it but the greatest peril still remained.

The parking area sat around eight feet higher than the water. A short serpentine path led down from the parking area to the dock entrance.

Sandy saw no shadowy figures in the half-empty lot which only held twenty or so spaces. No snipers atop the nearby shops or tucked back from the second story windows of the closed restaurant across the street.

At least none he could see. If they were any good, they'd be invisible.

"What are we waiting for?" Lita asked, pointing toward the dock. "There's the orange light."

Sandy saw it, too. Just a pinprick of vivid orange at a slip near the end of the dock, right where Dufresne's boat was supposed to be moored. The color reminded him of the coal of a cigarette flaring in the dark.

"Let's go," Sandy said, reaching for the door. "But *walk*.

Don't run unless I tell you."

Lita didn't answer but he knew she'd heard him.

They popped open the doors and started down the twisting path toward the dock. Sandy's leg throbbed with every limping step. He kept his eyes scanning, watching for any suspicious movement.

There wasn't anyone around. He wasn't sure if that should bother him or not. Was it normal for the docks to be this empty at this hour? Or had the locals been cleared out to lay a trap?

No, he decided. If Szoke's men had been lying in wait, they'd have sprung the ambush in the parking lot, as soon as he and Lita exited the car. The fact that had not happened told him something he didn't want to believe could come true.

They'd made it. They were home free.

Sandy stepped onto the wood of the dock, a spark of hope rising in him.

The roar of engines and the squeal of tires stamped out that ember.

Sandy whipped his head around to see multiple SUVs scream into the lot above and screech to a hard stop. Black-clad men spilled out of them while the vehicles were still rocking on their wheels. Within seconds, these figures had advanced toward Sandy, leveling MP5s toward him and Lita. A quick glance told him there were more than eight of them. Several were already shouting commands at him.

"Do not move!"

"Show me your hands!"

They had superior numbers, more firepower, and the high ground. He gauged the distance at around thirty yards. Not a bad range, but plenty of room for misses, both his and theirs.

"Do not move!" came another voice, different than the one who'd issued the same command a second earlier.

Sandy remained facing the approaching men. He didn't

recognize any of them though, in the dark at this distance, that was no surprise. Still, he didn't think these were Szoke's crew. Those men would have shot already.

"FBI, motherfucker!" shouted another man, one who seemed to have advanced closest to them. He stood near the top of the serpentine path that led down to dock. "Get your hands up in the air!"

Sandy didn't move. His gaze swept the assembled tactical team and saw no faces he knew, no familiar stances.

Surrender?

The thought danced in his head for a moment, as real as the go-fast boat next to the orange light at the end of the dock. If he surrendered to the FBI, would that put him and Lita beyond Szoke's grasp?

Maybe.

But maybe not Danforth's. The shadowy man's influence must run deep for this operation to have existed for so many years. And he didn't strike Sandy as someone willing to take a loss and move on.

Still…

"Do it now!" boomed the nearest agent.

Another vehicle whipped into the lot, slamming to a stop. Even at this distance, Sandy recognized Carter as she exited the driver's side. Szoke and another man in a suit got out as well.

In the same moment, he noticed several more black-clad figures creeping in on the extreme flanks of the FBI element that faced him. He didn't have time to look at their faces, but he recognized the slow, confident forward gait each of them used, like a cat easing up on a wounded bird.

"Get ready," he told Lita in a hushed voice.

She didn't answer.

Sandy began to walk slowly backwards onto the dock.

"Stay where you are!" the man yelled.

A Hard Favored Death

Sorry pal. That ain't happening.
Sandy took another step.

37

Carter took in the tense situation at a glance.

She didn't know whether or not Banks was considering surrender. He hadn't reached for a gun yet, so she took that as a positive sign.

At least until he started moving backwards onto the dock.

Shit.

"Stay where you are!" the FBI team leader roared at him.

On the edges of his group, Carter saw Szoke's men advancing, weapons raised. Beside her, Szoke raised his radio to his lips.

This is going to end badly, Carter realized. Before Szoke could speak a command, she stepped forward and shouted. "Banks!"

Banks didn't react, other than to take another slow, limping step backward. But she knew he heard her.

"What are you *doing?*" hissed Szoke, lowering the radio.

She ignored him and pushed onward. "Give up, Sandy! Give up and I guarantee she'll be safe. Do you hear me? You have my word."

"Shut up," Szoke told her. "This is a tactical situation now. Leave it to—"

"All out in the daylight, Banks!" Carter yelled. "All of it!"

Banks moved back another step.

"Why are you negotiating?" Maw asked her. "He's trapped. Out gunned. Let the team take him into custody."

Carter ignored Maw as well and tried once more to reach Banks. "She'll be *safe*. I promise."

Szoke lifted his small radio "Able Team," he murmured, "engage."

"No!" Carter yelled, but it was too late.

38

Sandy kept easing backward, one limping stride at a time. Carter hollered at him, exhorting him to surrender and promising Lita's safety if he did so.

Sandy took another step.

"Go," Sandy said. "Go now."

Lita hesitated.

Carter yelled something about daylight, but Sandy ignored her entreaties. He remained laser focused on the advancing men.

"Go!" he growled at Lita. "I'll be right behind you. Just like at the cemetery."

She still didn't move.

Another promise from Carter.

Sandy took another step backward.

Carter screamed, "No!"

Sandy reached for his gun.

Gunshots split the night.

Sandy shifted backward, bringing up his .45 and firing rapidly. Behind him, Lita wheeled around and sprinted down the dock toward the orange light. His foot caught something on the dock and he toppled hard to the wooden surface.

Immediately, he rolled to his right and sat up, continuing to return fire. The smell of salty brine and motor oil mixed in the air with the familiar scent of gunpowder. Sandy curled forward into a crouch as bullets bit into the wood next to him, sending splinters flying. He coiled his legs and sprang into the nearest boat, a modest fishing vessel with an open top.

He landed hard, bouncing off one of the seats and toppling to the deck. The smooth plastic was damp with the humid night air and smelled of fish and, more faintly, of chlorine. Sandy scrambled up to his knees. He cast a quick glance down the dock and saw Lita nearing the orange light. He thought he may have heard a male voice call out from the go-fast boat but, amidst all of the shouts coming from his attackers, it was too difficult to tell.

Sandy dropped the magazine and slammed in his second one. Then he popped up from cover to send several rounds towards the advancing men.

He had to keep them off the dock. Thirty seconds more. That was all Dufresne needed to be away.

That was his mission now.

Keep them off the dock.

Sandy let out a roar and fired rapidly, emptying the magazine in a flurry of shots.

The tactical team answered back, sending a hail of gunfire his way. He heard the bullets slap into the sides of the boat. Several passed by and struck the inside, below the water line. Instantly, sea water started streaming in, as if the boat had become a small fountain.

Sandy went through his reload action, his body acting on instinct. As he hammered the bottom of the mag with his free palm, he noticed blood dripping from his forearm. Yet, he felt no pain.

Before he could shoot again, another barrage pounded the small vessel, sounding like angry bits of hail against a metal shed. Sandy felt a small pinch in his abdomen. He glanced down. A dark red stain spread from the right side of his gut.

Keep them off the dock.

Sandy forced himself to spring upward, firing as he went.

He saw two men exiting the serpentine path, advancing in a crouching walk. He focused his fire on them. His own bullets tore into the lead man and sent the other scrambling.

He ducked down again.

"Son of a *bitch!*" someone hollered. The curse brought a grim smile to Sandy's lips.

The boat was rapidly filling with water. Already, when Sandy knelt down, it reached his thighs. Another minute and someone's retirement pastime was going to be underwater entirely.

A minute is more than I need, Sandy told himself.

He popped up and emptied the rest of the magazine, pointing randomly at anything moving. The tactical team returned fire. Several rounds buzzed angrily past his head. One clipped his ear, causing him to duck down again in reaction. Warm blood streamed down his cheek and neck.

Sandy hit the mag release lever with his thumb and dropped the empty. Then he slammed in a fresh magazine.

Last one.

Sandy took a deep, steadying breath. He let himself feel all of the pain in his body. His throbbing leg. His burning ear. The aching stiff soreness of the crease across his upper back. The strangely disconnected injuries to his arm and gut.

Sandy pushed away all the pain. He summoned all his rage, all his strength, in one more breath. Then he clambered over the side of the boat, hopped awkwardly onto the dock. Without pause, he advanced on the enemy at a steady, sure pace. Gun extended, he fired slowly now, methodically choosing his targets and hitting more often than he missed. He saw men fall under his gunfire. Others scrambled for cover.

Many returned fire.

Bullets tore and bit into his body. He absorbed them with the sort of distant objectivity that fatalism afforded him. Most hits felt more like dull punches than actual rounds. He grunted when they struck him and kept moving forward, firing his .45.

A short burst of automatic fire kicked up wood debris near his feet. A half-second later, a pulse of pain told him at least one round had hit home.

He gritted his teeth and took another step anyway. A man wound his way down the serpentine path, his MP5 at the ready. Sandy fired at him but the man didn't flinch, only raised his own weapon.

Sandy squeezed the trigger but his shot missed its target again. The slide of the .45 locked to the rear. Over the wisp of white smoke curling up from the empty chamber, Sandy saw the closest man fire.

A sharp pain lanced into his chest and he faltered.

Another burst tore into his knee and climbed up his thigh and Sandy went down. He collapsed onto his back.

Despite the pain, the strange disassociation remained. He imagined he heard the swelling roar of a go-fast boat engine screaming out to sea but, in the midst of gunfire, he couldn't be sure.

A moment later, the shooting tapered off and nearly stopped. A few stray rounds were fired. Someone—*Szoke? No, another voice*—called out to cease fire. Other men shouted and drew closer. The slight, easy sway of the dock beneath him suddenly shifted to erratic bounces.

Sandy ignored it all. He listened for the engine, and now he was almost certain he heard its telltale, snarling whine of speed in the distance.

She made it.

I'm sure of it.

He lay on his back and stared up at the dark night sky. He stared until the starry pinpricks splashed there first blurred, then expanded, and finally flooded his vision with nothing but light.

39

Carter saw it all happen. Not in slow motion, but rather in short staccato bursts of action, punctuated with a beat of stillness in between each.

Szoke's order to fire.

Banks reaching for his gun.

The girl—*Lita*, she reminded herself—bolting away on the docks.

Her own voice shouting out a denial, sounding too distant to have any impact on what was about to happen.

Then came the blasts of gunfire. When Banks toppled over backward, she thought he'd been hit. Maybe he had, but the man was resilient. He rolled away and came up shooting.

Next to her, Szoke and Maw ducked behind the safety of the SUV as shots rang out.

Carter moved forward.

She didn't draw her weapon. At this point, she saw how redundant an action that would be.

Instead, she bore witness.

Banks leapt into a small boat in a nearby slip, but Carter kept her eyes on Lita Delancey as the teenager—*barely a teen*, she thought wildly—ran down the docks. Chunks of wood leapt upward near her feet as she fled.

Carter swung her gaze around, looking for the source of those shots. In the chaos of the gunfight, she couldn't discern who had fired them. She wanted to yell again, shout out another denial, but knew it would do no good.

Szoke. The bastard had ordered his men to treat Lita the same as Banks. She recalled his sickening statement about her being "above the Escobar Line." Her lip curled in rage and disgust.

Banks returned fire from inside the fishing boat, forcing some of the tactical agents to take cover. When he ducked, they sent a barrage of rounds his way. The boat was riddled with bullets. It had to be taking on water. Soon it would sink, and Banks with it.

A head popped up and Banks sent another flurry of gunfire their direction.

Carter peered through the dimly lit night onto the docks to see Lita Delancey reach a slip with an orange light. She slowed, then was jerked forward onto the boat by a thin man in goggles.

Another volley of shots came from the FBI team and Szoke's squad, peppering the boat where Banks had taken refuge.

A brief second came, perhaps not even a complete one, of near silence, of stillness. Carter took a half step forward in that moment.

The engine of the go-fast boat rumbled to life.

Sandy Banks emerged over the edge of the boat, scrambling onto the dock. He didn't run, but instead began a slow, steady march toward their positions. Rather than fire wildly, he chose his shots with meticulous precision. In the weak apron of light cast by the nearby marina, she could see the right side of his face, painted with blood. His expression was calm and unyielding.

He is resolved, she realized. To die rather than lose. Or to die and to lose. She didn't know which but, even at this distance, she saw his own death in those eyes.

"Goddamnit!" Szoke cursed from behind her as the go-fast boat ripped its way out of the inlet and headed out of the harbor, its running lights dark.

A *rat-a-tat-tat* of automatic fire rang out to her right. She saw a spray of wooden debris kick up next to Banks' feet. A moment later, another burst slapped into his leg. A shot struck him in the chest and he toppled over backwards.

The shooting continued for several seconds longer before Maw bellowed out a ceasefire. Cautiously, the FBI tactical team approached Banks where he had fallen on the dock.

In the distance, the go-fast boat driver opened the engine up all the way, and Carter could hear the whining roar all the way from where she stood.

"Goddamnit!" Szoke shouted again.

Carter lost sight of the shadow on the water as it melted into the night.

"Alert the Coast Guard!" Szoke hollered.

Maw gaped at him. "You haven't done that yet?"

"Get them rolling," Szoke told Carter, ignoring the FBI supervisor.

Carter shook her head. "They'll never respond in time."

"Sure they will."

"That boat is going at least seventy miles an hour," Carter told him. "Probably more like a hundred or more since the driver is supremely motivated to get the fuck out of here. They'll be in international waters before the Coast Guard can get anywhere close."

"I don't care about international waters."

"The Coast Guard does," she said. "Do the math, Mark. It's over."

"It's not over." Szoke jabbed a finger at her, snarling, "*I want that kid.*"

Carter didn't move.

Szoke pulled a phone from his pocket and punched at the

screen.

Carter turned away from him. She started walking down the serpentine path toward Banks, but stopped halfway there. She stared at the man's crumpled, still form. Even in the dim apron of light beneath the dock pole lights, she could see Banks's bloody body was torn by bullets.

Is this justice, she wondered. If so, it felt hollow and wrong. If it wasn't, she decided, then maybe at least it was at an end.

Special Agent-in-Charge Edward Maw approached, stopping slightly behind her. Carter didn't bother looking at him. She just stared at Banks while the tactical team milled around, unsure how to proceed now that the shooting was over and their quarry had escaped.

"What a mess," Maw said quietly.

Carter nodded slowly.

"I'll tell you something else," he added. "This isn't over. I'm not finished with it. Not by a long shot."

Carter turned to face him. "Good," she said.

40

It took over a week to get Sandy Banks into the ground.

Carter herself had to make most of the arrangements. Szoke was at first dismissive of the idea, then consumed by other matters. She took on the task without resentment. In a very real way, it made a perfect kind of sense to her. So much of their journey had been intertwined. It only followed she should be here with him at the end.

She was the only one there that day, save for a groundskeeper and member of the clergy recommended by the funeral director she'd coordinated with for everything else.

There'd been no service before the burial. Therefore, the pastor gave a short eulogy at the graveside. He knew little about Sandy Banks, as Carter had shared virtually no information with him other than the man's name and age. Thus, the orator's statements were generalized, a real cut-and-paste tribute that could have applied to anyone.

Even so, Carter took some comfort from the platitudes. Banks, like her, had lived an abnormal life. Nothing said by anyone, clergy or lay person, could realistically approach putting the experience into words. Besides, there was no one to listen save her, and she was fine with the generic utterances made by the rental preacher. She stood erect at the side of the open grave, silent, thinking thoughts she could not likely share with anyone else in the world, and saying farewell in that way.

The pastor seemed to be wrapping up when a limousine wound its way along the narrow roadway to stop nearby. Carter turned to watch as a man in a dark suit got out and held the rear door open. Another, older man exited the back seat.

Danforth.

"You son of a bitch," she muttered.

The pastor stumbled in his address, looking at her in mild confusion. "Ma'am?"

"Sorry, pastor, not you." She twirled her finger. "Please, continue."

The pastor cleared his throat and resumed his platitudes. She only half-listened as she watched the old man make his way deliberately toward them. She hadn't seen Danforth in at least seven or eight years. The man had worked through Szoke for so long he had come to exist in her mind more as a symbol than a real person. But, as he wound his way around the grave markers, she saw he was very much real.

And older.

He walked deliberately, picking his way past obstacles. He carried a cane but did not use it. His shoulders were slightly hunched. She didn't remember that roundness to his posture before. When he drew close enough for her to see the lines in his face and the whiter shade of gray in his full goatee, the image was complete.

So, even the Prince of Darkness ages.

Danforth came to a stop next to her. Only then did he rest the tip of his cane on the grassy ground and lean onto it. Carter thought she might have detected a slight sigh as he did so.

Then he smiled at her.

The smile itself didn't surprise her. It was the lack of malice she'd expected to see that left her slightly reeling. She didn't smile back but gave Danforth a short nod.

Through it all, the pastor continued to recite some passage from the Bible that sounded vaguely familiar, before finally announcing his blessing on the soul of Sandy Banks and giving a hearty amen. He signaled the groundskeeper, who duly turned the lever that lowered the unadorned casket into the ground.

No one spoke until the casket reached its resting point. Then the pastor asked if anyone wished to speak. Carter shook her head. So did Danforth. The pastor nodded as if he'd expected that reply and snapped his Bible shut. "Then this concludes our service today."

"Thank you, Pastor," Carter said.

He stood by for a few moments and she wondered oddly if she was supposed to tip the man. Was this a common feeling among mourners? She'd already paid him what felt like a healthy sum. But the pastor stood watching her wordlessly, like a bellman unwilling to depart the hotel room after depositing the baggage.

Carter stared back, deciding not to budge. Besides, she wasn't carrying any cash.

After a short, awkward silence, the pastor dipped his chin again, turned and headed across the grass to his parked Oldsmobile.

The groundskeeper waited patiently for Carter and Danforth to follow suit, but the older man motioned toward him.

"Will you give us a few minutes, son?" he asked, sounding almost kindly.

"Of course," the groundskeeper said automatically. He turned and wandered away in roughly the same direction the pastor had gone.

Danforth waited until the man was out of earshot before speaking. He lifted his cane and pointed it toward the open grave. "How many deaths is it now for this one? Four? Five?"

Carter didn't try to tally up how many different incarnations of Sandy Banks had existed through the years, only to die a fictional death when it suited either him or his handlers.

"I think this one will take," she deadpanned.

Danforth chuckled at that. "I daresay."

They stood in silence, both looking downward. Finally, Carter asked, "Why are you here?"

"To pay my respects," said Danforth. "Banks may have been a pain in the ass but, whatever else happened, he was a useful pain in the ass. His actions served this nation well."

Carter was tired of games and the lies that came with them. "Excuse me, sir, but that's bullshit."

"Ha!" Danforth wagged a bony finger at her. "There's the Lori Carter I know."

"You don't know me."

"Sure, I do."

"Go fuck yourself."

"I'm sure I will, at some point," Danforth said. "We all do. Seems to be in our collective nature to be instrumental in our own downfall."

"Fuck your philosophy, too," Carter said. She turned to face the old man, glaring at him with naked anger. "This is over. I don't know what happens next but, I'll tell you this, whatever it is—I'm not taking your shit or anyone else's anymore."

"Good." A slight grin played at the corners of Danforth's mouth. "That's good."

"What are you smiling about? Your operation just got torched."

Danforth waved a hand. "Not really. Oh, your peacock of a SAC has the FBI poking its nose under my tent, that's true. He's a real noisemaker, that one."

"He sees it as a way to revitalize his career."

"I'm sure he's right. But people like him are easy to deal with."

"Oh, really?"

"Certainly. He's not an idealist. Not a crusader. All he wants is to resuscitate a stalled climb up the ladder. Well, that is easily provided."

"You think you can just make this go away?"

"I know I can," said Danforth. "Not easily, and not without casualties, but it will be resolved."

"Casualties?" Carter drew herself up and eyed him with suspicion. "You're throwing me to the wolves, aren't you?"

"Certainly not. No, we'll have to sacrifice Szoke at the altar on this one. He'll take the hit for the team. We'll give your man Maw the mobile command center as evidence, too. Along with Szoke served up on a platter, that'll provide him with more than enough props to finish the production he's planning."

"Good. This operation is long past its sell-by date."

Danforth's lips tilted upward into a knowing grin. "Not quite yet. We'll still have the HQ in Idaho and all my contacts. The good work will go on."

"Without Mark?"

"Sadly, yes."

"What happens to him?"

Danforth shrugged. "A few months in federal prison before he's quietly transferred to a separate location he won't actually ever arrive at."

"Tying up loose ends?"

"If you mean by giving him a comfortable pension under an assumed name, then yes." He gave her a meaningful look. "I take care of my people."

Carter glanced down at the open ground in front of her. "Like him?"

"Banks refused to be a team player. His end was sadly predictable. But, as a well-known risk management guru is wont to say, predictable is preventable." He tapped his cane on the sod when he spoke the final three words. Then he added, "I'd like to think you'll be able to prevent anything like this occurring on your watch."

"Me?"

"Yes, of course, you."

She shook her head firmly. "No. I'm out."

Danforth's grim smile returned. "No one is ever out, Lori. They are just further in." He reached out to touch her on the arm but she recoiled. Danforth stopped, holding his hand in mid-air for a moment before dropping it. "The work we do will always be needed. But we are entering a more nuanced time in our nation's history," he said. "We'll need to solve problems more creatively. Perhaps… perhaps sometimes less permanently."

She stared at him, not believing the words she was hearing.

"Szoke was a cudgel," Danforth continued, "at a time when a cudgel was necessary. You, on the other hand, are a scalpel. A scalpel is both a weapon and a tool, capable of cutting as the situation requires. I'm certain you have the creativity to lead the unit through this adaptation."

"No," Carter said firmly. "I'm done."

"No," Danforth echoed. "You're not. But we'll talk about the details back at HQ in a few days. Meanwhile, enjoy a little free time. Have a nice meal. Read a book. Or find some brief form of companionship. Whatever you like." He smiled primly. "And then, after that, we have work to do, you and I."

Without another word, the man turned away from her. She watched as he headed back to his car, wending his way past the grave markers, holding his cane but not using it. She wanted to shout after him but, in that moment, she'd lost all of her power of denial.

Instead, she whispered, "I'm out," even though she knew it wasn't true.

EPILOGUE

42 months later

The day was not unlike the hundreds they had spent together before but, at the same time, it felt special. Most of it passed quietly, both of them reading and following the sun along with the pair of cats Alexander Dimitrakos had taken in over the past several years. Later, they celebrated with a small dinner, just the two of them, and baklava for dessert.

Seventeen was an interesting age. Dimitrakos had seen boys and girls who were still almost children when they reached this birthday. Others seemed to already be an adult by the time they hit this age.

Angela fell in the latter category. Truth be told, this was true almost from the moment he spotted her waiting near the fountain in Plaza de La Vigia in Mantanzas, Cuba. She'd been accompanied by a ragged-looking boat pilot who looked more than a little forlorn at the fact he wouldn't be able to return to the U.S. for at least a little while.

Angela appeared almost waifish that night, though her hard expression belied her age. Now, she looked every bit a grown woman with a sharp mind to match. He felt a strange tinge of pride in that, though he knew he had little to nothing to do with it.

They sat on the small balcony, sipping wine and looking out over the sea. Angela, already a reserved person, remained even more quiet than usual. Dimitrakos didn't mind. He'd come to appreciate her company, perhaps even to love her as a wayward, adoptive uncle might. He enjoyed the calm of the late afternoon, the satisfying fullness of his belly, and the pleasant hum the wine gave him.

When the sun began to dip low on the horizon, threatening to touch the sea, Angela finally spoke. "I miss her," she said. She spoke nearly perfect Greek now. Her accent had diminished to the point of being barely evident.

"Your mother?"

She nodded once, not looking his way.

"I imagine so," Dimitrakos said. "I also imagine she would be quite proud of the woman you've become."

"That's part of why I miss her."

"And what about him?"

"My father?"

"Yes."

She shrugged. "I miss the person he showed to me. I know it was only a small slice of who he really was. Or maybe it was entirely manufactured, a façade. Who can say?"

"Who can say about any us on that count?"

"I can say it about you, Alex. You are exactly who you show me to be."

"Perhaps," he allowed. "But we all have our secret selves. Our deep mistakes. Our terrible regrets."

"Why are you talking this way?" she asked, smiling slightly. "It's my birthday."

"So it is. But you're a grown woman, so I'm speaking to you as one."

A shadow passed over her face.

"What is it?" he asked.

She shook her head. "Nothing. Just something similar someone once said to me."

He hesitated, thinking. Then he said, "I think I can guess

who."

"We don't need to talk about him," Angela said.

"No, we don't. Do you still hate him, though?"

"Absolutely."

He heard something reluctant in her voice, so he pressed. "Perhaps not quite so completely as that, it sounds to me."

"He was a bad man," she said simply.

"Who made at least one good choice when he helped you."

"That was only necessary because of his own bad actions," she said, her voice tightening. "He killed my father. I know he was no saint, but he was still my father, and this man took him away from me. Forever. And that decision, that action, resulted in my mother being killed, too." Angela's eyes became glassy and her voice shook. "Which was much worse."

Dimitrakos nodded at her words. "He was a bad man, certainly. But maybe there was also some good in him. That's how the world is, isn't it? No one is purely good any more than they are purely evil."

"I never said he was purely evil. But what he did..." She trailed off, glancing out at the glass-like waters of the Aegean.

"What he did was horrible," Dimitrakos said.

"But?"

"There is no but."

"I can sense one lingering there in your tone, Alex."

She is getting too wise for her years, he mused.

"It is only a thought," he said.

"Then tell me."

He was quiet for a few moments, looking out over the water while he considered how to express the sentiment. Finally, he settled on simplicity.

"You said I was exactly who I showed you I was, yes?"

She nodded.

"You're right about that," he said. "But I wasn't always this man. Or, I was, but I took actions back then that put me directly in the path of this man you still hate. Yet, he showed mercy that day."

Angela watched him, saying nothing.

"I don't regret my activism," Dimitrakos continued, "though I have long since left it behind. However, it was a combination of my decisions and his that made it possible for you to be sitting here today."

"So, I should be grateful he killed my father? That he caused the death of my mother?" Angela's voice took on an edge.

"No, of course not."

"Then what are you saying?"

"I'm saying, we all make our choices in this world," Dimitrakos said. "We live with those choices. This man we speak of made a choice. You must live with it." He reached out and rested his hand over the top of hers. "But he also made another choice, didn't he? And you *get* to live because of that one."

Angela took in his words. "It still isn't fair," she murmured, seeming to be a much younger version of herself for a moment. Tears shimmered in her eyes.

"It isn't," Dimitrakos agreed. He patted her hand, then pulled away to lift his glass from the table. He raised it to the sea, made a silent toast to all of the fallen, and took a sip. He held the crisp wine in his mouth for a moment before swallowing.

"No, it is not fair," he repeated. "But it is life."

Acknowledgments

I'd like to thank:

Mike Black, for taking a look at the first eight thousand words and offering some excellent critiques.

Colin Conway, for taking the first run at the story and offering some important fixes.

Paula Dunn, for being the alpha reader of all alpha readers.

Members of the Beta Squad, who caught the mistakes I missed: John Emery, Ron Sarich, Beth Camp, Suzanne Peckham, Steve Guerra, and Brad Hallock. A special shout out to Elena E. Smith for finding some late-standing story and character issues and offering some splendid solutions.

Lastly, Kristi. You're still my girl.

Frank Zafiro
August 2025
Redmond, Oregon

ABOUT THE AUTHOR

Frank Zafiro writes gritty crime fiction from both sides of the badge. He was a police officer from 1993 to 2013, holding many different positions and ranks. He retired as a captain.

Frank is the author of over fifty novels, most of them crime fiction. He also writes heartwarming humor as Frank Scalise and science fiction and fantasy as Frank Saverio. In addition to writing, Frank has hosted the crime fiction podcast *Wrong Place, Write Crime* since 2017. He is a martial artist, an avid hockey fan, and a tortured guitarist.

He currently lives in Redmond, Oregon, with his wife Kristi and two cats, Pasta and Gary. Only one of the three is at all impressed with his literary career.

You can keep up with him at http://frankzafiro.com.

www.ingramcontent.com/pod-product-compliance
Lightning Source LLC
LaVergne TN
LVHW012035070526
838202LV00056B/5502